THE CREEPS

NIGHT OF THE
FRANKENFROGS

Chris Schweizer

AMULET BOOKS
NEW YORK

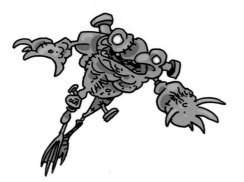

Library of Congress Control Number: 2014955691

Hardcover ISBN: 978-1-4197-1379-8
Paperback ISBN: 978-1-4197-1766-6

Book design by Pamela Notarantonio

Printed and bound in China
10 9 8 7 6 5 4 3 2 1

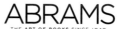

ABRAMS
THE ART OF BOOKS SINCE 1949
115 West 18th Street
New York, NY 10011
www.abramsbooks.com

TO PENNY, MY FAVORITE READER

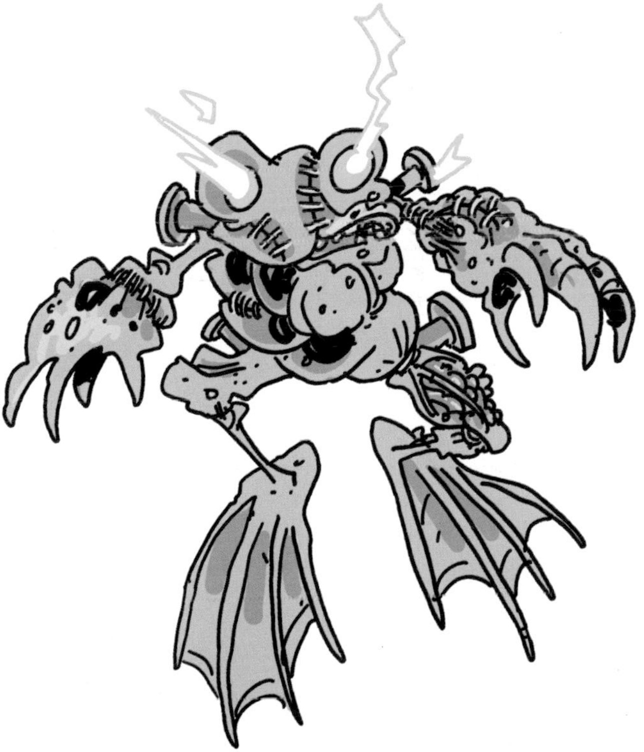

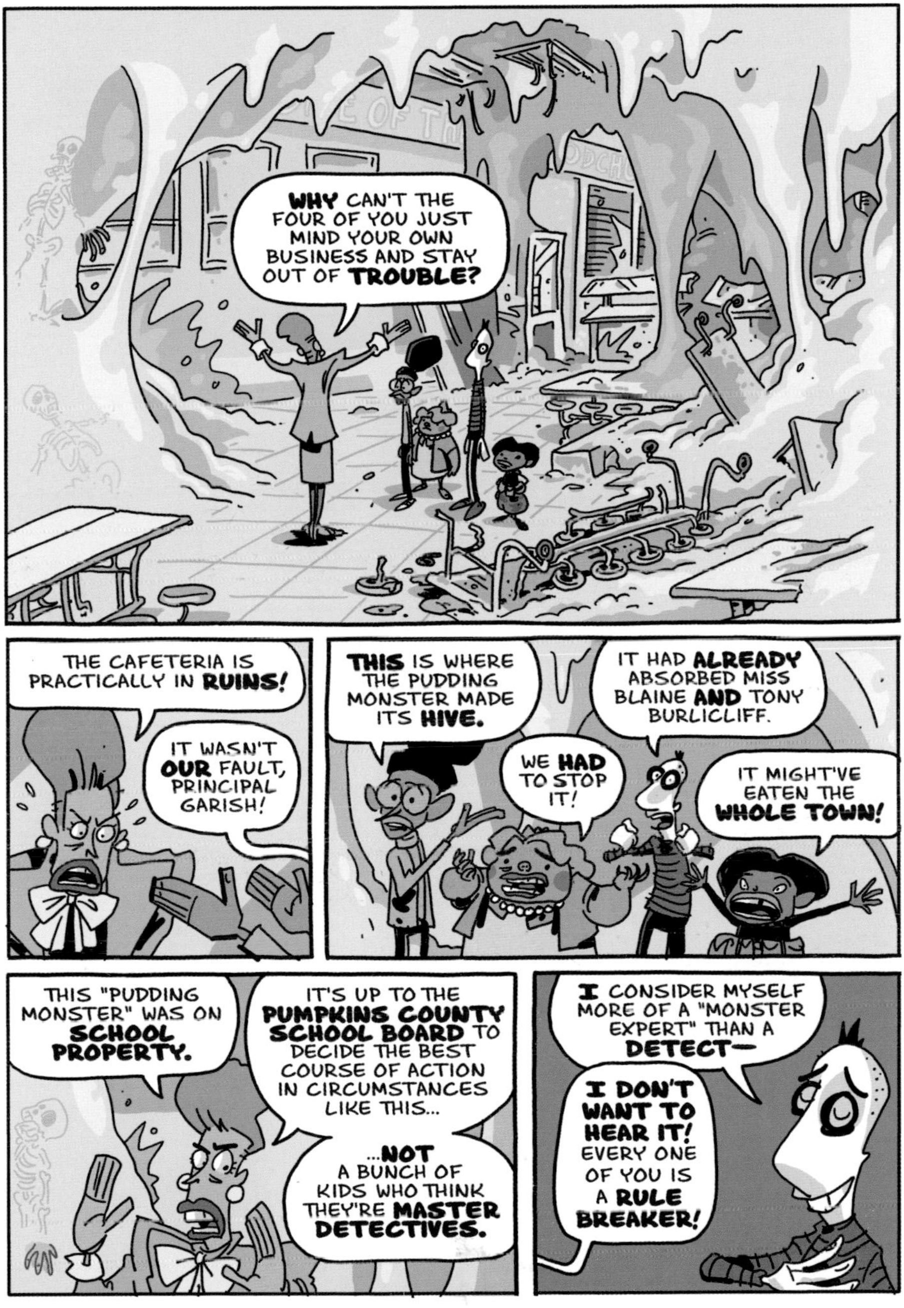
WHY CAN'T THE FOUR OF YOU JUST MIND YOUR OWN BUSINESS AND STAY OUT OF TROUBLE?
THE CAFETERIA IS PRACTICALLY IN RUINS!
IT WASN'T OUR FAULT, PRINCIPAL GARISH!
THIS IS WHERE THE PUDDING MONSTER MADE ITS HIVE.
IT HAD ALREADY ABSORBED MISS BLAINE AND TONY BURLICLIFF.
WE HAD TO STOP IT!
IT MIGHT'VE EATEN THE WHOLE TOWN!
THIS "PUDDING MONSTER" WAS ON SCHOOL PROPERTY.
IT'S UP TO THE PUMPKINS COUNTY SCHOOL BOARD TO DECIDE THE BEST COURSE OF ACTION IN CIRCUMSTANCES LIKE THIS...
...NOT A BUNCH OF KIDS WHO THINK THEY'RE MASTER DETECTIVES.
I CONSIDER MYSELF MORE OF A "MONSTER EXPERT" THAN A DETECT—
I DON'T WANT TO HEAR IT! EVERY ONE OF YOU IS A RULE BREAKER!

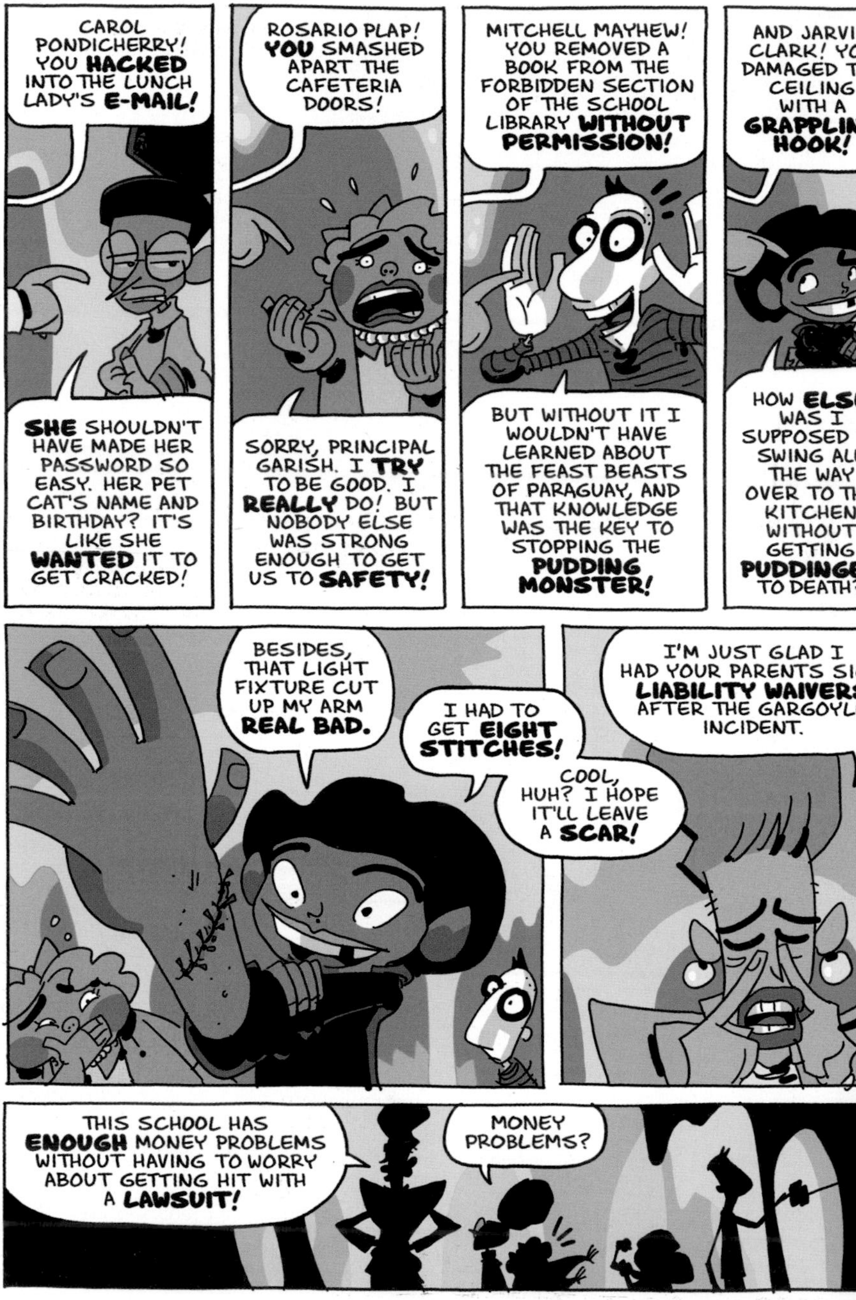
CAROL PONDICHERRY! YOU **HACKED** INTO THE LUNCH LADY'S **E-MAIL!**
SHE SHOULDN'T HAVE MADE HER PASSWORD SO EASY. HER PET CAT'S NAME AND BIRTHDAY? IT'S LIKE SHE **WANTED** IT TO GET CRACKED!
ROSARIO PLAP! **YOU** SMASHED APART THE CAFETERIA DOORS!
SORRY, PRINCIPAL GARISH. I **TRY** TO BE GOOD. I **REALLY** DO! BUT NOBODY ELSE WAS STRONG ENOUGH TO GET US TO **SAFETY!**
MITCHELL MAYHEW! YOU REMOVED A BOOK FROM THE FORBIDDEN SECTION OF THE SCHOOL LIBRARY **WITHOUT PERMISSION!**
BUT WITHOUT IT I WOULDN'T HAVE LEARNED ABOUT THE FEAST BEASTS OF PARAGUAY, AND THAT KNOWLEDGE WAS THE KEY TO STOPPING THE **PUDDING MONSTER!**
AND JARVIS CLARK! YOU DAMAGED THE CEILING WITH A **GRAPPLING HOOK!**
HOW **ELSE** WAS I SUPPOSED TO SWING ALL THE WAY OVER TO THE KITCHEN WITHOUT GETTING **PUDDINGED** TO DEATH?
BESIDES, THAT LIGHT FIXTURE CUT UP MY ARM **REAL BAD.**
I HAD TO GET **EIGHT STITCHES!**
COOL, HUH? I HOPE IT'LL LEAVE A **SCAR!**
I'M JUST GLAD I HAD YOUR PARENTS SIGN **LIABILITY WAIVERS** AFTER THE GARGOYLE INCIDENT.
THIS SCHOOL HAS **ENOUGH** MONEY PROBLEMS WITHOUT HAVING TO WORRY ABOUT GETTING HIT WITH A **LAWSUIT!**
MONEY PROBLEMS?

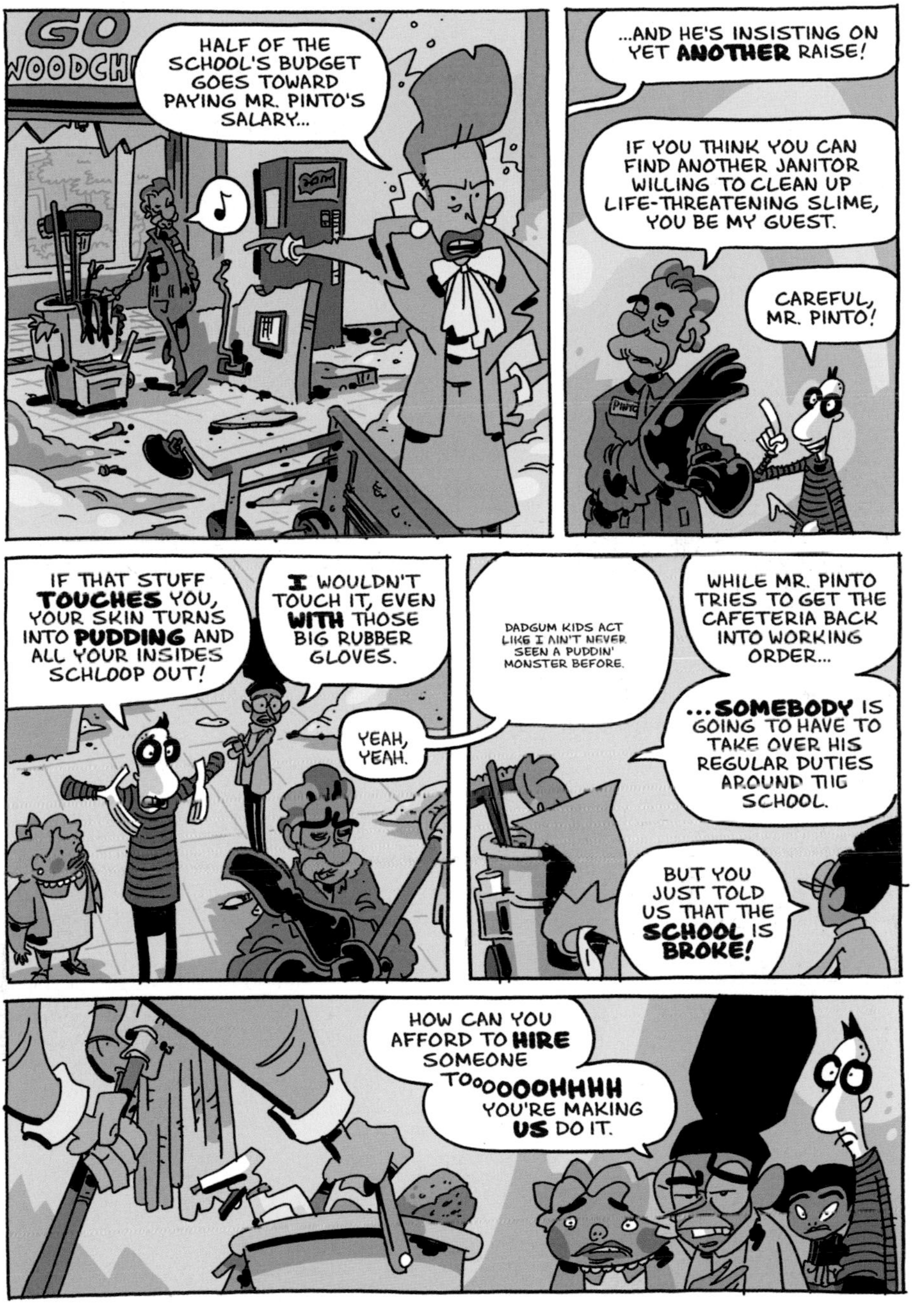
GO
HALF OF THE SCHOOL'S BUDGET GOES TOWARD PAYING MR. PINTO'S SALARY...
♪
...AND HE'S INSISTING ON YET **ANOTHER** RAISE!
IF YOU THINK YOU CAN FIND ANOTHER JANITOR WILLING TO CLEAN UP LIFE-THREATENING SLIME, YOU BE MY GUEST.
PINTO
CAREFUL, MR. PINTO!
IF THAT STUFF **TOUCHES** YOU, YOUR SKIN TURNS INTO **PUDDING** AND ALL YOUR INSIDES SCHLOOP OUT!
I WOULDN'T TOUCH IT, EVEN **WITH** THOSE BIG RUBBER GLOVES.
YEAH, YEAH.
DADGUM KIDS ACT LIKE I AIN'T NEVER SEEN A PUDDIN' MONSTER BEFORE.
WHILE MR. PINTO TRIES TO GET THE CAFETERIA BACK INTO WORKING ORDER...
...**SOMEBODY** IS GOING TO HAVE TO TAKE OVER HIS REGULAR DUTIES AROUND THE SCHOOL.
BUT YOU JUST TOLD US THAT THE **SCHOOL** IS **BROKE!**
HOW CAN YOU AFFORD TO **HIRE** SOMEONE TOoooOOHHHH YOU'RE MAKING **US** DO IT.

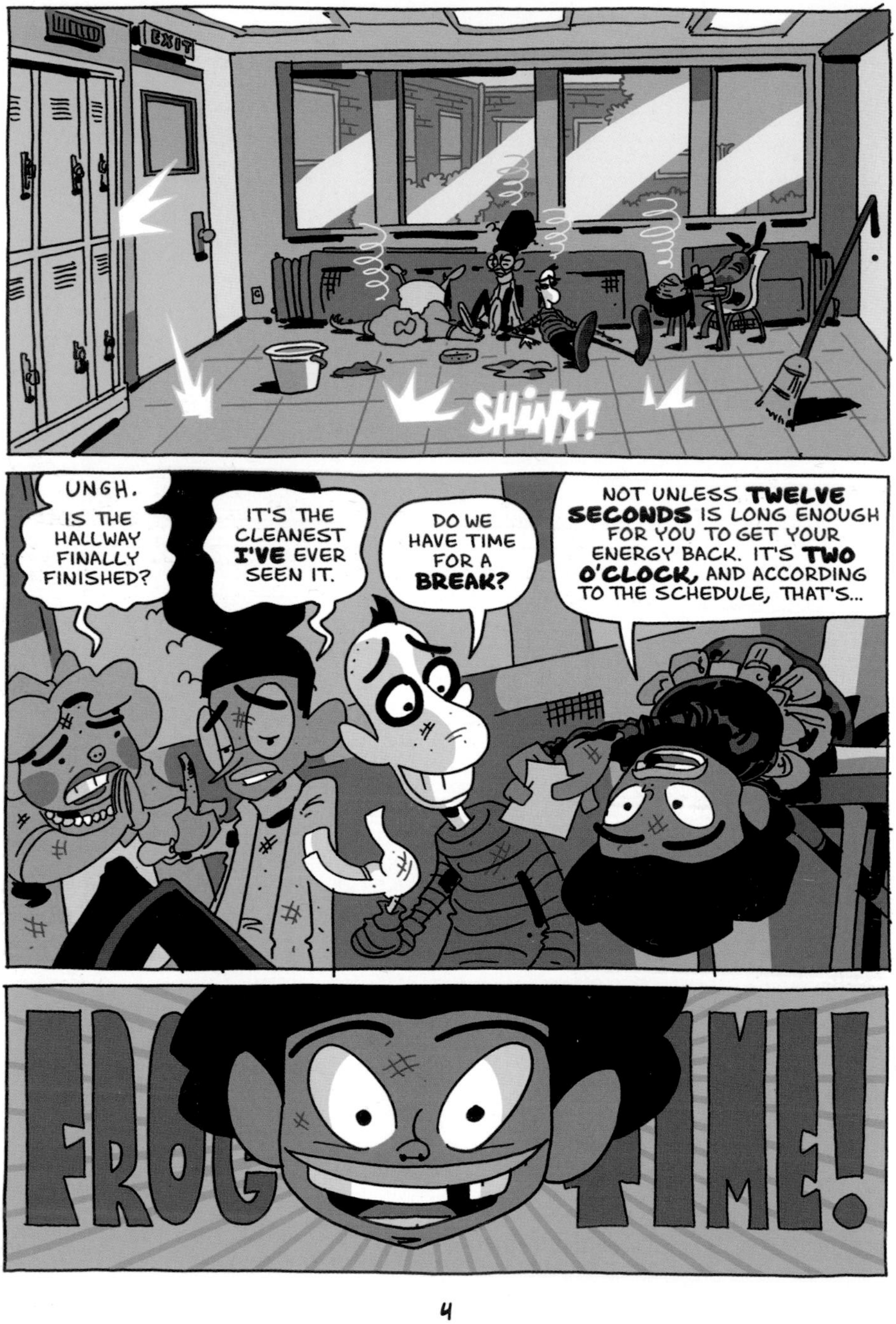
EXIT
SHINY!
UNGH. IS THE HALLWAY FINALLY FINISHED?
IT'S THE CLEANEST I'VE EVER SEEN IT.
DO WE HAVE TIME FOR A BREAK?
NOT UNLESS TWELVE SECONDS IS LONG ENOUGH FOR YOU TO GET YOUR ENERGY BACK. IT'S TWO O'CLOCK, AND ACCORDING TO THE SCHEDULE, THAT'S...
FROG TIME!

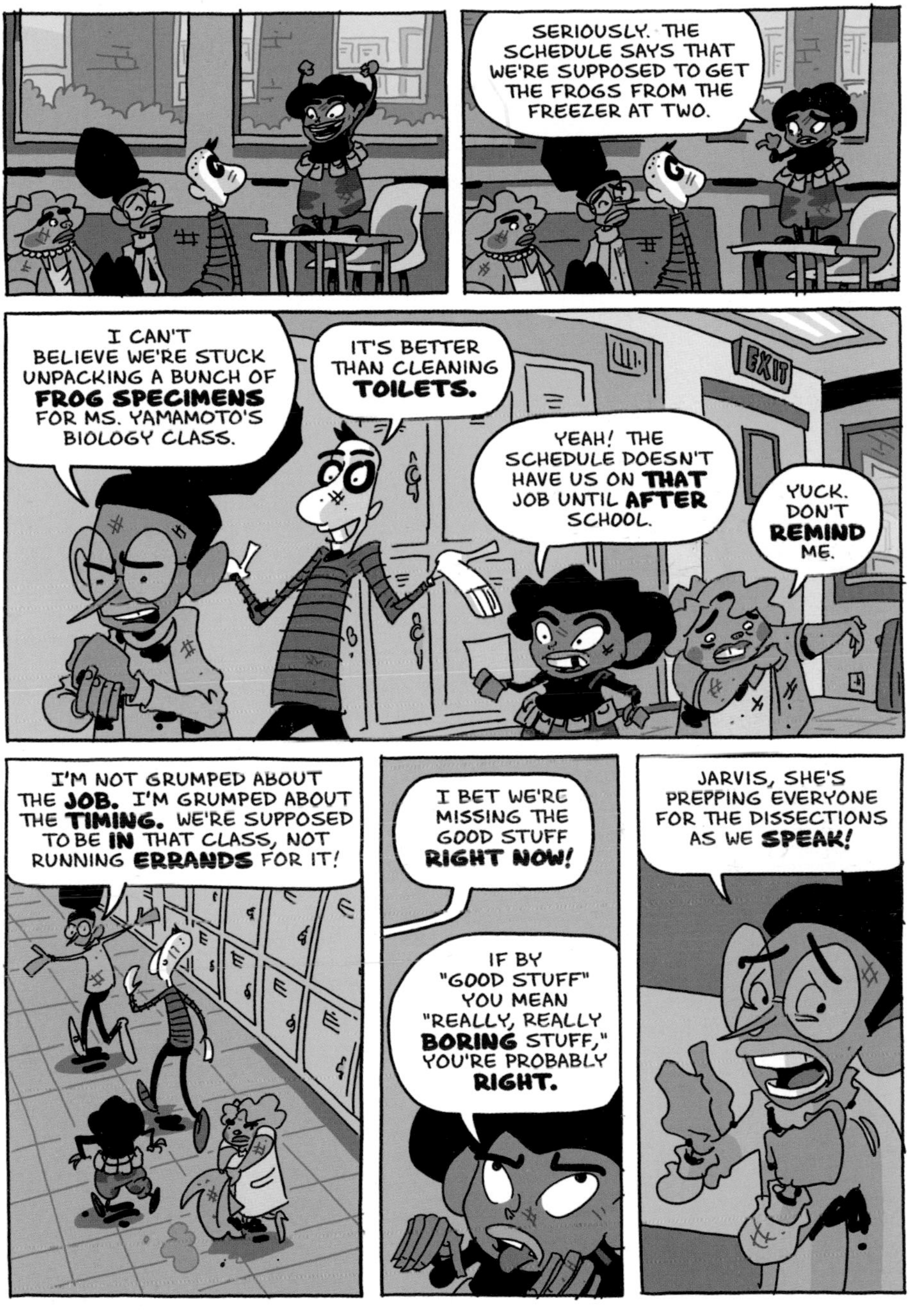

SERIOUSLY. THE SCHEDULE SAYS THAT WE'RE SUPPOSED TO GET THE FROGS FROM THE FREEZER AT TWO.
I CAN'T BELIEVE WE'RE STUCK UNPACKING A BUNCH OF **FROG SPECIMENS** FOR MS. YAMAMOTO'S BIOLOGY CLASS.
IT'S BETTER THAN CLEANING **TOILETS.**
EXIT
YEAH! THE SCHEDULE DOESN'T HAVE US ON **THAT** JOB UNTIL **AFTER** SCHOOL.
YUCK. DON'T **REMIND** ME.
I'M NOT GRUMPED ABOUT THE **JOB.** I'M GRUMPED ABOUT THE **TIMING.** WE'RE SUPPOSED TO BE **IN** THAT CLASS, NOT RUNNING **ERRANDS** FOR IT!
I BET WE'RE MISSING THE GOOD STUFF **RIGHT NOW!**
IF BY "GOOD STUFF" YOU MEAN "REALLY, REALLY **BORING** STUFF," YOU'RE PROBABLY **RIGHT.**
JARVIS, SHE'S PREPPING EVERYONE FOR THE DISSECTIONS AS WE **SPEAK!**

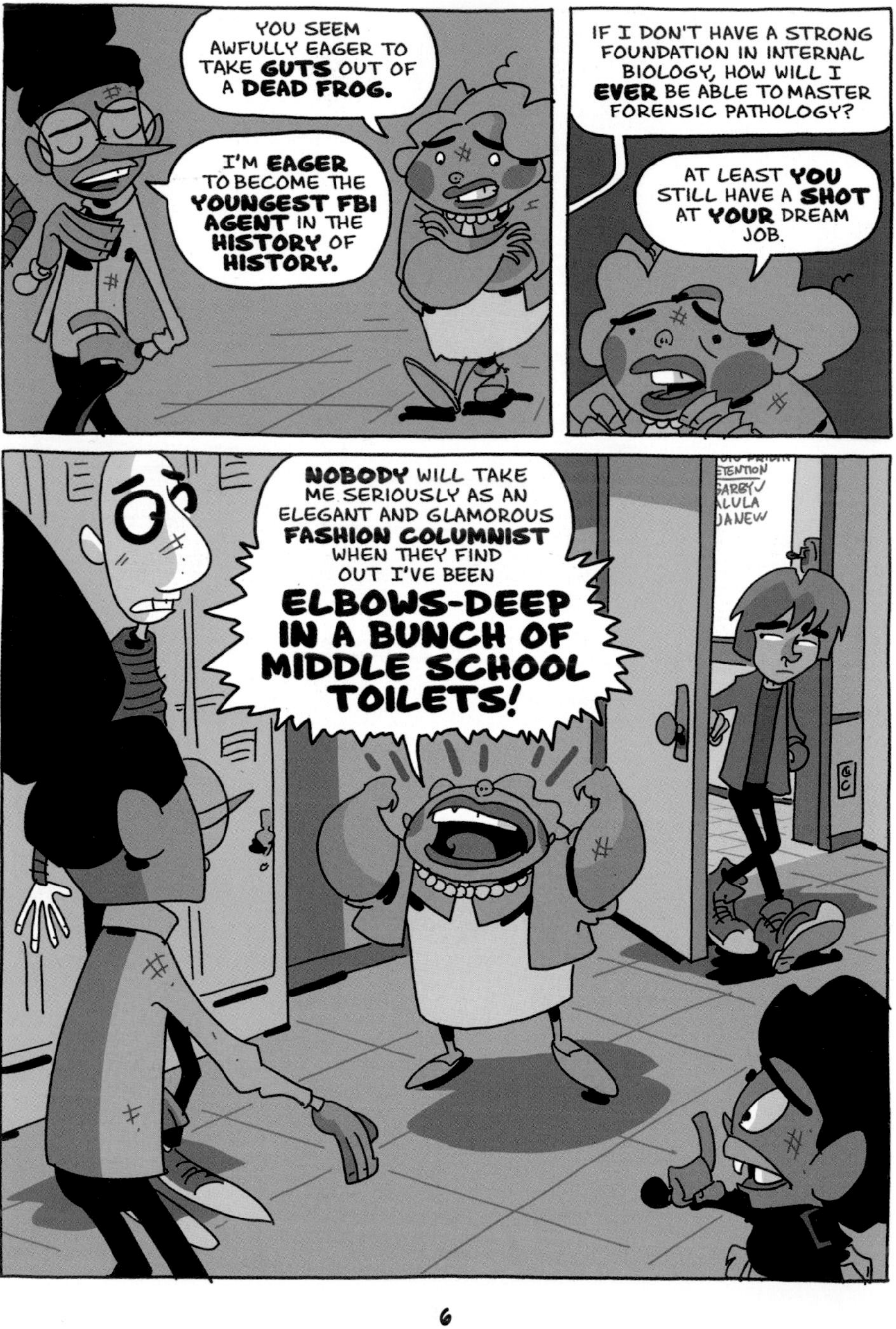

YOU SEEM AWFULLY EAGER TO TAKE **GUTS** OUT OF A **DEAD FROG.**
I'M **EAGER** TO BECOME THE **YOUNGEST FBI AGENT** IN THE **HISTORY** OF **HISTORY.**
IF I DON'T HAVE A STRONG FOUNDATION IN INTERNAL BIOLOGY, HOW WILL I **EVER** BE ABLE TO MASTER FORENSIC PATHOLOGY?
AT LEAST **YOU** STILL HAVE A **SHOT** AT **YOUR** DREAM JOB.
NOBODY WILL TAKE ME SERIOUSLY AS AN ELEGANT AND GLAMOROUS **FASHION COLUMNIST** WHEN THEY FIND OUT I'VE BEEN **ELBOWS-DEEP IN A BUNCH OF MIDDLE SCHOOL TOILETS!**

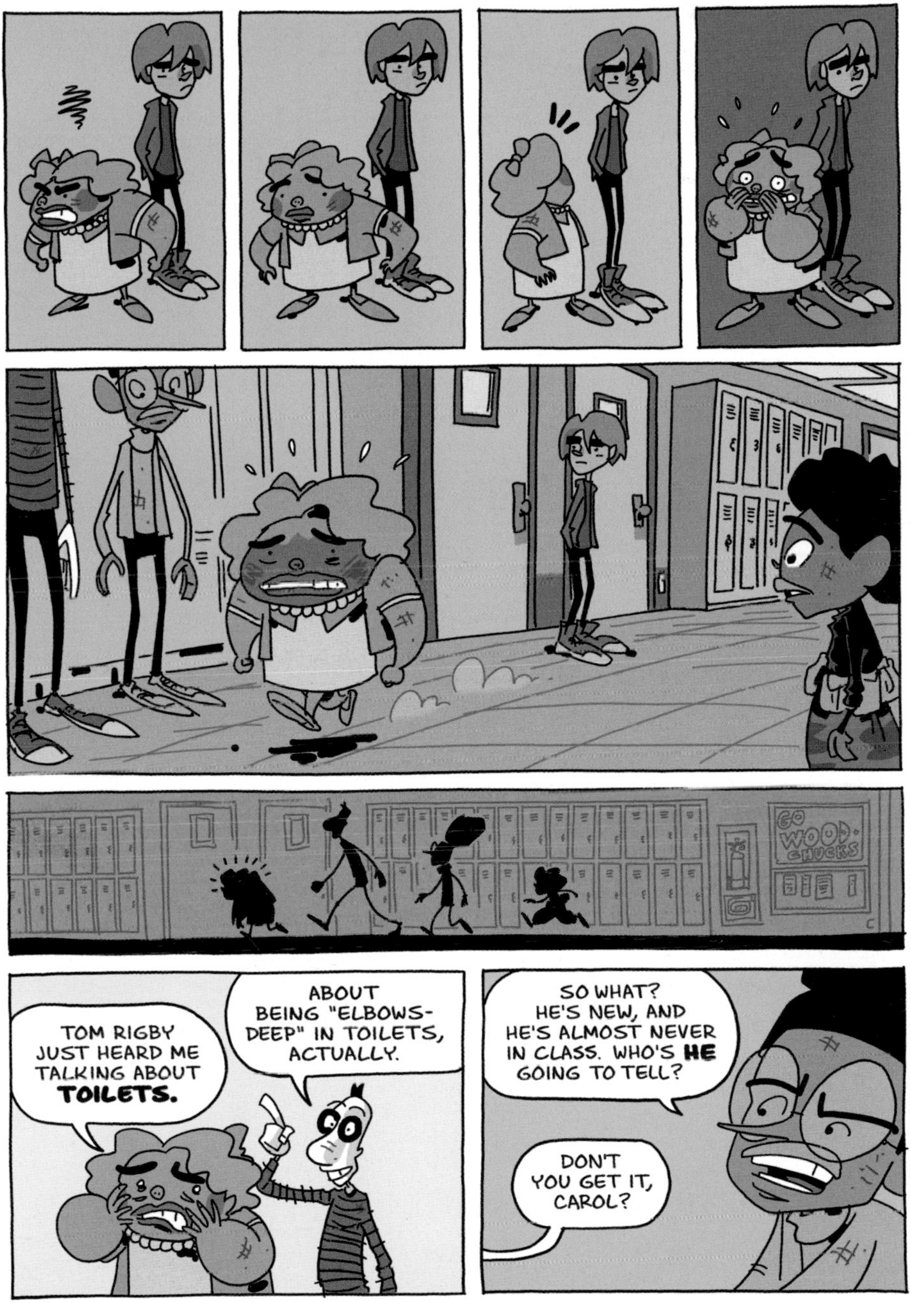
GO WOOD-CHUCKS
TOM RIGBY JUST HEARD ME TALKING ABOUT **TOILETS.**
ABOUT BEING "ELBOWS-DEEP" IN TOILETS, ACTUALLY.
SO WHAT? HE'S NEW, AND HE'S ALMOST NEVER IN CLASS. WHO'S **HE** GOING TO TELL?
DON'T YOU GET IT, CAROL?

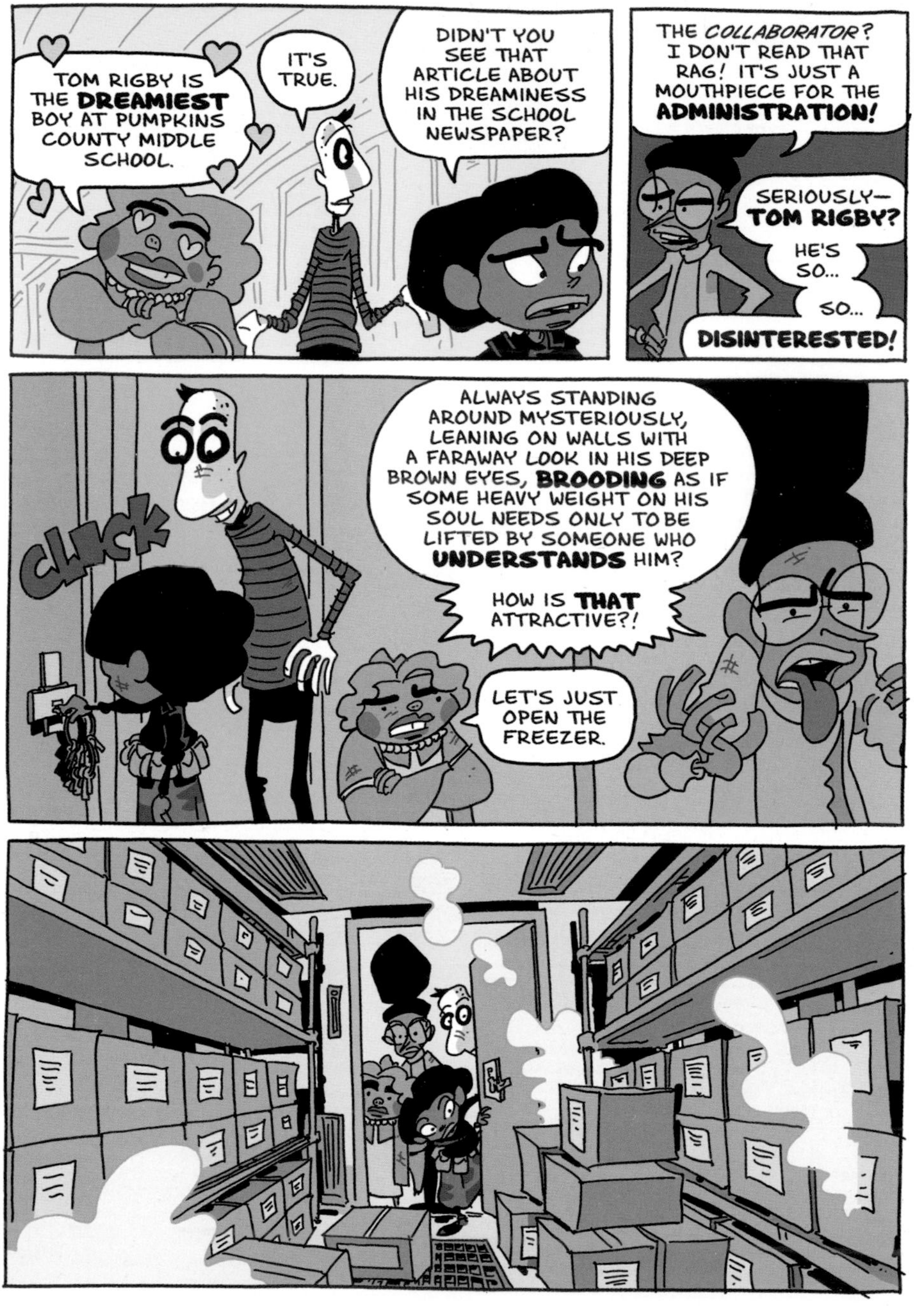
TOM RIGBY IS THE **DREAMIEST** BOY AT PUMPKINS COUNTY MIDDLE SCHOOL.
IT'S TRUE.
DIDN'T YOU SEE THAT ARTICLE ABOUT HIS DREAMINESS IN THE SCHOOL NEWSPAPER?
THE *COLLABORATOR*? I DON'T READ THAT RAG! IT'S JUST A MOUTHPIECE FOR THE **ADMINISTRATION!**
SERIOUSLY— **TOM RIGBY?**
HE'S SO...
SO...
DISINTERESTED!
CLICK
ALWAYS STANDING AROUND MYSTERIOUSLY, LEANING ON WALLS WITH A FARAWAY LOOK IN HIS DEEP BROWN EYES, **BROODING** AS IF SOME HEAVY WEIGHT ON HIS SOUL NEEDS ONLY TO BE LIFTED BY SOMEONE WHO **UNDERSTANDS** HIM?
HOW IS **THAT** ATTRACTIVE?!
LET'S JUST OPEN THE FREEZER.

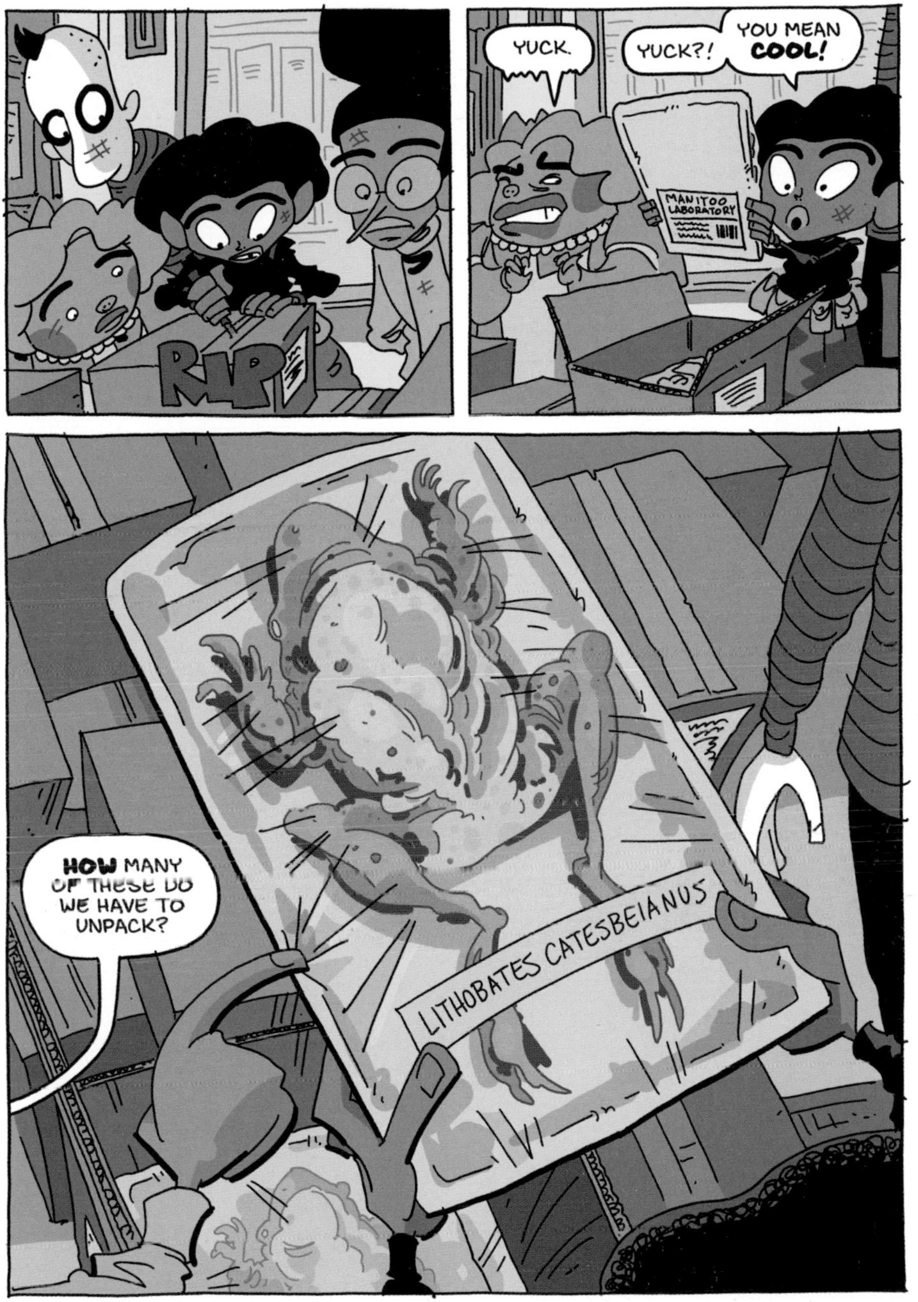
RIP
YUCK.
YUCK?!
YOU MEAN COOL!
MANITOO LABORATORY
HOW MANY OF THESE DO WE HAVE TO UNPACK?
LITHOBATES CATESBEIANUS

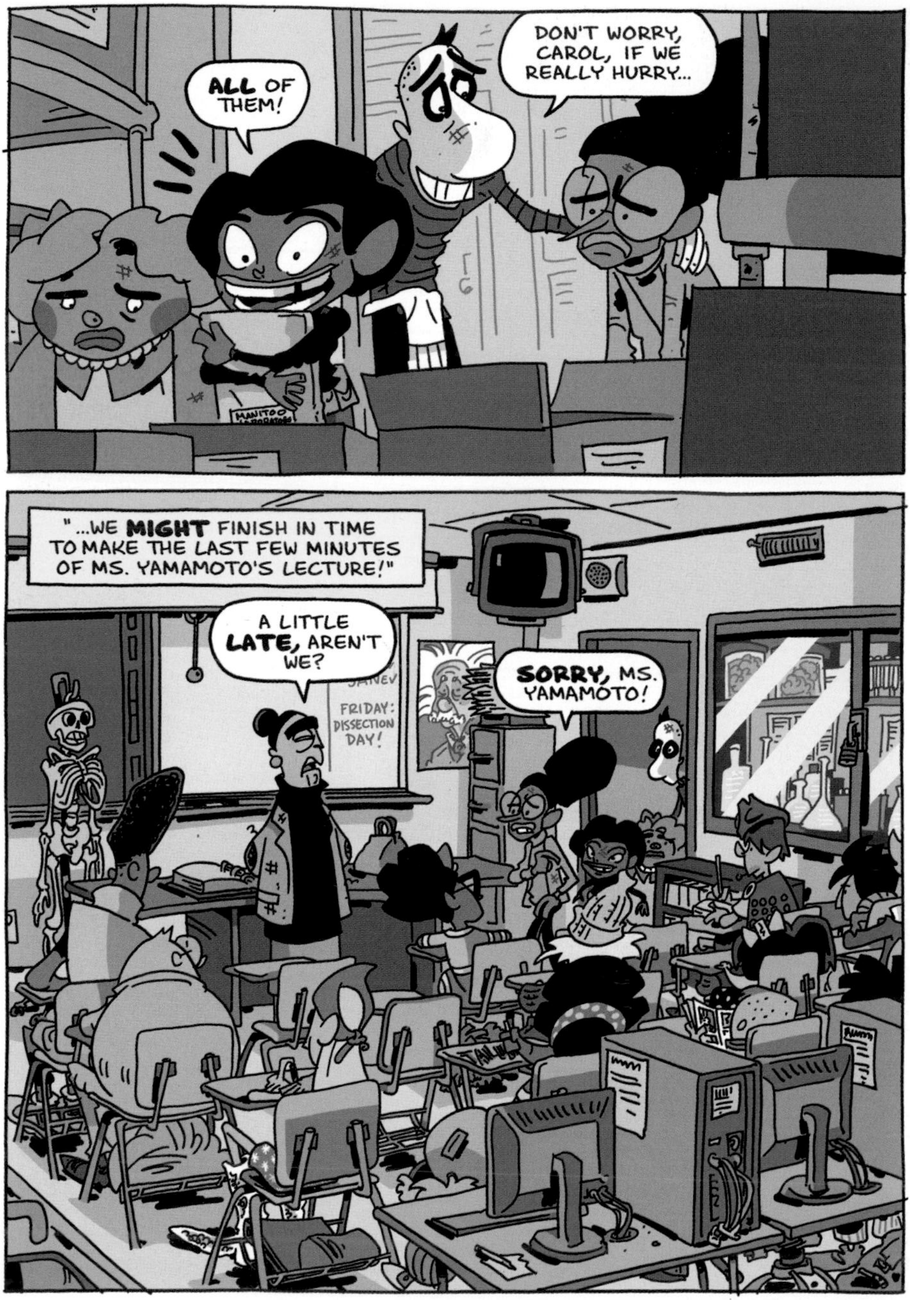
ALL OF THEM!
DON'T WORRY, CAROL, IF WE REALLY HURRY...
"...WE **MIGHT** FINISH IN TIME TO MAKE THE LAST FEW MINUTES OF MS. YAMAMOTO'S LECTURE!"
A LITTLE **LATE,** AREN'T WE?
FRIDAY: DISSECTION DAY!
SORRY, MS. YAMAMOTO!

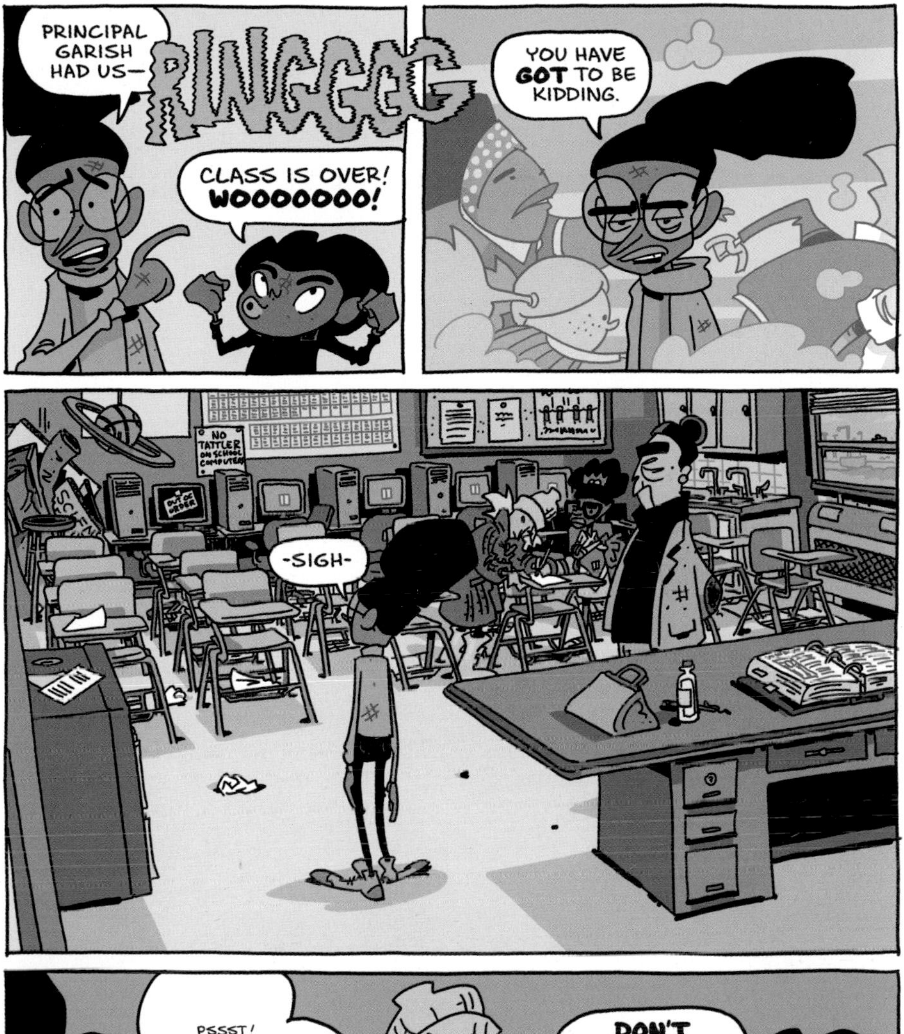
PRINCIPAL GARISH HAD US—
RINGGGG
CLASS IS OVER! WOOOOOOO!
YOU HAVE GOT TO BE KIDDING.
NO TATTLER ON SCHOOL COMPUTERS
-SIGH-
PSSST!
HEY, SIGN THIS!
DON'T GIVE THAT TO THEM!

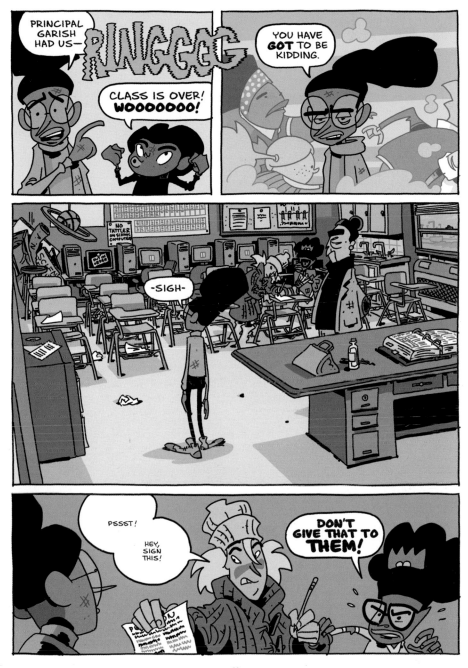

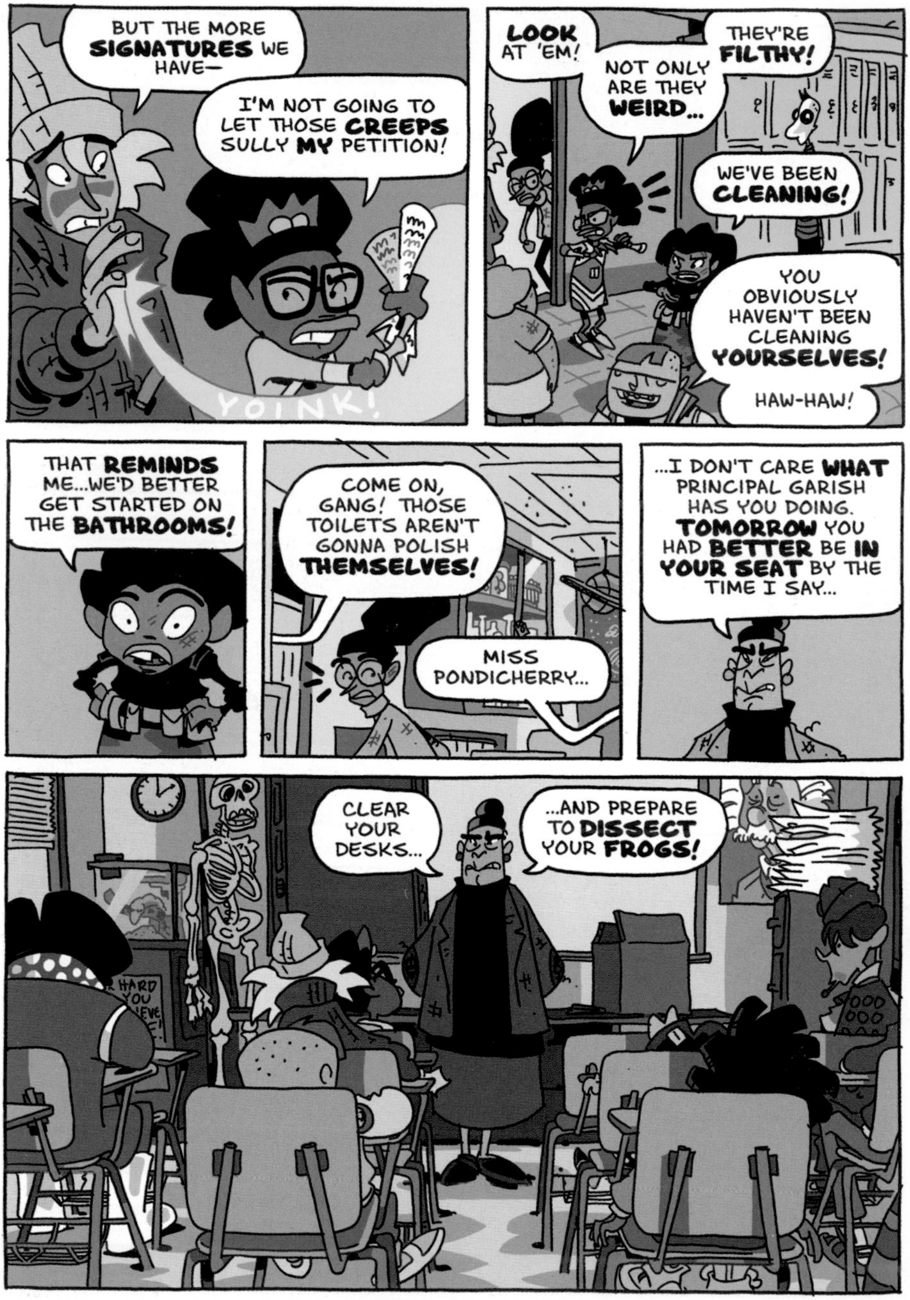
BUT THE MORE **SIGNATURES** WE HAVE—
I'M NOT GOING TO LET THOSE **CREEPS** SULLY **MY** PETITION!
YOINK!
LOOK AT 'EM!
NOT ONLY ARE THEY **WEIRD**...
THEY'RE **FILTHY**!
WE'VE BEEN **CLEANING**!
YOU OBVIOUSLY HAVEN'T BEEN CLEANING **YOURSELVES**!
HAW-HAW!
THAT **REMINDS** ME...WE'D BETTER GET STARTED ON THE **BATHROOMS**!
COME ON, GANG! THOSE TOILETS AREN'T GONNA POLISH **THEMSELVES**!
MISS PONDICHERRY...
...I DON'T CARE **WHAT** PRINCIPAL GARISH HAS YOU DOING. **TOMORROW** YOU HAD **BETTER** BE **IN YOUR SEAT** BY THE TIME I SAY...
CLEAR YOUR DESKS...
...AND PREPARE TO **DISSECT** YOUR **FROGS**!

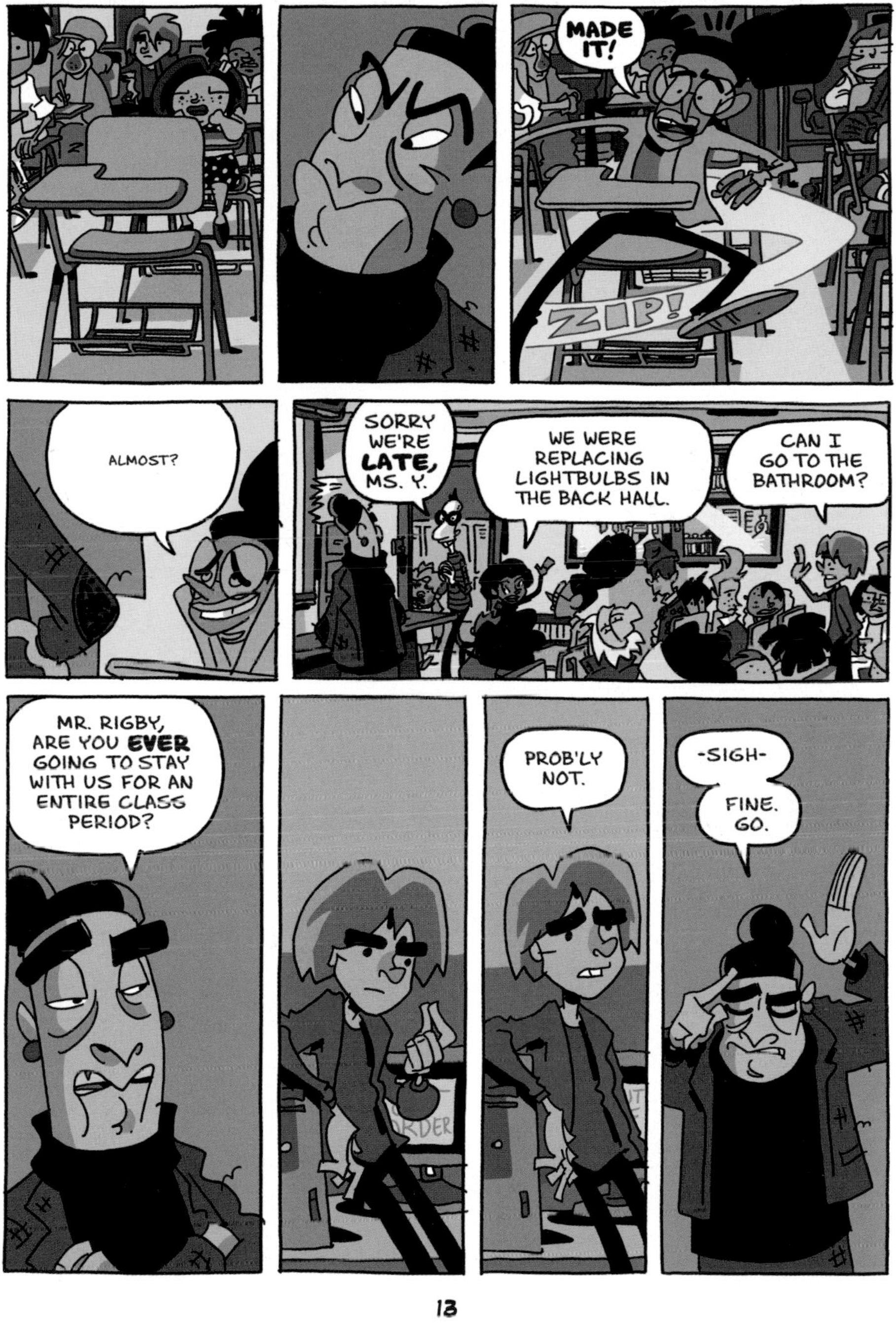

MADE IT!
ZIP!
ALMOST?
SORRY WE'RE **LATE,** MS. Y.
WE WERE REPLACING LIGHTBULBS IN THE BACK HALL.
CAN I GO TO THE BATHROOM?
MR. RIGBY, ARE YOU **EVER** GOING TO STAY WITH US FOR AN ENTIRE CLASS PERIOD?
PROB'LY NOT.
-SIGH-
FINE. GO.

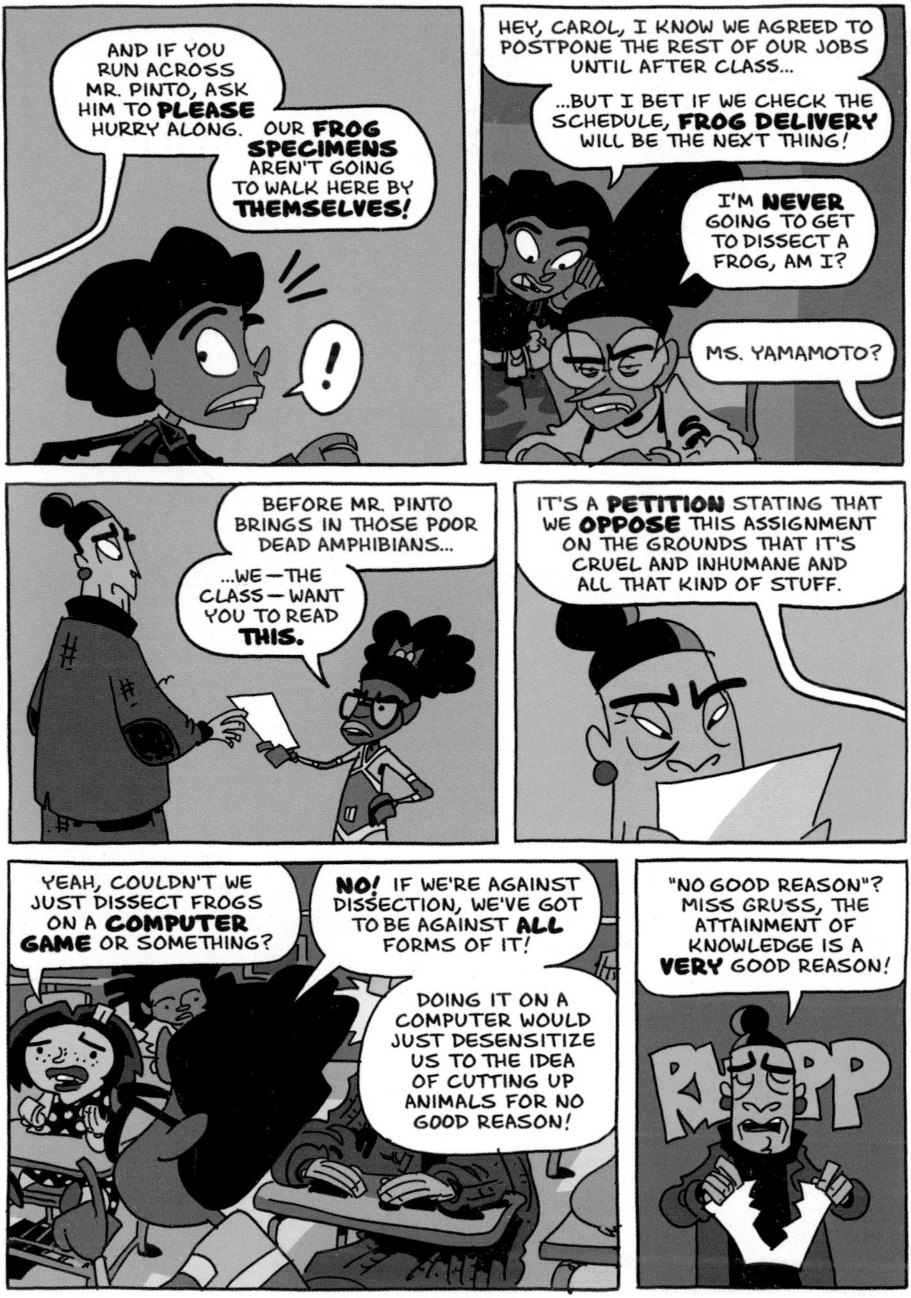
AND IF YOU RUN ACROSS MR. PINTO, ASK HIM TO **PLEASE** HURRY ALONG.
OUR **FROG SPECIMENS** AREN'T GOING TO WALK HERE BY **THEMSELVES!**
!
HEY, CAROL, I KNOW WE AGREED TO POSTPONE THE REST OF OUR JOBS UNTIL AFTER CLASS...
...BUT I BET IF WE CHECK THE SCHEDULE, **FROG DELIVERY** WILL BE THE NEXT THING!
I'M **NEVER** GOING TO GET TO DISSECT A FROG, AM I?
MS. YAMAMOTO?
BEFORE MR. PINTO BRINGS IN THOSE POOR DEAD AMPHIBIANS...
...WE—THE CLASS—WANT YOU TO READ **THIS.**
IT'S A **PETITION** STATING THAT WE **OPPOSE** THIS ASSIGNMENT ON THE GROUNDS THAT IT'S CRUEL AND INHUMANE AND ALL THAT KIND OF STUFF.
YEAH, COULDN'T WE JUST DISSECT FROGS ON A **COMPUTER GAME** OR SOMETHING?
NO! IF WE'RE AGAINST DISSECTION, WE'VE GOT TO BE AGAINST **ALL** FORMS OF IT!
DOING IT ON A COMPUTER WOULD JUST DESENSITIZE US TO THE IDEA OF CUTTING UP ANIMALS FOR NO GOOD REASON!
"NO GOOD REASON"? MISS GRUSS, THE ATTAINMENT OF KNOWLEDGE IS A **VERY** GOOD REASON!
RIPPP

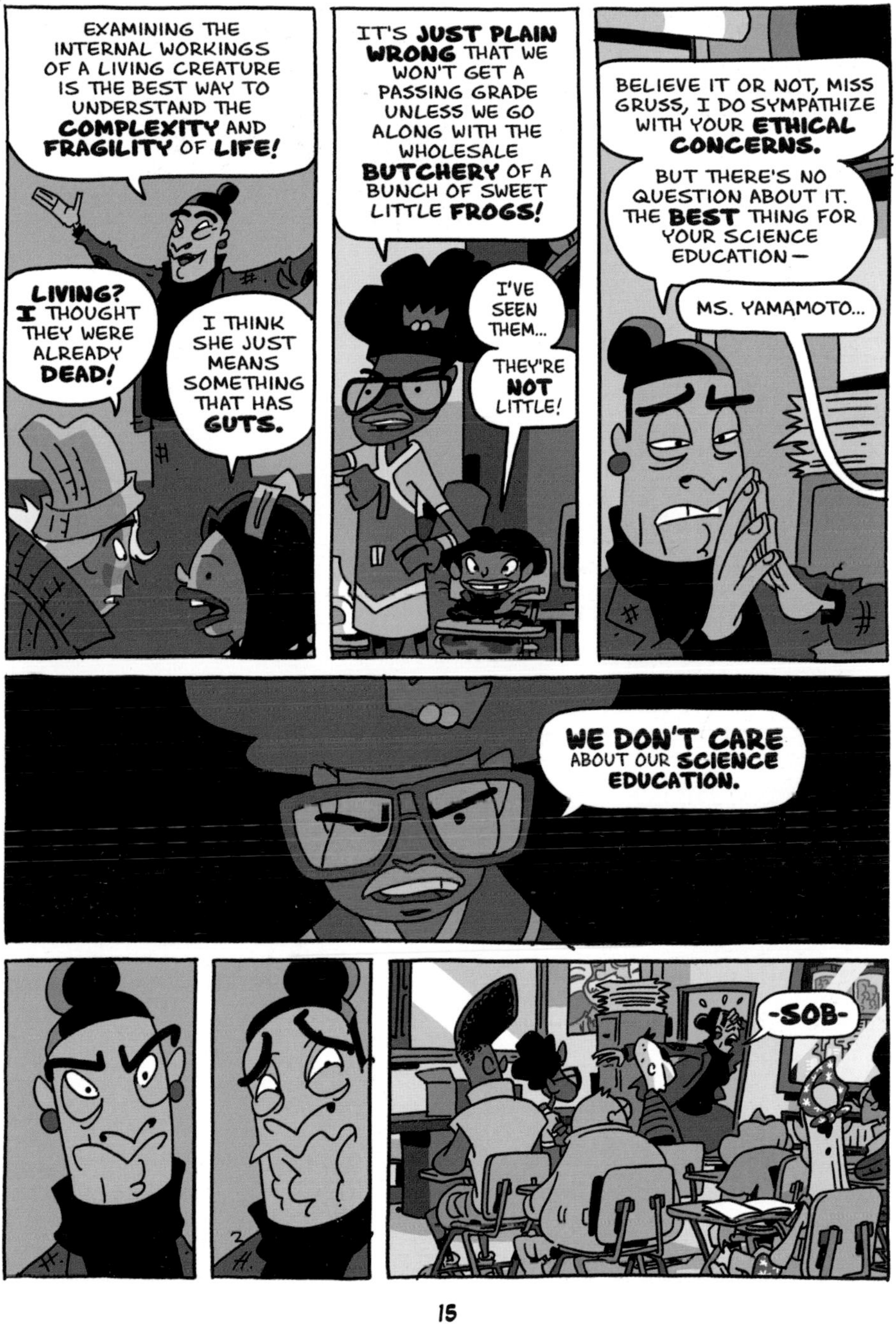
EXAMINING THE INTERNAL WORKINGS OF A LIVING CREATURE IS THE BEST WAY TO UNDERSTAND THE COMPLEXITY AND FRAGILITY OF LIFE!
LIVING? I THOUGHT THEY WERE ALREADY DEAD!
I THINK SHE JUST MEANS SOMETHING THAT HAS GUTS.
IT'S JUST PLAIN WRONG THAT WE WON'T GET A PASSING GRADE UNLESS WE GO ALONG WITH THE WHOLESALE BUTCHERY OF A BUNCH OF SWEET LITTLE FROGS!
I'VE SEEN THEM...
THEY'RE NOT LITTLE!
BELIEVE IT OR NOT, MISS GRUSS, I DO SYMPATHIZE WITH YOUR ETHICAL CONCERNS.
BUT THERE'S NO QUESTION ABOUT IT. THE BEST THING FOR YOUR SCIENCE EDUCATION—
MS. YAMAMOTO...
WE DON'T CARE ABOUT OUR SCIENCE EDUCATION.
-SOB-

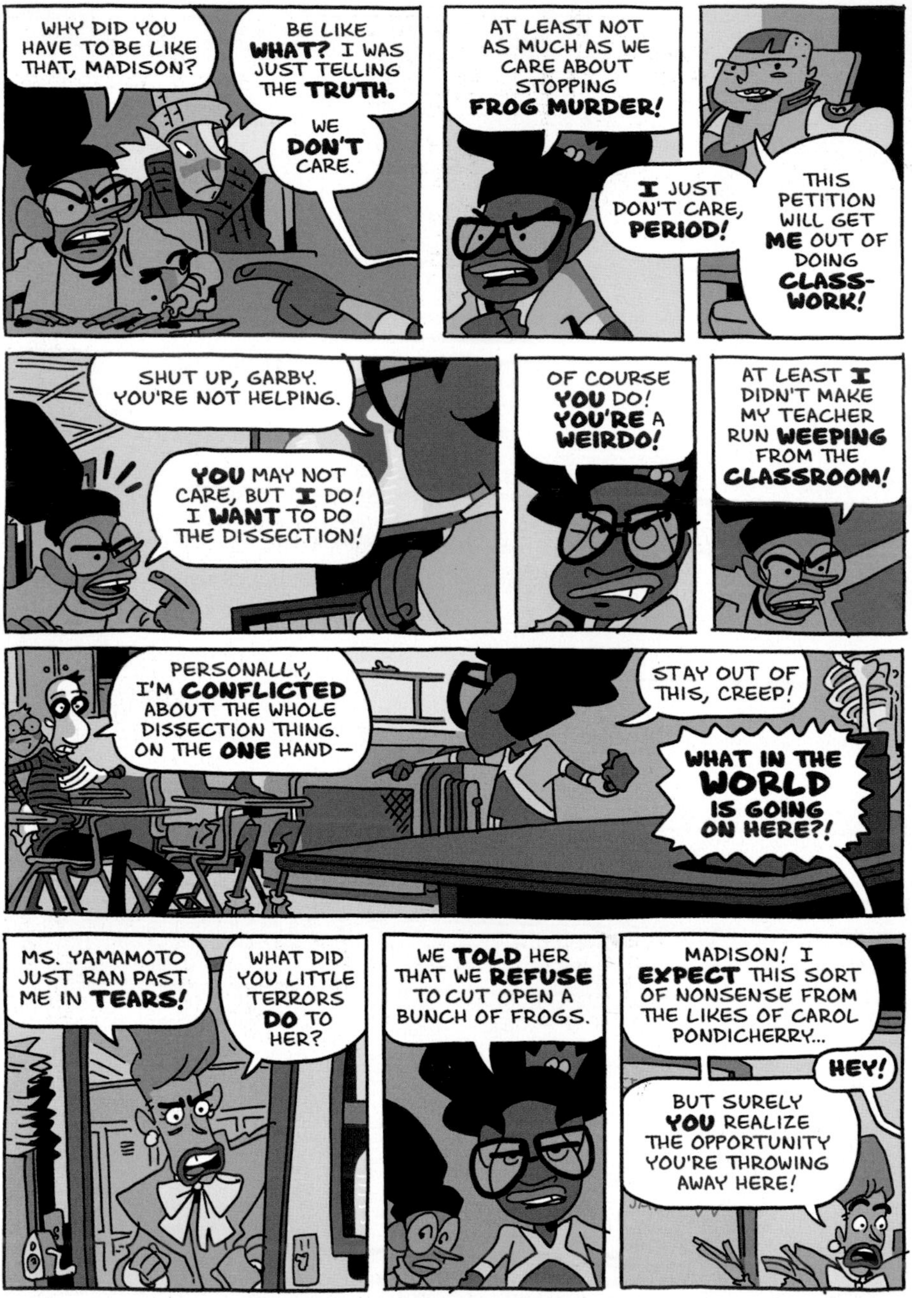
WHY DID YOU HAVE TO BE LIKE THAT, MADISON?
BE LIKE WHAT? I WAS JUST TELLING THE TRUTH.
WE DON'T CARE.
AT LEAST NOT AS MUCH AS WE CARE ABOUT STOPPING FROG MURDER!
I JUST DON'T CARE, PERIOD!
THIS PETITION WILL GET ME OUT OF DOING CLASS-WORK!
SHUT UP, GARBY. YOU'RE NOT HELPING.
YOU MAY NOT CARE, BUT I DO! I WANT TO DO THE DISSECTION!
OF COURSE YOU DO! YOU'RE A WEIRDO!
AT LEAST I DIDN'T MAKE MY TEACHER RUN WEEPING FROM THE CLASSROOM!
PERSONALLY, I'M CONFLICTED ABOUT THE WHOLE DISSECTION THING. ON THE ONE HAND—
STAY OUT OF THIS, CREEP!
WHAT IN THE WORLD IS GOING ON HERE?!
MS. YAMAMOTO JUST RAN PAST ME IN TEARS!
WHAT DID YOU LITTLE TERRORS DO TO HER?
WE TOLD HER THAT WE REFUSE TO CUT OPEN A BUNCH OF FROGS.
MADISON! I EXPECT THIS SORT OF NONSENSE FROM THE LIKES OF CAROL PONDICHERRY...
HEY!
BUT SURELY YOU REALIZE THE OPPORTUNITY YOU'RE THROWING AWAY HERE!

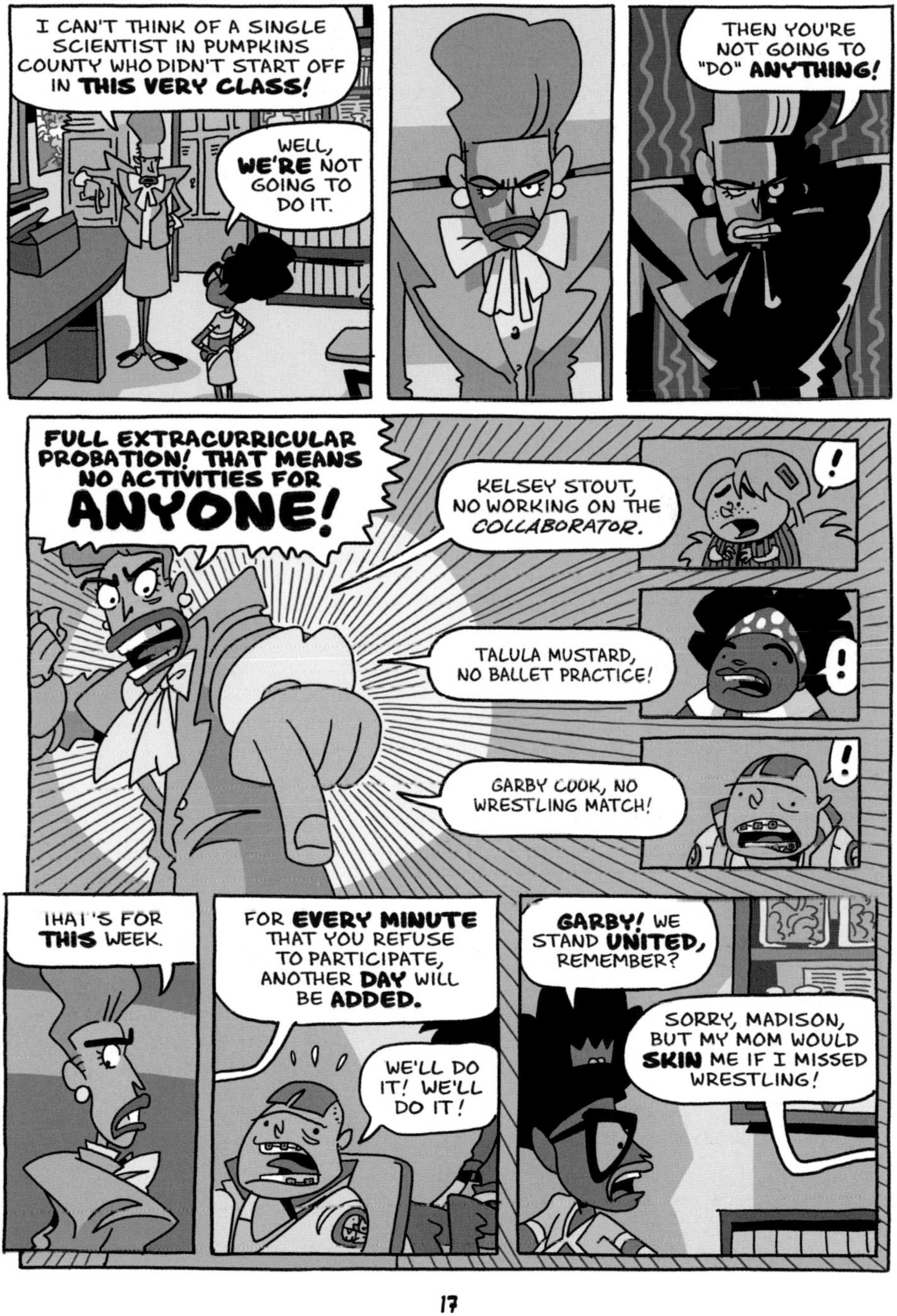
I CAN'T THINK OF A SINGLE SCIENTIST IN PUMPKINS COUNTY WHO DIDN'T START OFF IN **THIS VERY CLASS!**
WELL, **WE'RE** NOT GOING TO DO IT.
THEN YOU'RE NOT GOING TO "DO" **ANYTHING!**
FULL EXTRACURRICULAR PROBATION! THAT MEANS NO ACTIVITIES FOR ANYONE!
KELSEY STOUT, NO WORKING ON THE *COLLABORATOR*.
!
TALULA MUSTARD, NO BALLET PRACTICE!
!
GARBY COOK, NO WRESTLING MATCH!
!
THAT'S FOR **THIS** WEEK.
FOR **EVERY MINUTE** THAT YOU REFUSE TO PARTICIPATE, ANOTHER **DAY** WILL BE **ADDED.**
WE'LL DO IT! WE'LL DO IT!
GARBY! WE STAND **UNITED,** REMEMBER?
SORRY, MADISON, BUT MY MOM WOULD **SKIN** ME IF I MISSED WRESTLING!

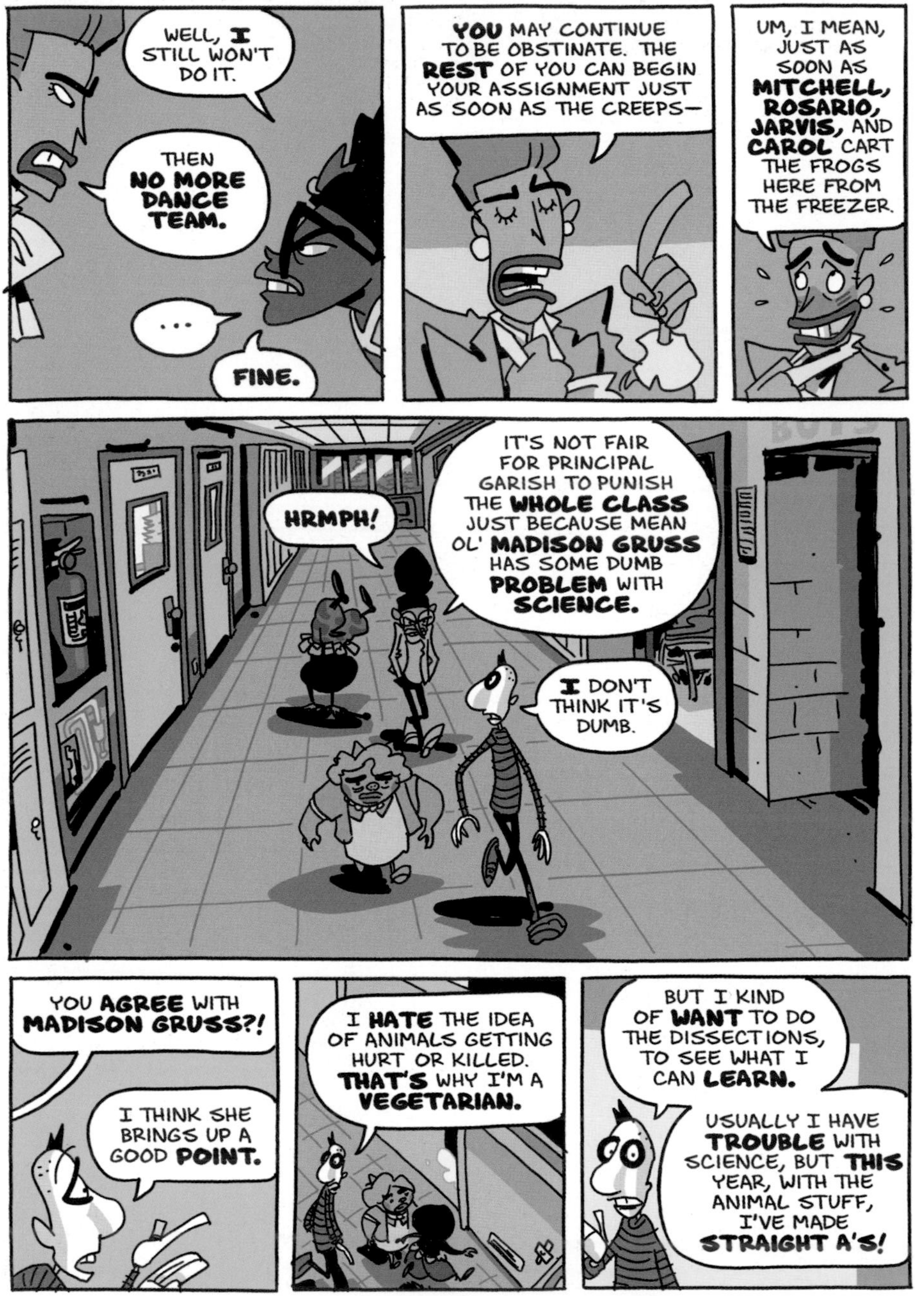
WELL, I STILL WON'T DO IT.
THEN NO MORE DANCE TEAM.
...
FINE.
YOU MAY CONTINUE TO BE OBSTINATE. THE REST OF YOU CAN BEGIN YOUR ASSIGNMENT JUST AS SOON AS THE CREEPS—
UM, I MEAN, JUST AS SOON AS MITCHELL, ROSARIO, JARVIS, AND CAROL CART THE FROGS HERE FROM THE FREEZER.
HRMPH!
IT'S NOT FAIR FOR PRINCIPAL GARISH TO PUNISH THE WHOLE CLASS JUST BECAUSE MEAN OL' MADISON GRUSS HAS SOME DUMB PROBLEM WITH SCIENCE.
I DON'T THINK IT'S DUMB.
YOU AGREE WITH MADISON GRUSS?!
I THINK SHE BRINGS UP A GOOD POINT.
I HATE THE IDEA OF ANIMALS GETTING HURT OR KILLED. THAT'S WHY I'M A VEGETARIAN.
BUT I KIND OF WANT TO DO THE DISSECTIONS, TO SEE WHAT I CAN LEARN.
USUALLY I HAVE TROUBLE WITH SCIENCE, BUT THIS YEAR, WITH THE ANIMAL STUFF, I'VE MADE STRAIGHT A'S!

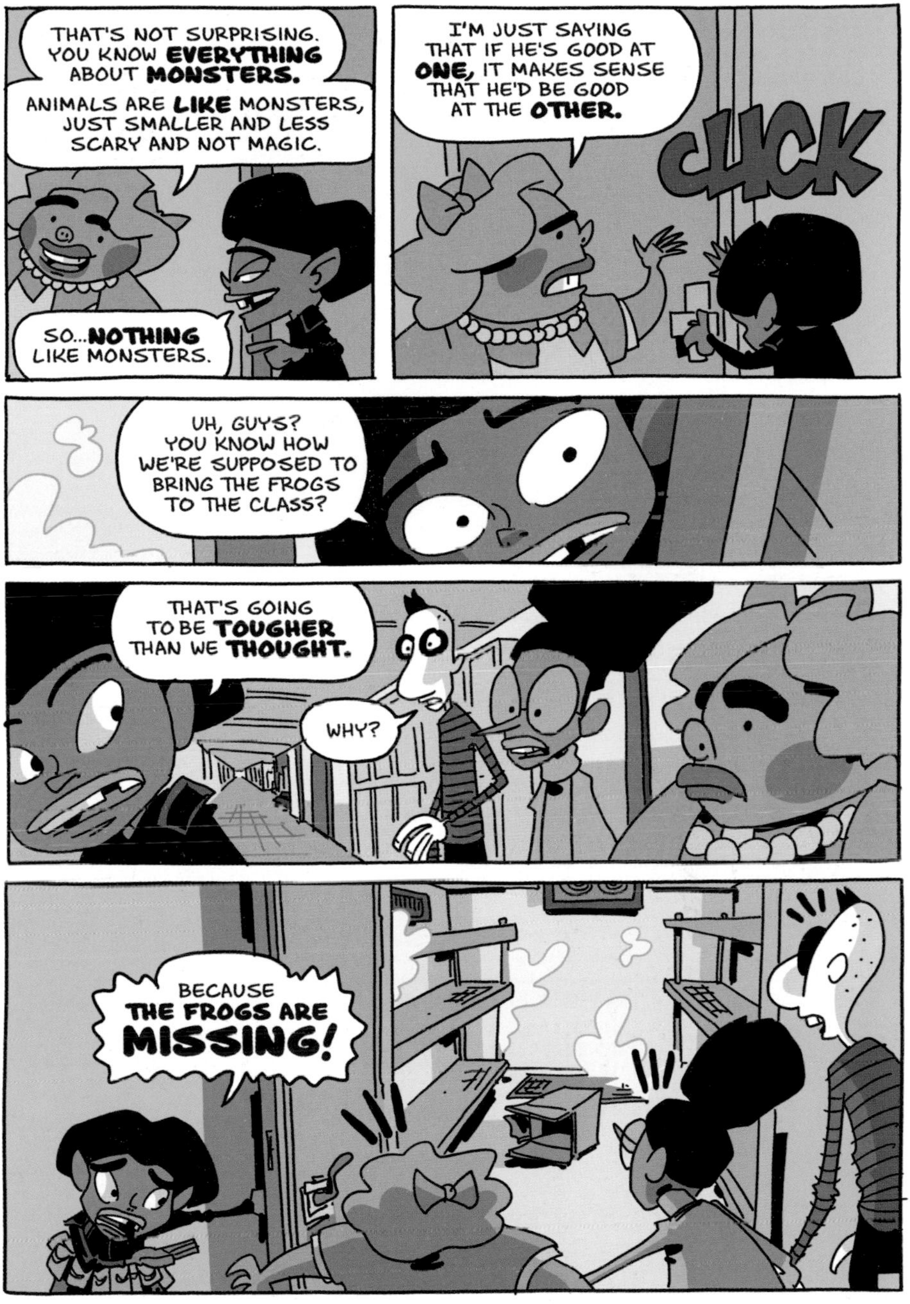
THAT'S NOT SURPRISING. YOU KNOW **EVERYTHING** ABOUT **MONSTERS.**
ANIMALS ARE **LIKE** MONSTERS, JUST SMALLER AND LESS SCARY AND NOT MAGIC.
SO... **NOTHING** LIKE MONSTERS.
I'M JUST SAYING THAT IF HE'S GOOD AT **ONE,** IT MAKES SENSE THAT HE'D BE GOOD AT THE **OTHER.**
CLICK
UH, GUYS? YOU KNOW HOW WE'RE SUPPOSED TO BRING THE FROGS TO THE CLASS?
THAT'S GOING TO BE **TOUGHER** THAN WE **THOUGHT.**
WHY?
BECAUSE **THE FROGS ARE MISSING!**

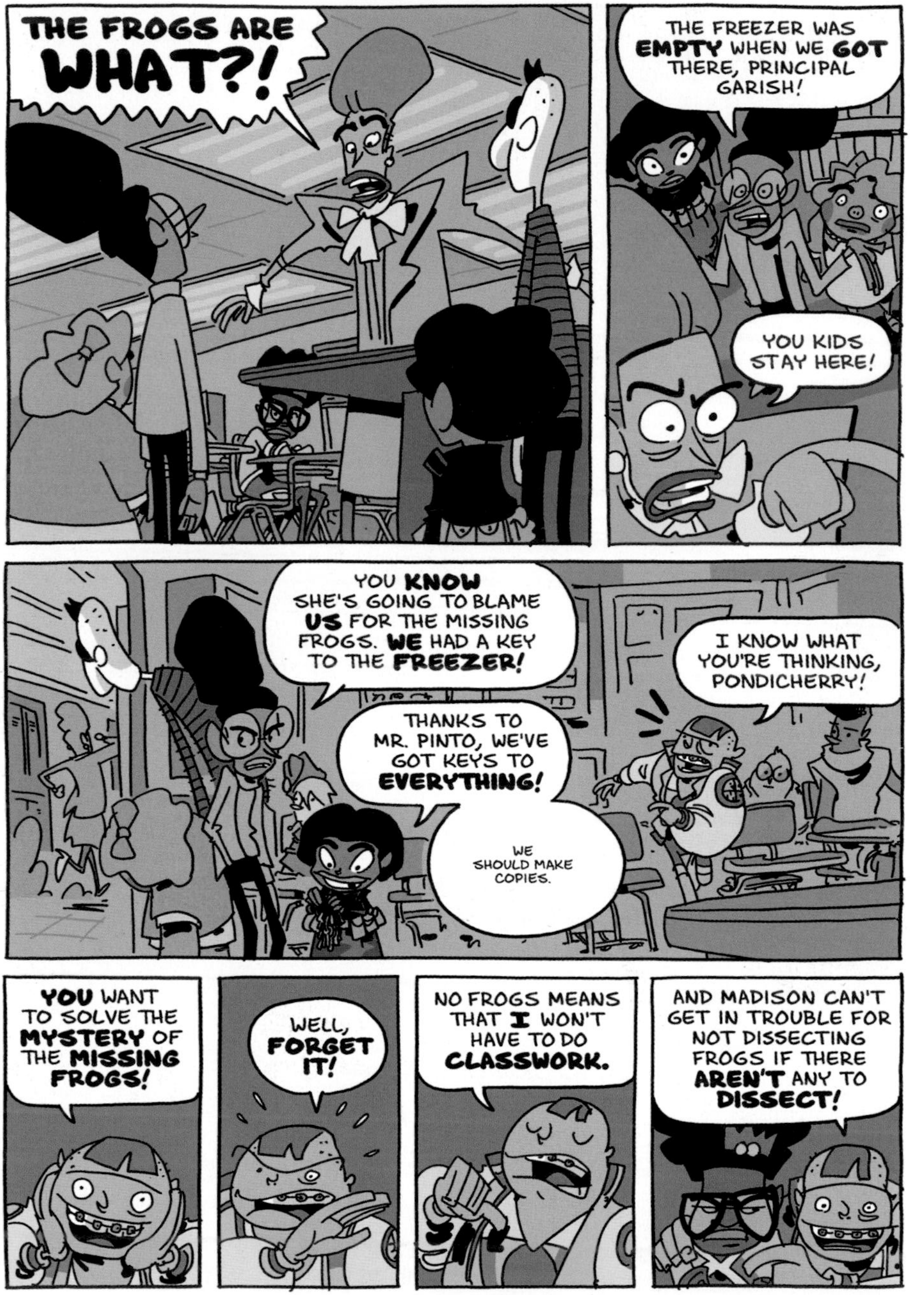
THE FROGS ARE WHAT?!
THE FREEZER WAS EMPTY WHEN WE GOT THERE, PRINCIPAL GARISH!
YOU KIDS STAY HERE!
YOU KNOW SHE'S GOING TO BLAME US FOR THE MISSING FROGS. WE HAD A KEY TO THE FREEZER!
I KNOW WHAT YOU'RE THINKING, PONDICHERRY!
THANKS TO MR. PINTO, WE'VE GOT KEYS TO EVERYTHING!
WE SHOULD MAKE COPIES.
YOU WANT TO SOLVE THE MYSTERY OF THE MISSING FROGS!
WELL, FORGET IT!
NO FROGS MEANS THAT I WON'T HAVE TO DO CLASSWORK.
AND MADISON CAN'T GET IN TROUBLE FOR NOT DISSECTING FROGS IF THERE AREN'T ANY TO DISSECT!

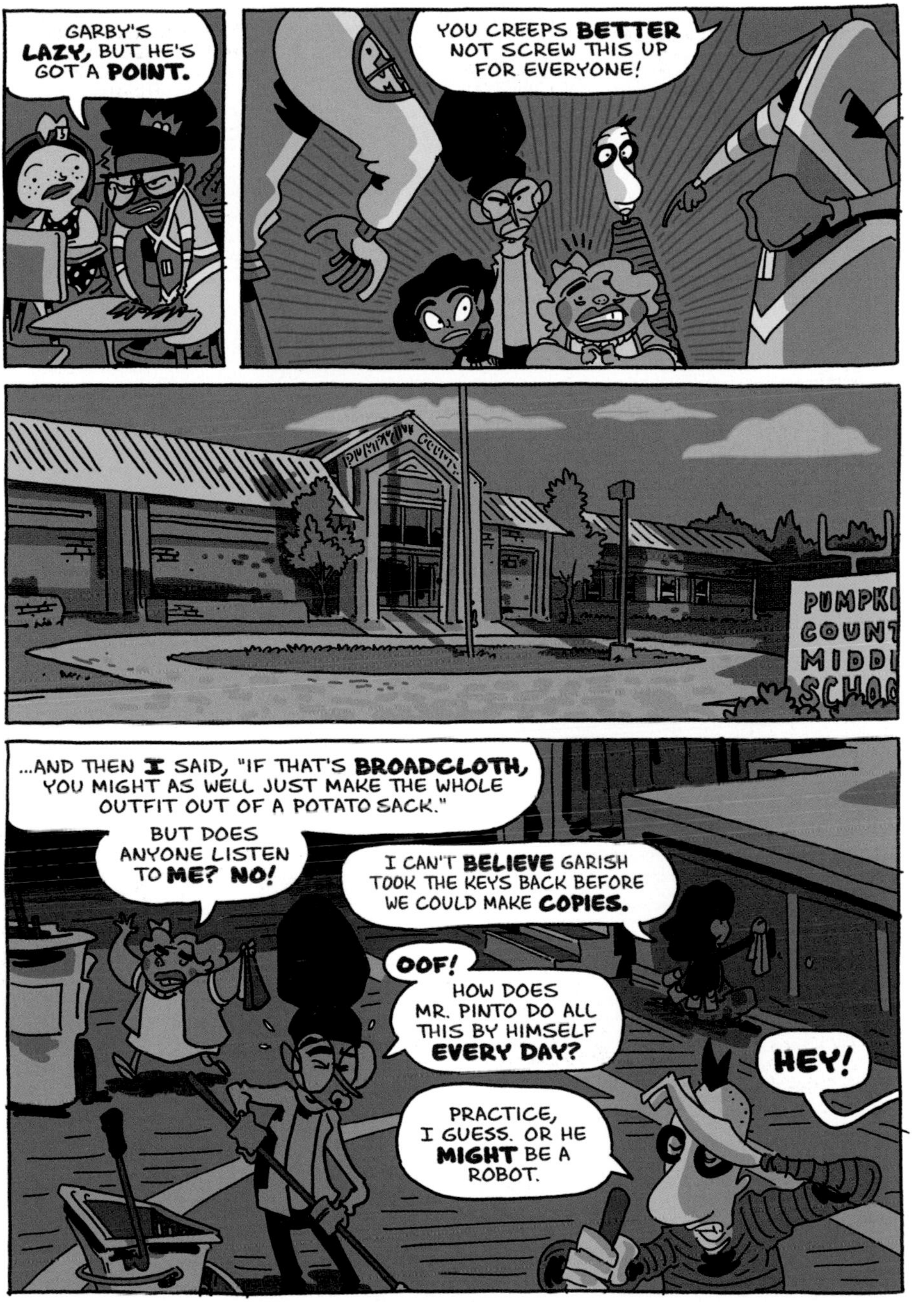
GARBY'S **LAZY,** BUT HE'S GOT A **POINT.**
YOU CREEPS **BETTER** NOT SCREW THIS UP FOR EVERYONE!
PUMPKI COUNT MIDDI SCHO
...AND THEN **I** SAID, "IF THAT'S **BROADCLOTH,** YOU MIGHT AS WELL JUST MAKE THE WHOLE OUTFIT OUT OF A POTATO SACK."
BUT DOES ANYONE LISTEN TO **ME? NO!**
I CAN'T **BELIEVE** GARISH TOOK THE KEYS BACK BEFORE WE COULD MAKE **COPIES.**
OOF!
HOW DOES MR. PINTO DO ALL THIS BY HIMSELF **EVERY DAY?**
PRACTICE, I GUESS. OR HE **MIGHT** BE A ROBOT.
HEY!

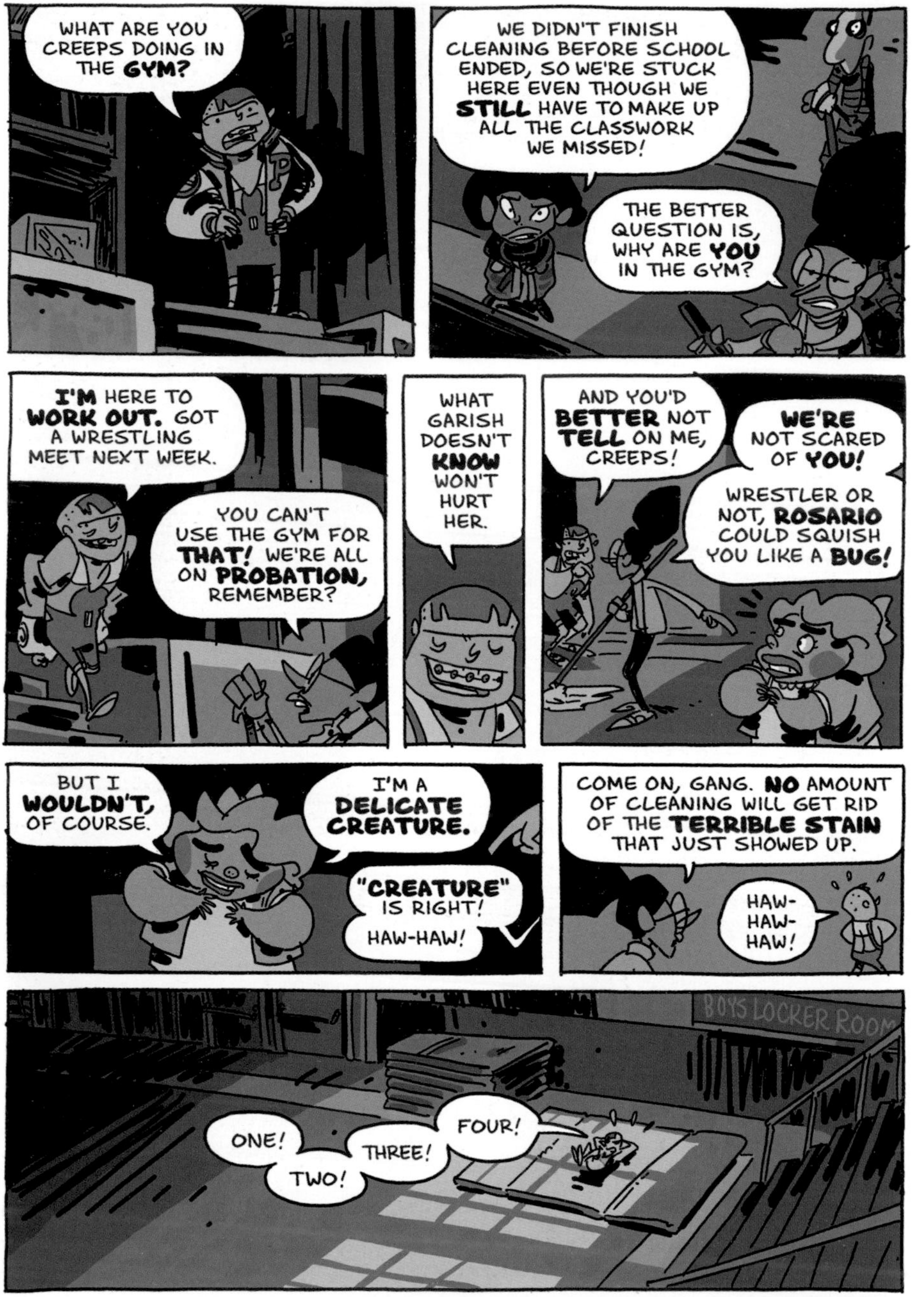
WHAT ARE YOU CREEPS DOING IN THE GYM?
WE DIDN'T FINISH CLEANING BEFORE SCHOOL ENDED, SO WE'RE STUCK HERE EVEN THOUGH WE STILL HAVE TO MAKE UP ALL THE CLASSWORK WE MISSED!
THE BETTER QUESTION IS, WHY ARE YOU IN THE GYM?
I'M HERE TO WORK OUT. GOT A WRESTLING MEET NEXT WEEK.
YOU CAN'T USE THE GYM FOR THAT! WE'RE ALL ON PROBATION, REMEMBER?
WHAT GARISH DOESN'T KNOW WON'T HURT HER.
AND YOU'D BETTER NOT TELL ON ME, CREEPS!
WE'RE NOT SCARED OF YOU!
WRESTLER OR NOT, ROSARIO COULD SQUISH YOU LIKE A BUG!
BUT I WOULDN'T, OF COURSE.
I'M A DELICATE CREATURE.
"CREATURE" IS RIGHT!
HAW-HAW!
COME ON, GANG. NO AMOUNT OF CLEANING WILL GET RID OF THE TERRIBLE STAIN THAT JUST SHOWED UP.
HAW-HAW-HAW!
BOYS LOCKER ROOM
ONE!
TWO!
THREE!
FOUR!

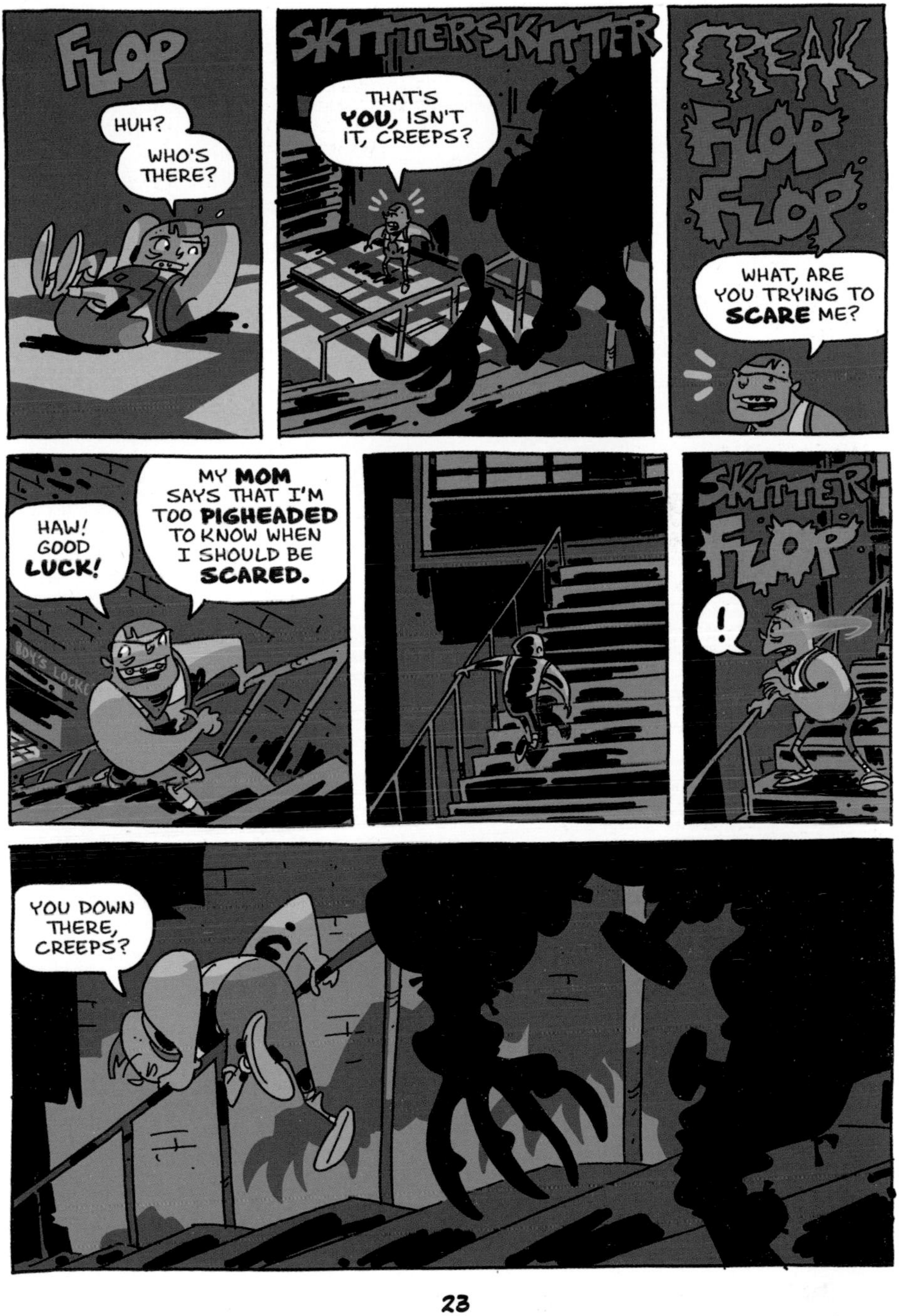
FLOP
HUH?
WHO'S THERE?
SKITTERSKITTER
THAT'S YOU, ISN'T IT, CREEPS?
CREAK
FLOP
FLOP
WHAT, ARE YOU TRYING TO SCARE ME?
HAW! GOOD LUCK!
MY MOM SAYS THAT I'M TOO PIGHEADED TO KNOW WHEN I SHOULD BE SCARED.
SKITTER
FLOP
!
YOU DOWN THERE, CREEPS?

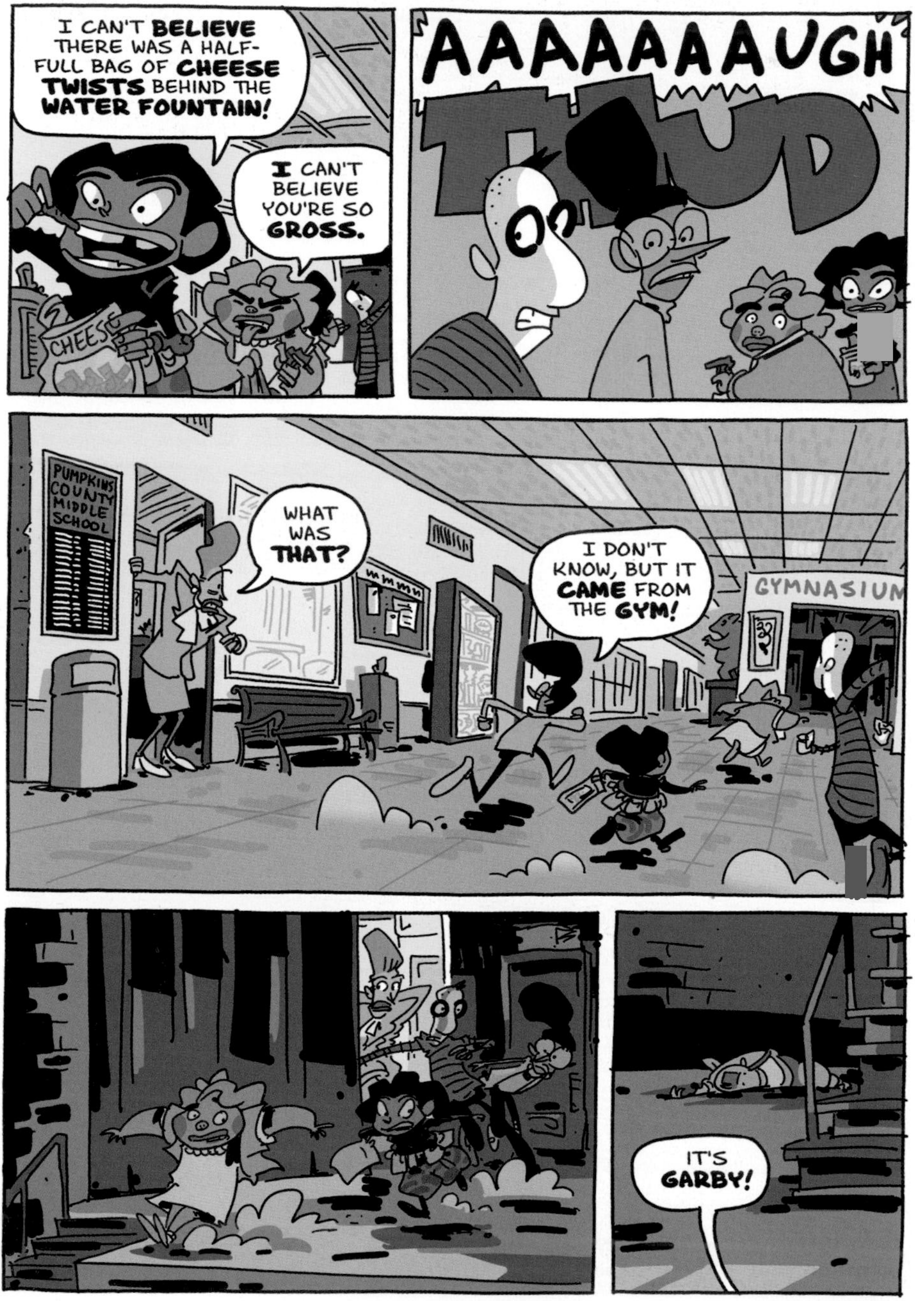
I CAN'T **BELIEVE** THERE WAS A HALF-FULL BAG OF **CHEESE TWISTS** BEHIND THE **WATER FOUNTAIN!**
I CAN'T BELIEVE YOU'RE SO **GROSS.**
CHEESE
AAAAAAAUGH
THUD
PUMPKINS COUNTY MIDDLE SCHOOL
WHAT WAS **THAT?**
I DON'T KNOW, BUT IT **CAME** FROM THE **GYM!**
GYMNASIUM
IT'S **GARBY!**

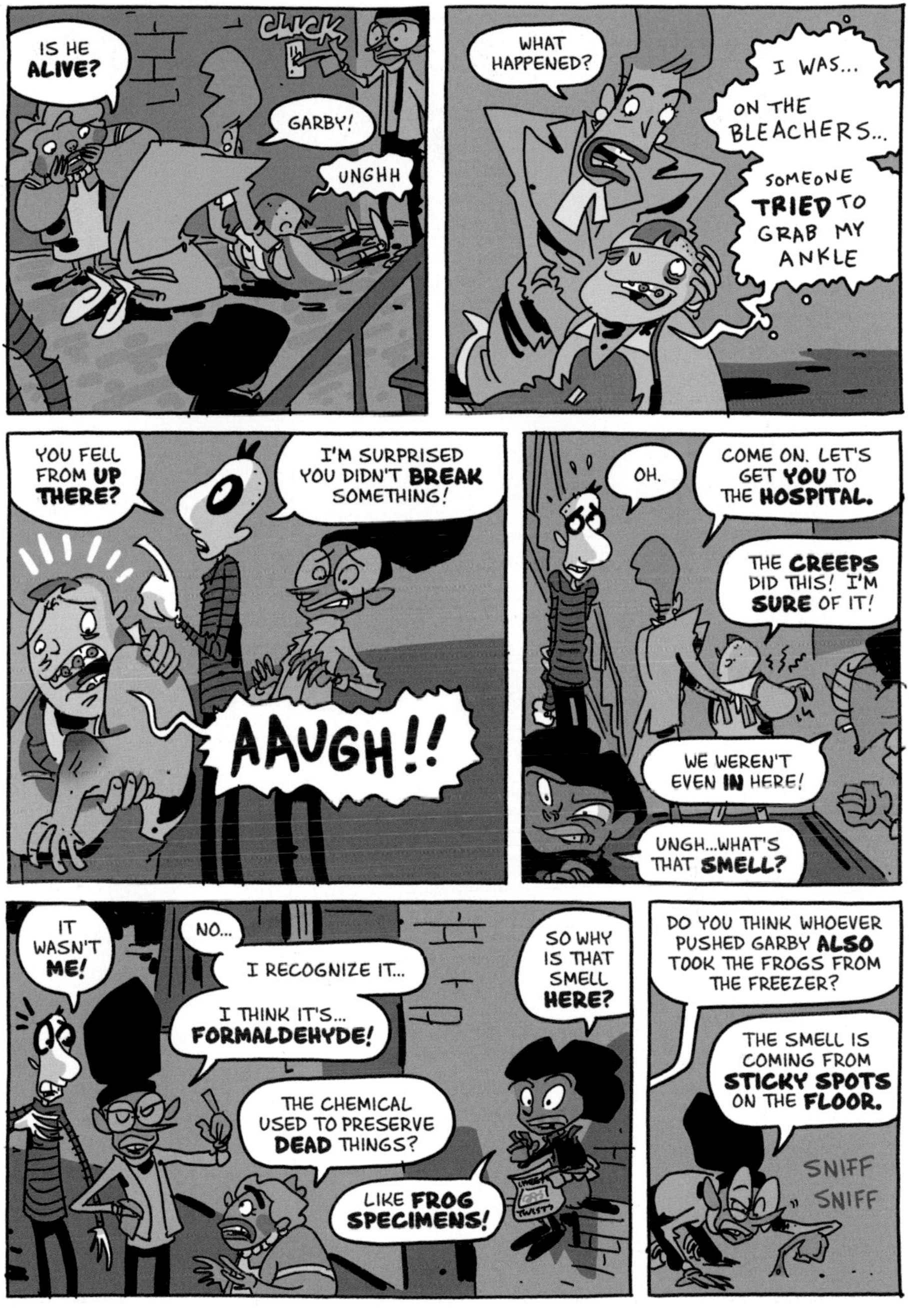

CLICK
IS HE ALIVE?
GARBY!
UNGHH
WHAT HAPPENED?
I WAS...
ON THE BLEACHERS...
SOMEONE TRIED TO GRAB MY ANKLE
YOU FELL FROM UP THERE?
I'M SURPRISED YOU DIDN'T BREAK SOMETHING!
AAUGH!!
OH.
COME ON. LET'S GET YOU TO THE HOSPITAL.
THE CREEPS DID THIS! I'M SURE OF IT!
WE WEREN'T EVEN IN HERE!
UNGH...WHAT'S THAT SMELL?
IT WASN'T ME!
NO...
I RECOGNIZE IT...
I THINK IT'S... FORMALDEHYDE!
THE CHEMICAL USED TO PRESERVE DEAD THINGS?
LIKE FROG SPECIMENS!
SO WHY IS THAT SMELL HERE?
DO YOU THINK WHOEVER PUSHED GARBY ALSO TOOK THE FROGS FROM THE FREEZER?
THE SMELL IS COMING FROM STICKY SPOTS ON THE FLOOR.
SNIFF SNIFF

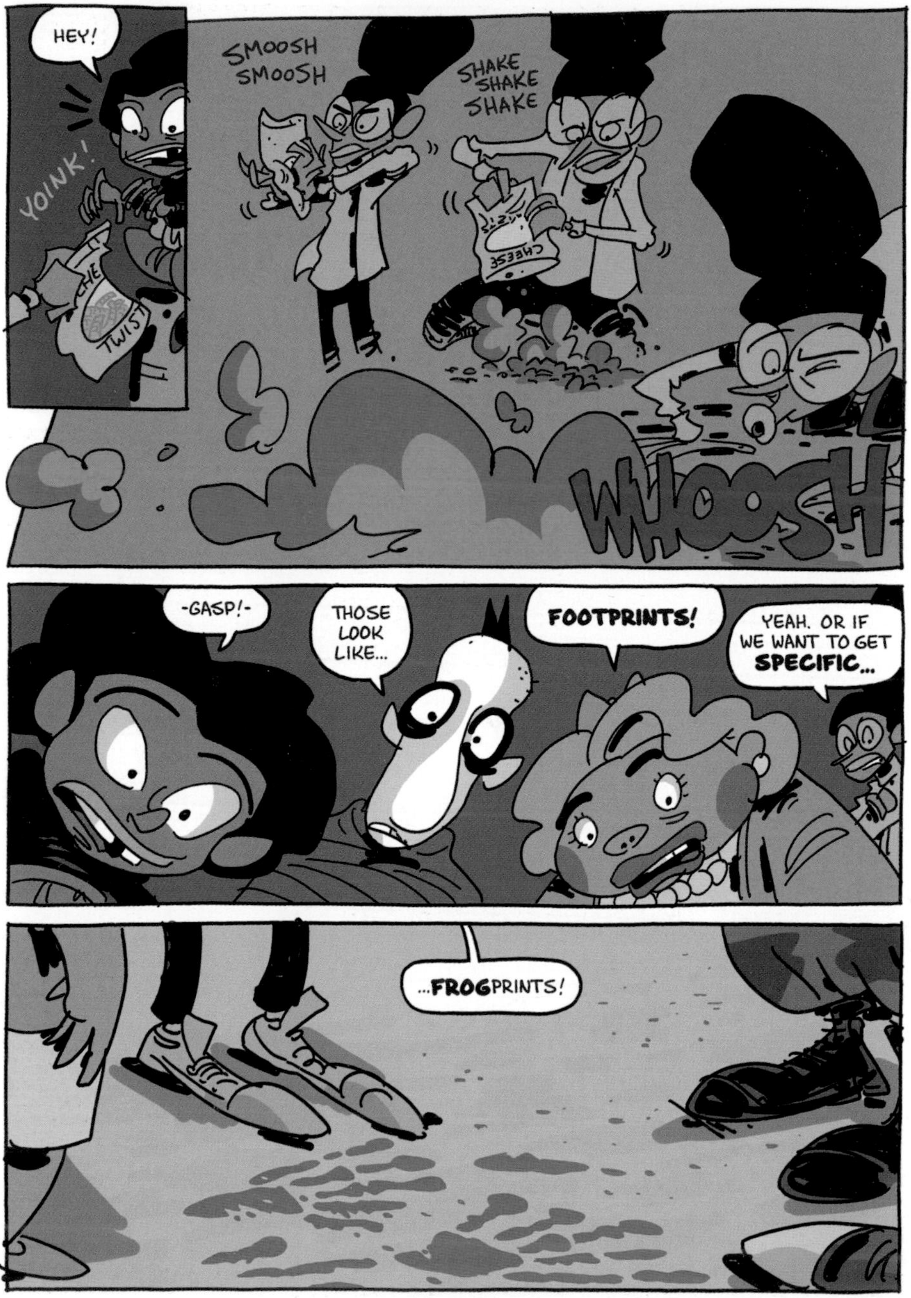
HEY!
YOINK!
SMOOSH
SMOOSH
SHAKE
SHAKE
SHAKE
WHOOSH
-GASP!-
THOSE LOOK LIKE...
FOOTPRINTS!
YEAH. OR IF WE WANT TO GET **SPECIFIC...**
...**FROG**PRINTS!

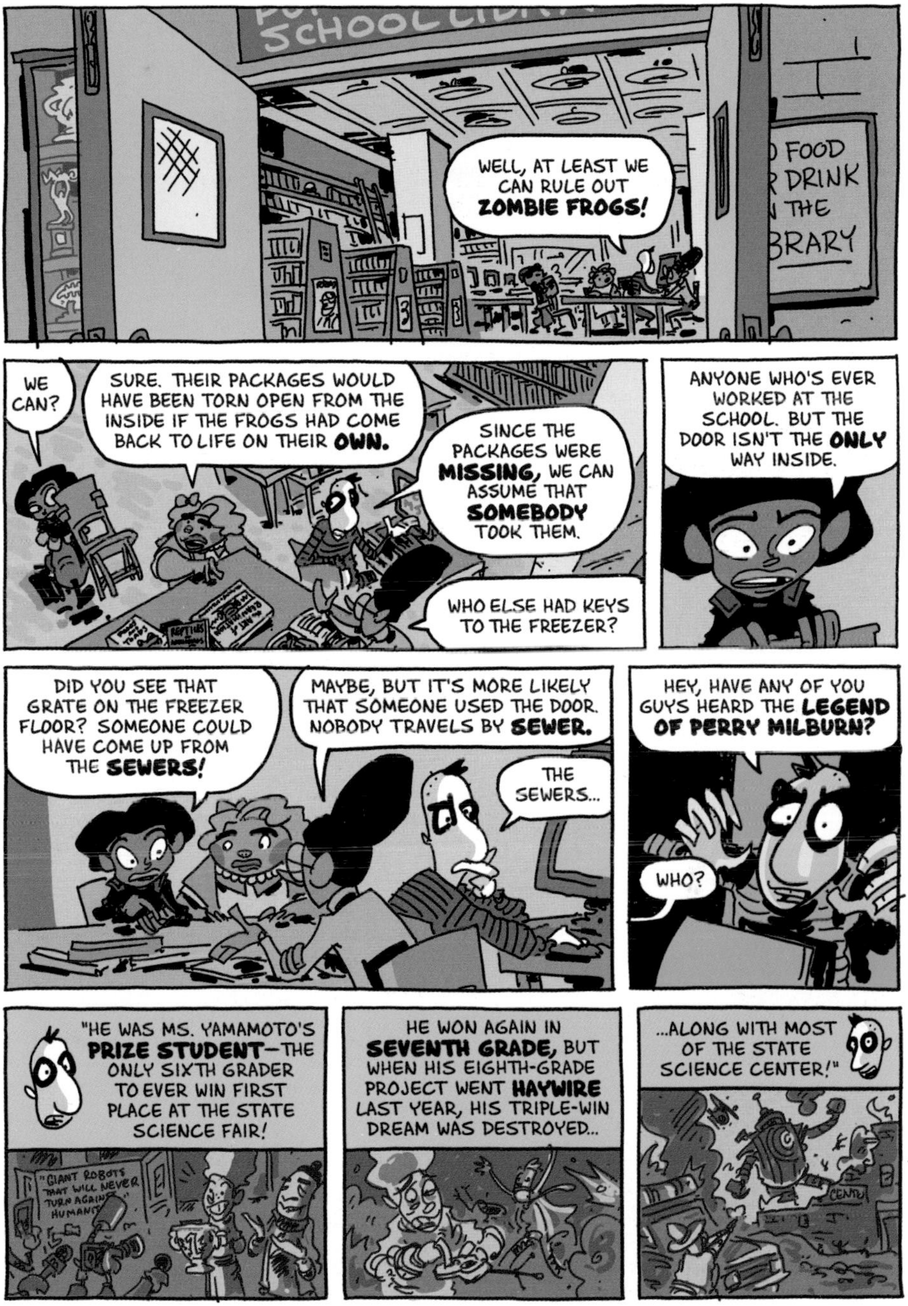
SCHOOL LIBR
D FOOD
R DRINK
N THE
BRARY
WELL, AT LEAST WE CAN RULE OUT **ZOMBIE FROGS!**
WE CAN?
SURE. THEIR PACKAGES WOULD HAVE BEEN TORN OPEN FROM THE INSIDE IF THE FROGS HAD COME BACK TO LIFE ON THEIR **OWN.**
SINCE THE PACKAGES WERE **MISSING,** WE CAN ASSUME THAT **SOMEBODY** TOOK THEM.
WHO ELSE HAD KEYS TO THE FREEZER?
ANYONE WHO'S EVER WORKED AT THE SCHOOL. BUT THE DOOR ISN'T THE **ONLY** WAY INSIDE.
DID YOU SEE THAT GRATE ON THE FREEZER FLOOR? SOMEONE COULD HAVE COME UP FROM THE **SEWERS!**
MAYBE, BUT IT'S MORE LIKELY THAT SOMEONE USED THE DOOR. NOBODY TRAVELS BY **SEWER.**
THE SEWERS...
HEY, HAVE ANY OF YOU GUYS HEARD THE **LEGEND OF PERRY MILBURN?**
WHO?
"HE WAS MS. YAMAMOTO'S **PRIZE STUDENT**—THE ONLY SIXTH GRADER TO EVER WIN FIRST PLACE AT THE STATE SCIENCE FAIR!
"GIANT ROBOTS THAT WILL NEVER TURN AGAINST HUMANITY"
HE WON AGAIN IN **SEVENTH GRADE,** BUT WHEN HIS EIGHTH-GRADE PROJECT WENT **HAYWIRE** LAST YEAR, HIS TRIPLE-WIN DREAM WAS DESTROYED...
...ALONG WITH MOST OF THE STATE SCIENCE CENTER!"

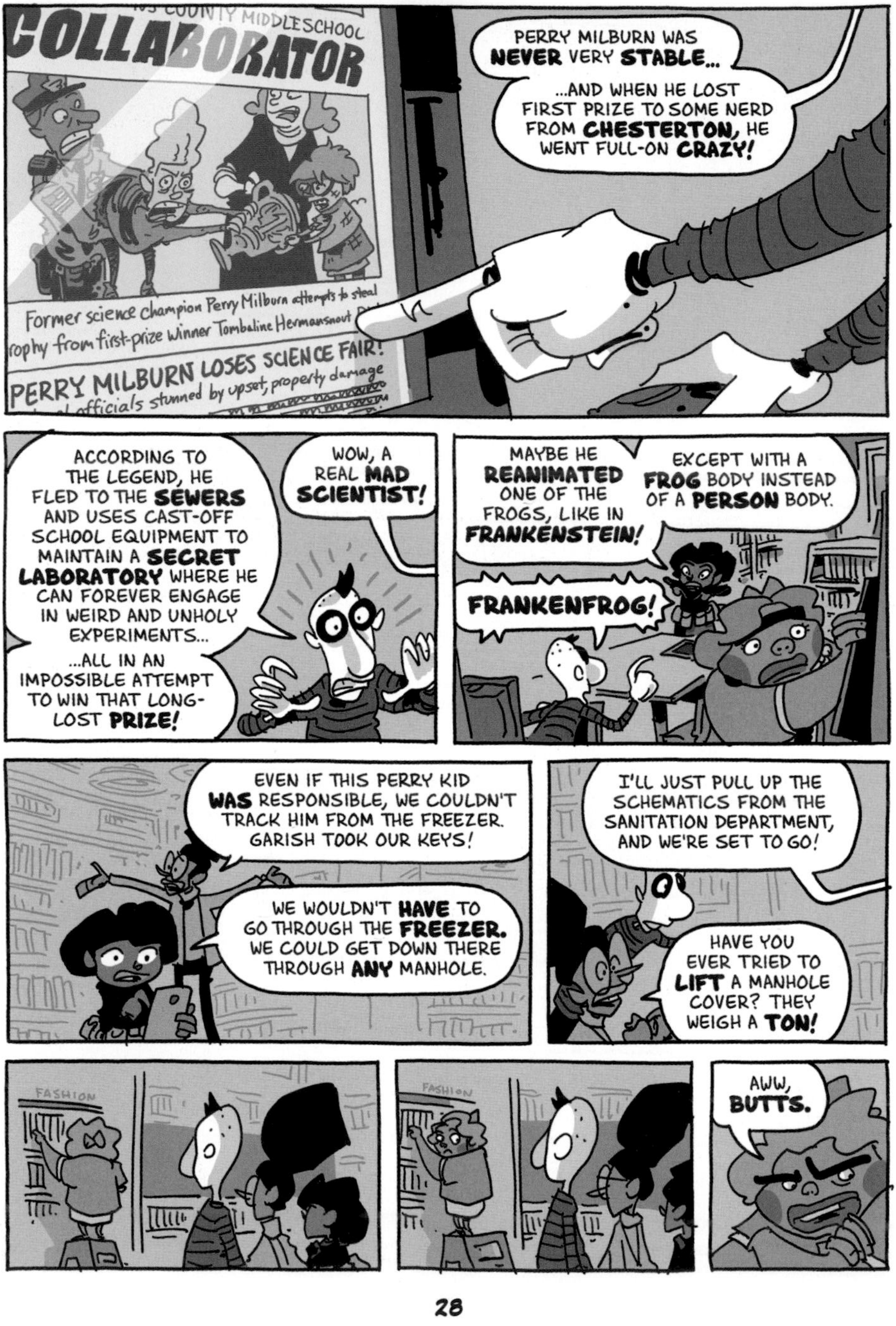
COUNTY MIDDLESCHOOL
COLLABORATOR
Former science champion Perry Milburn attempts to steal trophy from first-prize winner Tombaline Hermansnout
PERRY MILBURN LOSES SCIENCE FAIR!
officials stunned by upset, property damage
PERRY MILBURN WAS NEVER VERY STABLE...
...AND WHEN HE LOST FIRST PRIZE TO SOME NERD FROM CHESTERTON, HE WENT FULL-ON CRAZY!
ACCORDING TO THE LEGEND, HE FLED TO THE SEWERS AND USES CAST-OFF SCHOOL EQUIPMENT TO MAINTAIN A SECRET LABORATORY WHERE HE CAN FOREVER ENGAGE IN WEIRD AND UNHOLY EXPERIMENTS...
...ALL IN AN IMPOSSIBLE ATTEMPT TO WIN THAT LONG-LOST PRIZE!
WOW, A REAL MAD SCIENTIST!
MAYBE HE REANIMATED ONE OF THE FROGS, LIKE IN FRANKENSTEIN!
EXCEPT WITH A FROG BODY INSTEAD OF A PERSON BODY.
FRANKENFROG!
EVEN IF THIS PERRY KID WAS RESPONSIBLE, WE COULDN'T TRACK HIM FROM THE FREEZER. GARISH TOOK OUR KEYS!
WE WOULDN'T HAVE TO GO THROUGH THE FREEZER. WE COULD GET DOWN THERE THROUGH ANY MANHOLE.
I'LL JUST PULL UP THE SCHEMATICS FROM THE SANITATION DEPARTMENT, AND WE'RE SET TO GO!
HAVE YOU EVER TRIED TO LIFT A MANHOLE COVER? THEY WEIGH A TON!
FASHION
FASHION
AWW, BUTTS.

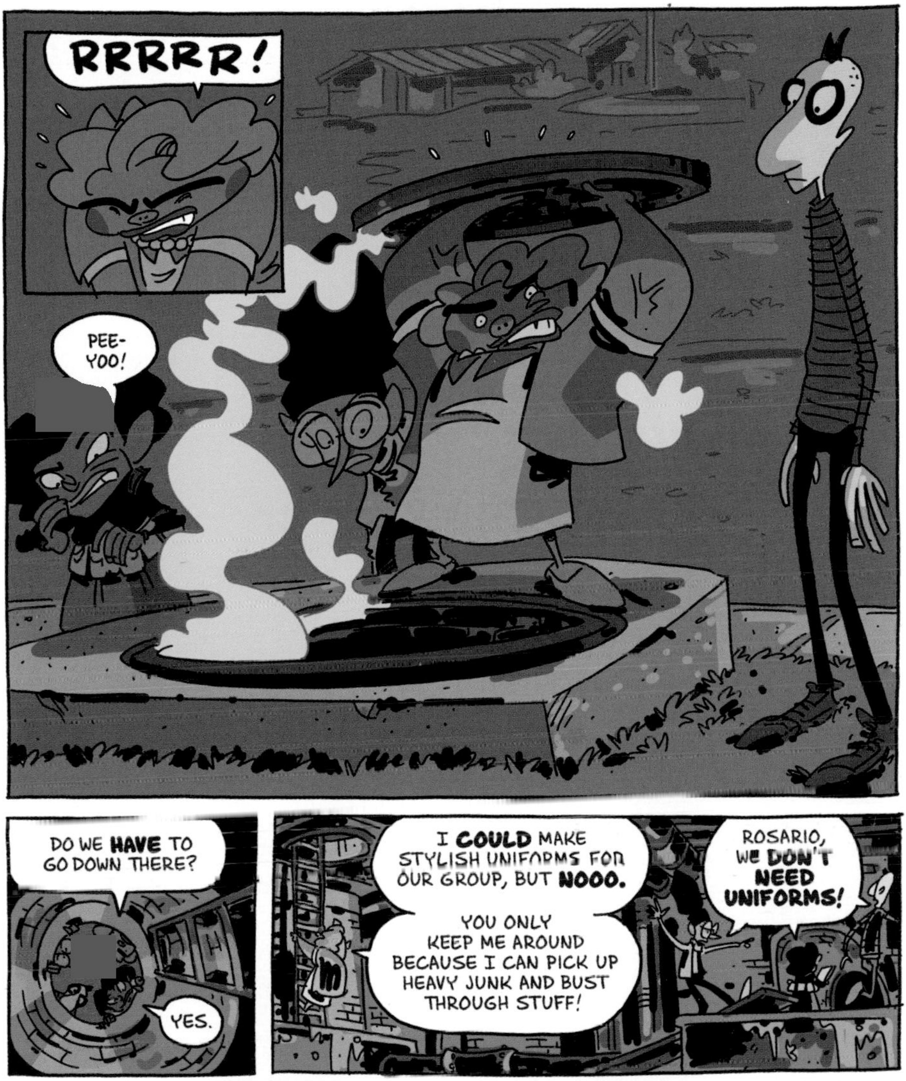
RRRRR!
PEE-YOO!
DO WE HAVE TO GO DOWN THERE?
YES.
I COULD MAKE STYLISH UNIFORMS FOR OUR GROUP, BUT NOOO.
YOU ONLY KEEP ME AROUND BECAUSE I CAN PICK UP HEAVY JUNK AND BUST THROUGH STUFF!
ROSARIO, WE DON'T NEED UNIFORMS!
I JUST THINK THAT IF WE ALL WORE PINK—
SOMETHING RAN PAST MY FOOT!
DON'T WORRY. IT WAS PROBABLY JUST A RAT.

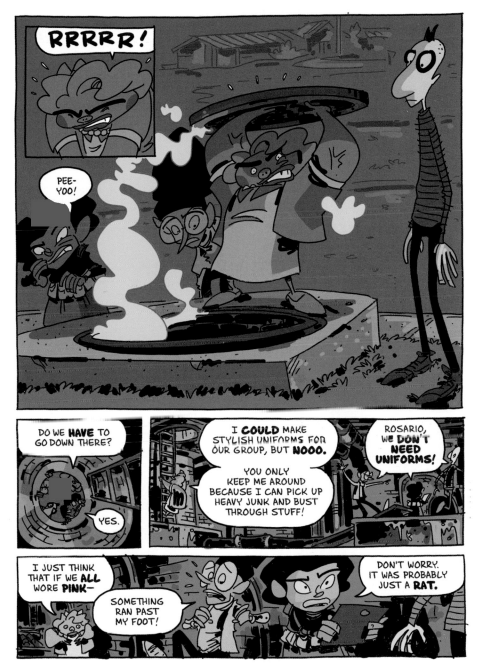

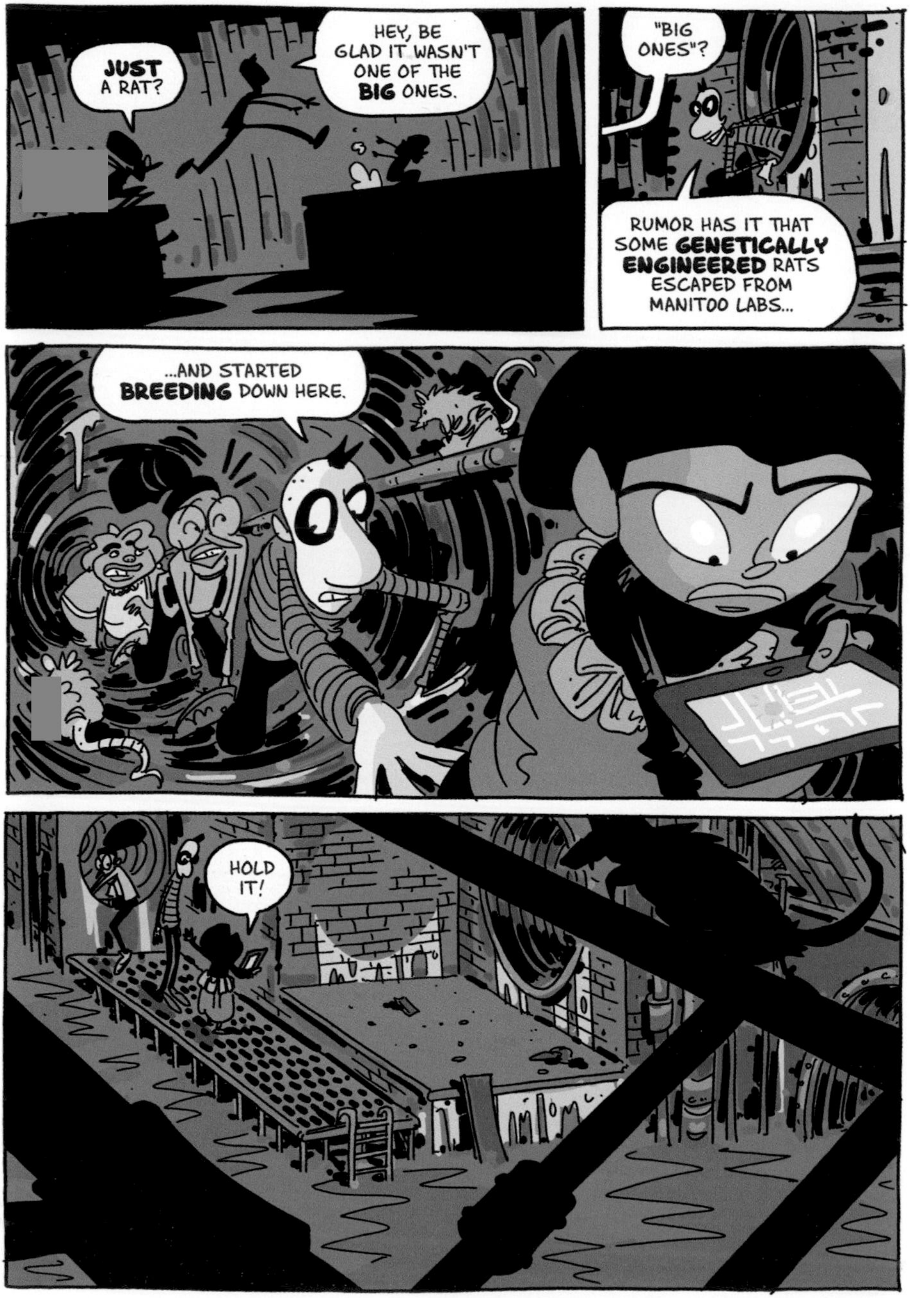
JUST A RAT?
HEY, BE GLAD IT WASN'T ONE OF THE BIG ONES.
"BIG ONES"?
RUMOR HAS IT THAT SOME GENETICALLY ENGINEERED RATS ESCAPED FROM MANITOO LABS...
...AND STARTED BREEDING DOWN HERE.
HOLD IT!

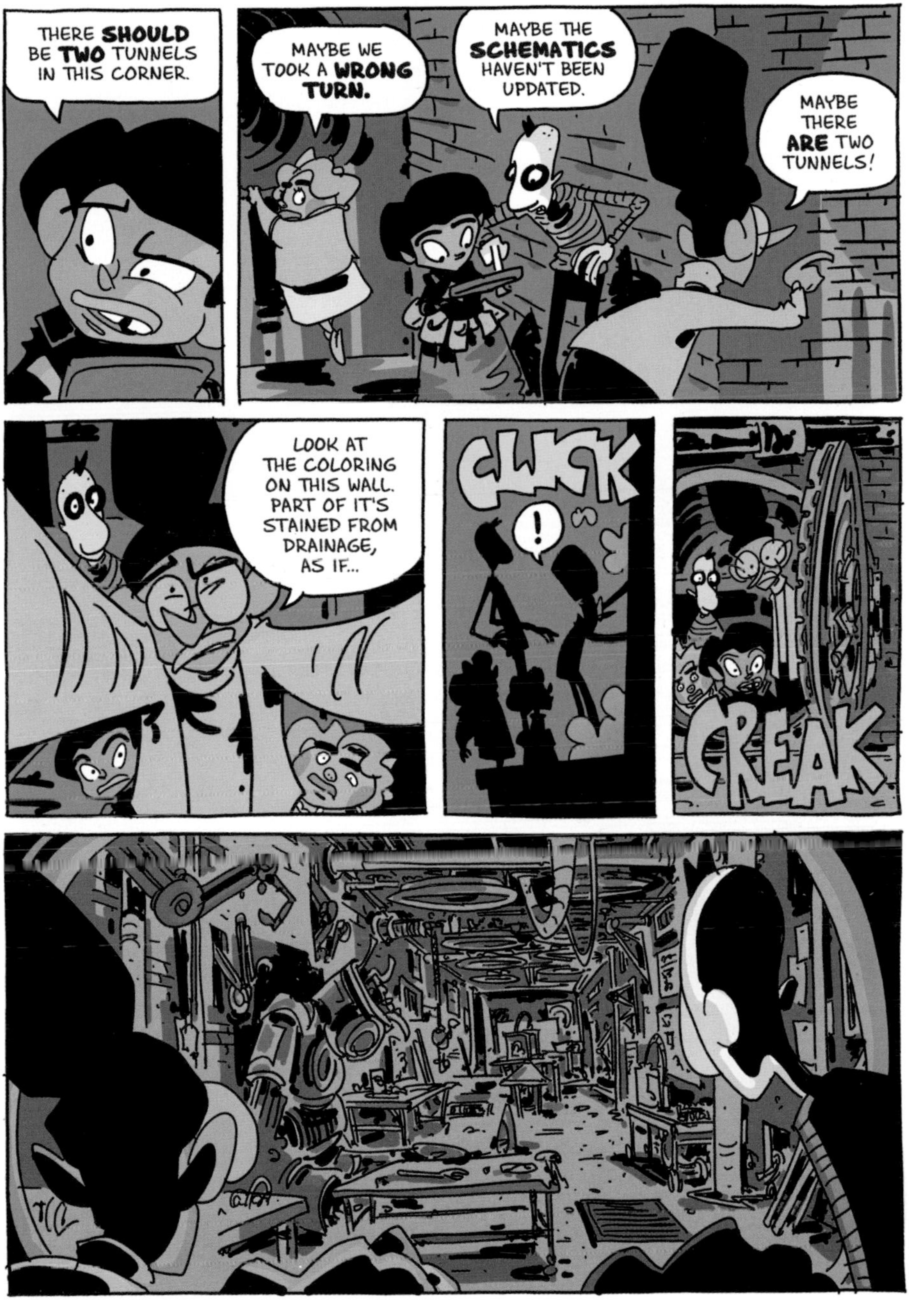
THERE **SHOULD** BE **TWO** TUNNELS IN THIS CORNER.
MAYBE WE TOOK A **WRONG TURN.**
MAYBE THE **SCHEMATICS** HAVEN'T BEEN UPDATED.
MAYBE THERE **ARE** TWO TUNNELS!
LOOK AT THE COLORING ON THIS WALL. PART OF IT'S STAINED FROM DRAINAGE, AS IF...
CLICK
!
CREAK

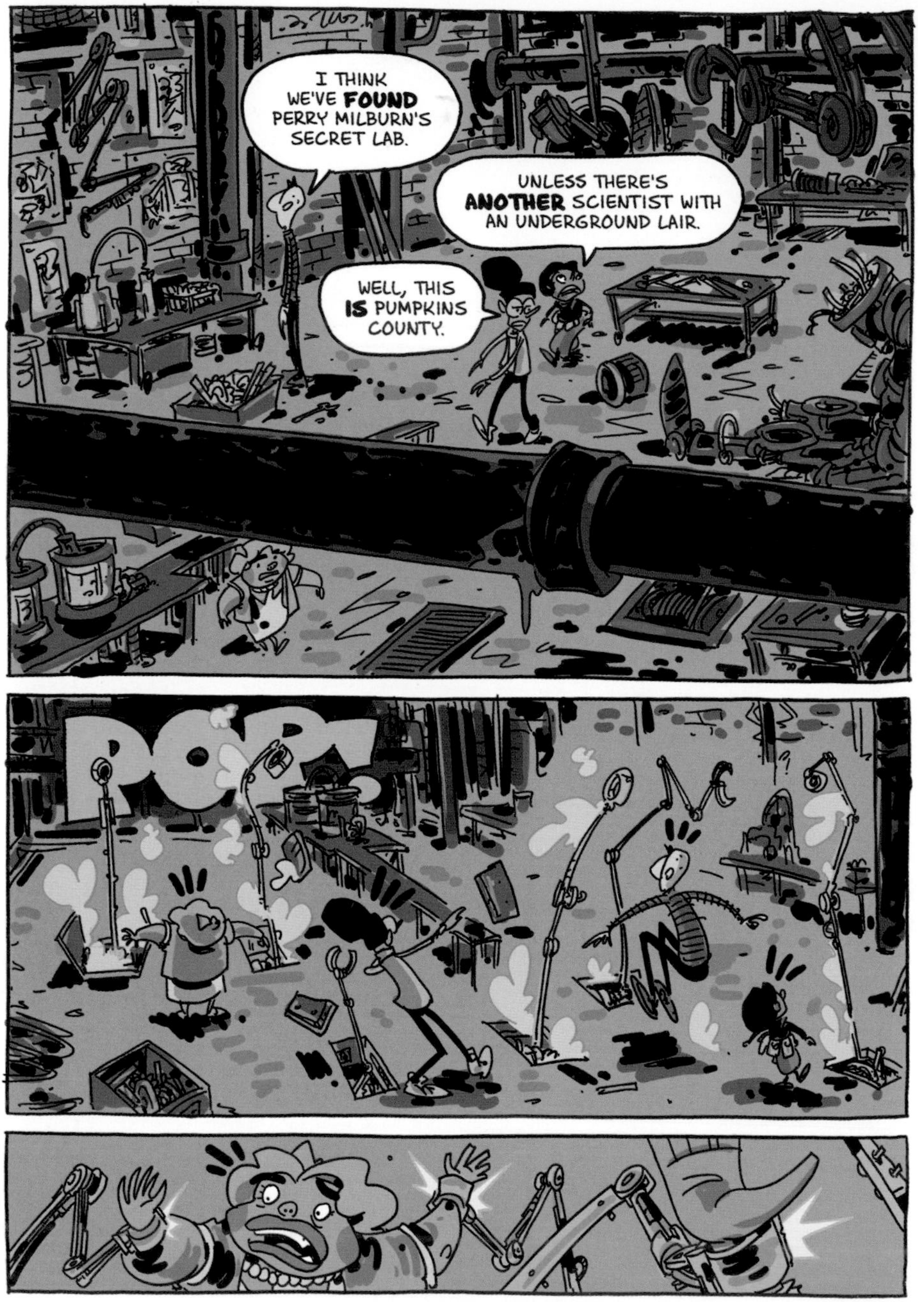
I THINK WE'VE **FOUND** PERRY MILBURN'S SECRET LAB.
UNLESS THERE'S **ANOTHER** SCIENTIST WITH AN UNDERGROUND LAIR.
WELL, THIS **IS** PUMPKINS COUNTY.
POP

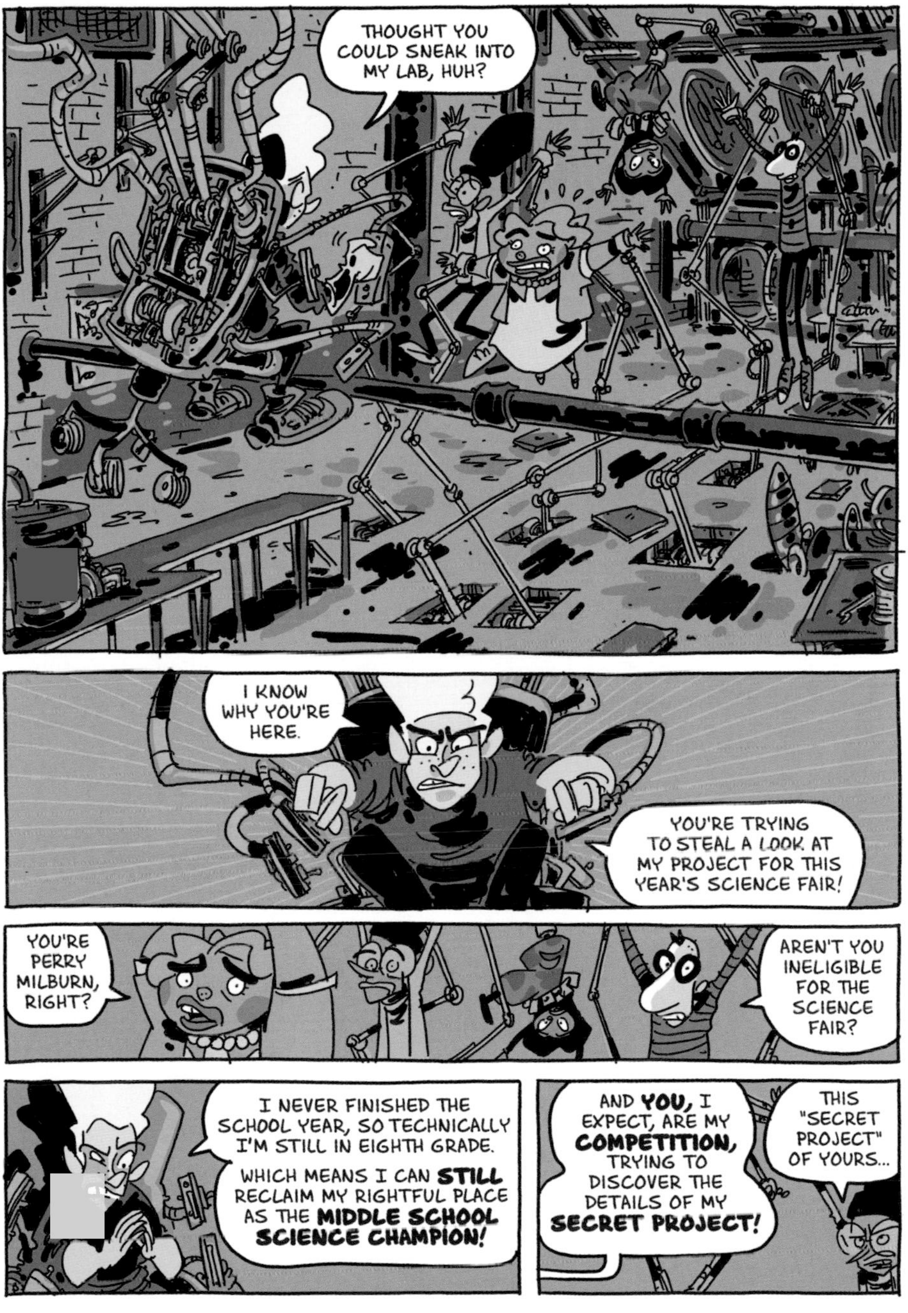
THOUGHT YOU COULD SNEAK INTO MY LAB, HUH?
I KNOW WHY YOU'RE HERE.
YOU'RE TRYING TO STEAL A LOOK AT MY PROJECT FOR THIS YEAR'S SCIENCE FAIR!
YOU'RE PERRY MILBURN, RIGHT?
AREN'T YOU INELIGIBLE FOR THE SCIENCE FAIR?
I NEVER FINISHED THE SCHOOL YEAR, SO TECHNICALLY I'M STILL IN EIGHTH GRADE.
WHICH MEANS I CAN **STILL** RECLAIM MY RIGHTFUL PLACE AS THE **MIDDLE SCHOOL SCIENCE CHAMPION!**
AND **YOU,** I EXPECT, ARE MY **COMPETITION,** TRYING TO DISCOVER THE DETAILS OF MY **SECRET PROJECT!**
THIS "SECRET PROJECT" OF YOURS...

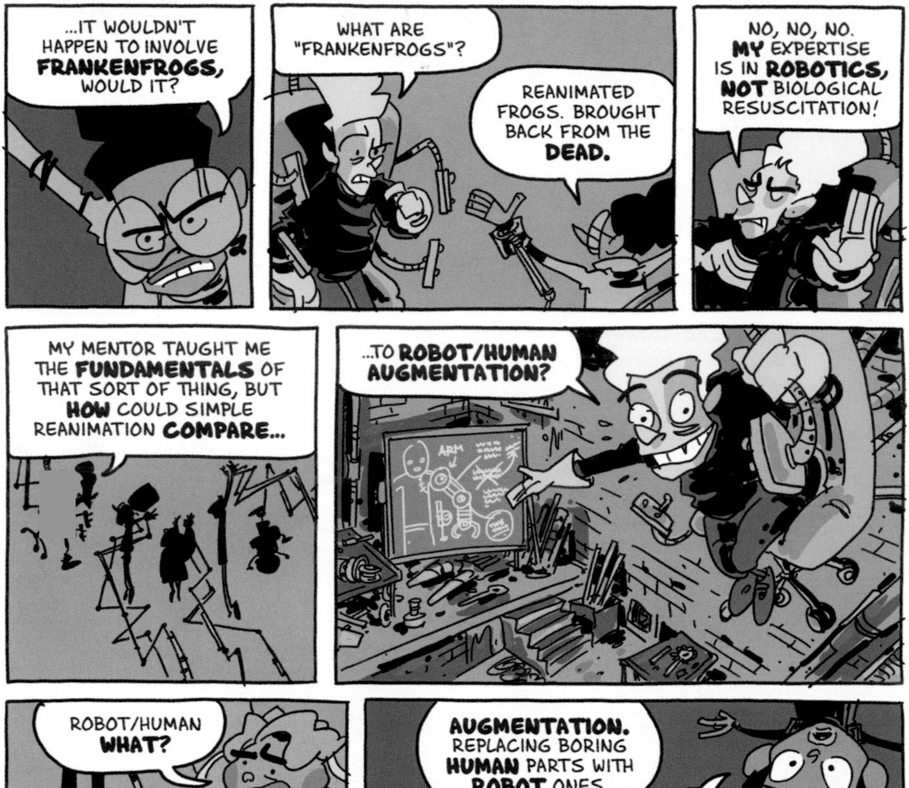
...IT WOULDN'T HAPPEN TO INVOLVE FRANKENFROGS, WOULD IT?
WHAT ARE "FRANKENFROGS"?
REANIMATED FROGS. BROUGHT BACK FROM THE DEAD.
NO, NO, NO. MY EXPERTISE IS IN ROBOTICS, NOT BIOLOGICAL RESUSCITATION!
MY MENTOR TAUGHT ME THE FUNDAMENTALS OF THAT SORT OF THING, BUT HOW COULD SIMPLE REANIMATION COMPARE...
...TO ROBOT/HUMAN AUGMENTATION?
ARM
ROBOT/HUMAN WHAT?
AUGMENTATION. REPLACING BORING HUMAN PARTS WITH ROBOT ONES.
COOL!
BUT NOW THAT YOU KNOW WHAT I'M WORKING ON...
CLICK
...I CAN'T LET YOU LEAVE HERE ALIVE!
WAIT!
BZZZ

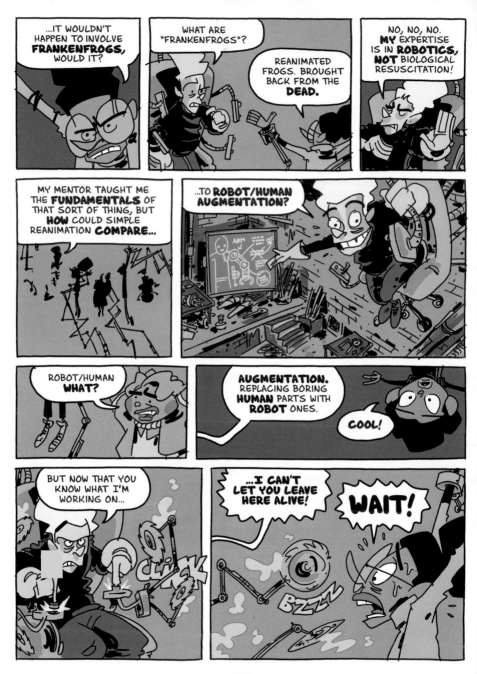

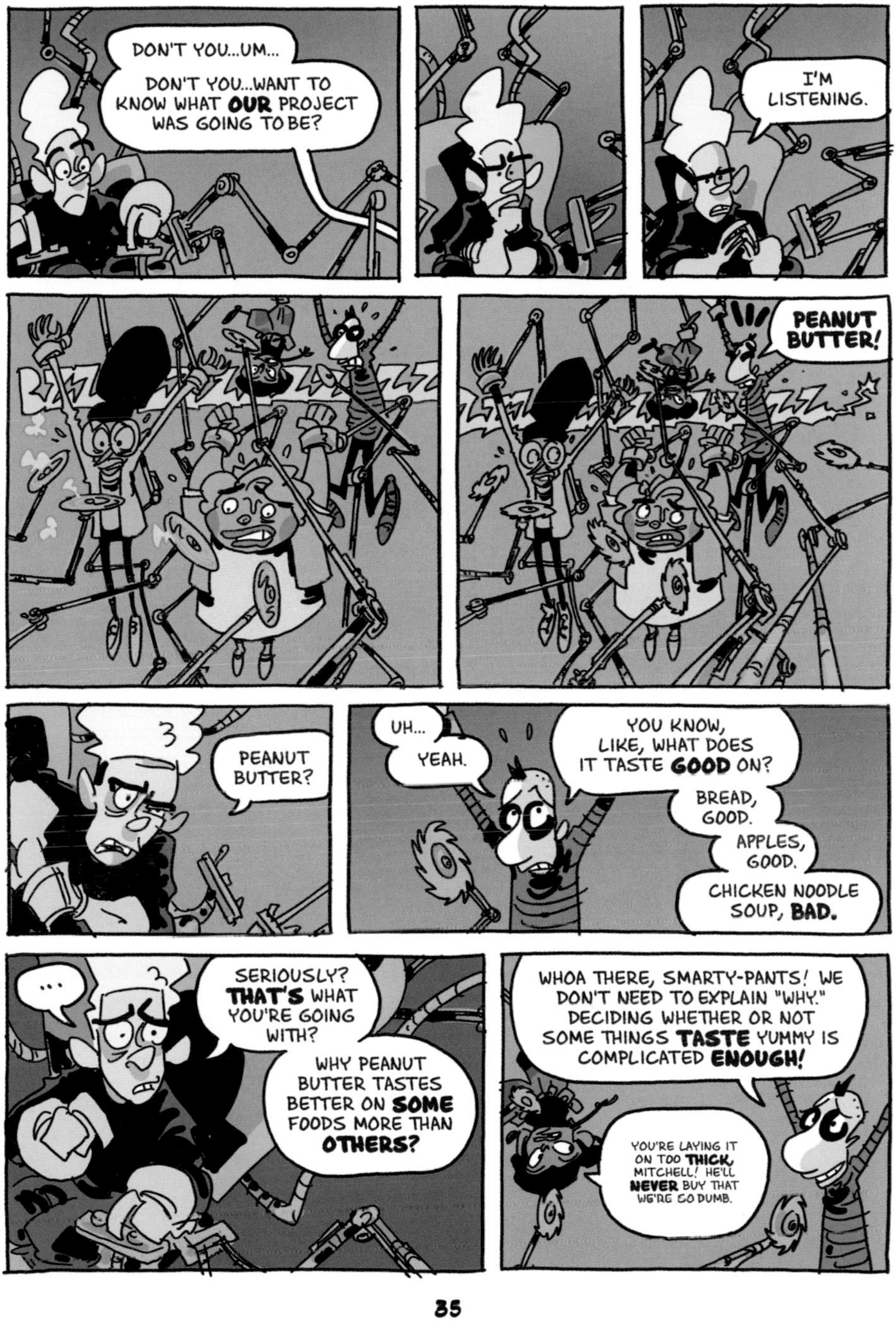

DON'T YOU...UM...
DON'T YOU...WANT TO KNOW WHAT **OUR** PROJECT WAS GOING TO BE?
I'M LISTENING.
PEANUT BUTTER!
PEANUT BUTTER?
UH...
YEAH.
YOU KNOW, LIKE, WHAT DOES IT TASTE **GOOD** ON?
BREAD, GOOD.
APPLES, GOOD.
CHICKEN NOODLE SOUP, **BAD.**
...
SERIOUSLY? **THAT'S** WHAT YOU'RE GOING WITH?
WHY PEANUT BUTTER TASTES BETTER ON **SOME** FOODS MORE THAN **OTHERS?**
WHOA THERE, SMARTY-PANTS! WE DON'T NEED TO EXPLAIN "WHY." DECIDING WHETHER OR NOT SOME THINGS **TASTE** YUMMY IS COMPLICATED **ENOUGH!**
YOU'RE LAYING IT ON TOO **THICK,** MITCHELL! HE'LL **NEVER** BUY THAT WE'RE SO DUMB.

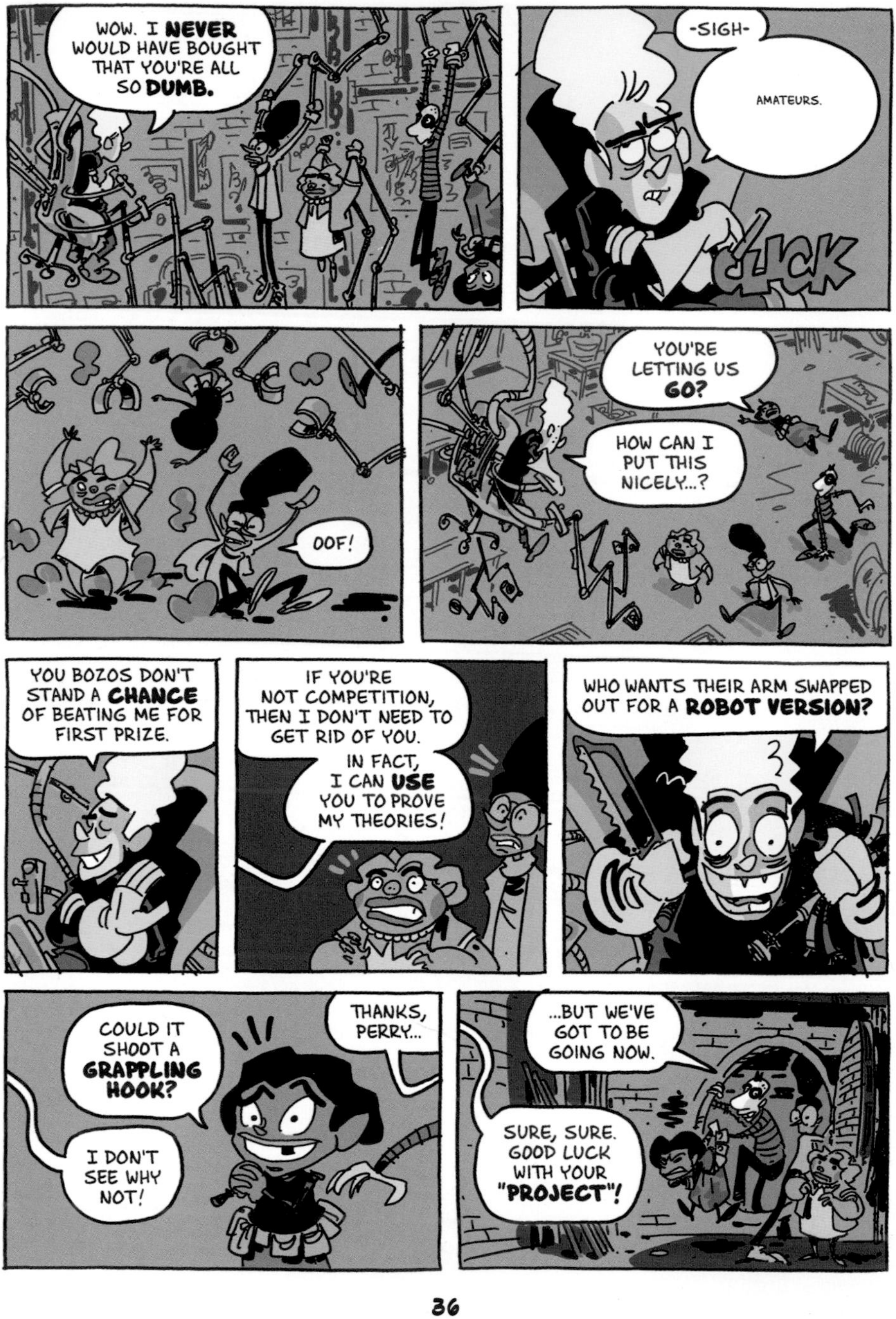
WOW. I **NEVER** WOULD HAVE BOUGHT THAT YOU'RE ALL SO **DUMB.**
-SIGH-
AMATEURS.
CLICK
OOF!
YOU'RE LETTING US **GO?**
HOW CAN I PUT THIS NICELY...?
YOU BOZOS DON'T STAND A **CHANCE** OF BEATING ME FOR FIRST PRIZE.
IF YOU'RE NOT COMPETITION, THEN I DON'T NEED TO GET RID OF YOU.
IN FACT, I CAN **USE** YOU TO PROVE MY THEORIES!
WHO WANTS THEIR ARM SWAPPED OUT FOR A **ROBOT VERSION?**
COULD IT SHOOT A **GRAPPLING HOOK?**
I DON'T SEE WHY NOT!
THANKS, PERRY...
...BUT WE'VE GOT TO BE GOING NOW.
SURE, SURE. GOOD LUCK WITH YOUR "**PROJECT**"!

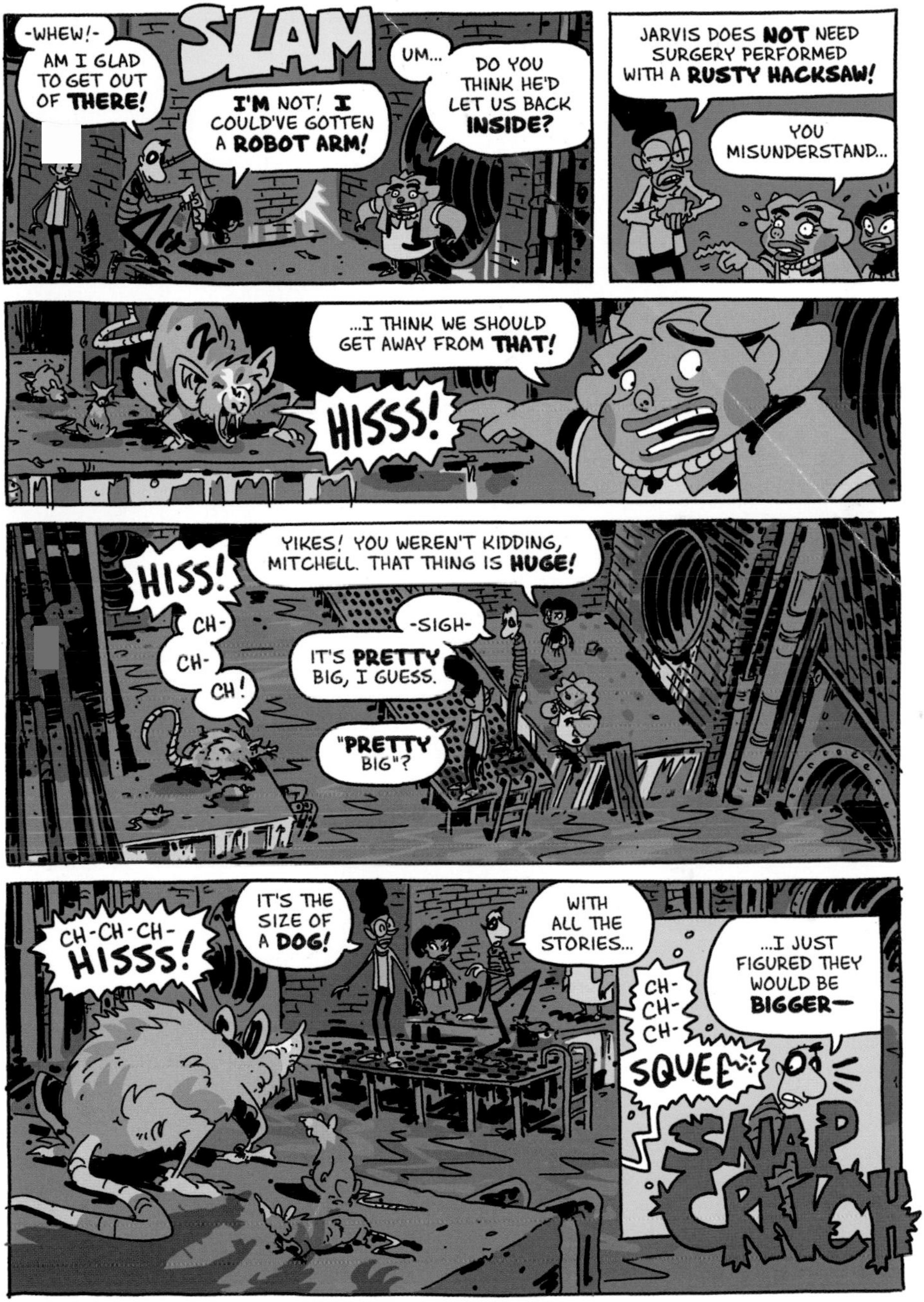
-WHEW!-
AM I GLAD TO GET OUT OF THERE!
SLAM
I'M NOT! I COULD'VE GOTTEN A ROBOT ARM!
UM...
DO YOU THINK HE'D LET US BACK INSIDE?
JARVIS DOES NOT NEED SURGERY PERFORMED WITH A RUSTY HACKSAW!
YOU MISUNDERSTAND...
...I THINK WE SHOULD GET AWAY FROM THAT!
HISSS!
HISS!
YIKES! YOU WEREN'T KIDDING, MITCHELL. THAT THING IS HUGE!
CH- CH- CH!
-SIGH-
IT'S PRETTY BIG, I GUESS.
"PRETTY BIG"?
CH-CH-CH-HISSS!
IT'S THE SIZE OF A DOG!
WITH ALL THE STORIES...
...I JUST FIGURED THEY WOULD BE BIGGER—
CH- CH- CH-
SQUEE
SNAP
CRNCH

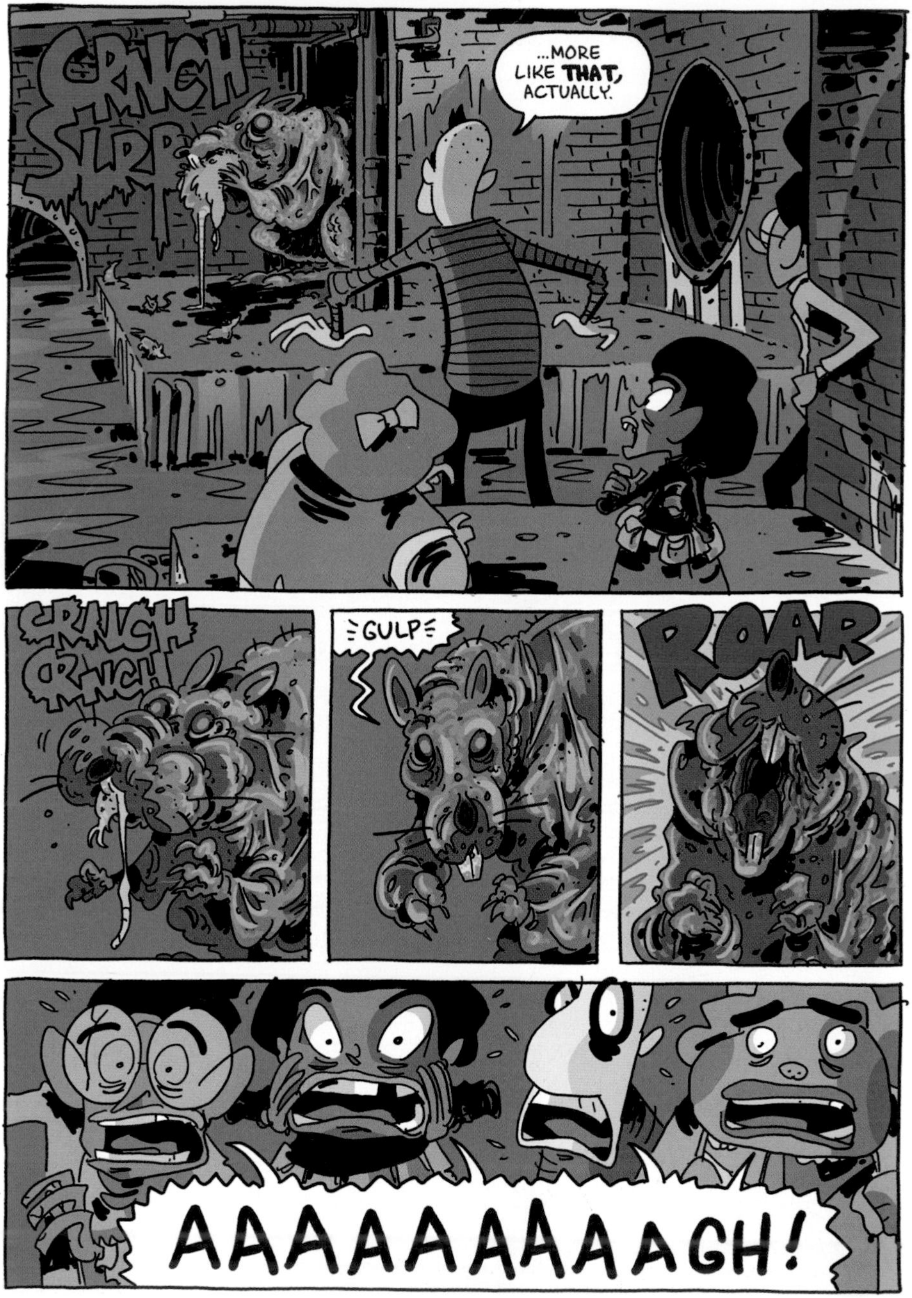

CRUNCH
SLRP
...MORE LIKE THAT, ACTUALLY.
CRUNCH
CRUNCH
GULP
ROAR
AAAAAAAAAAGH!

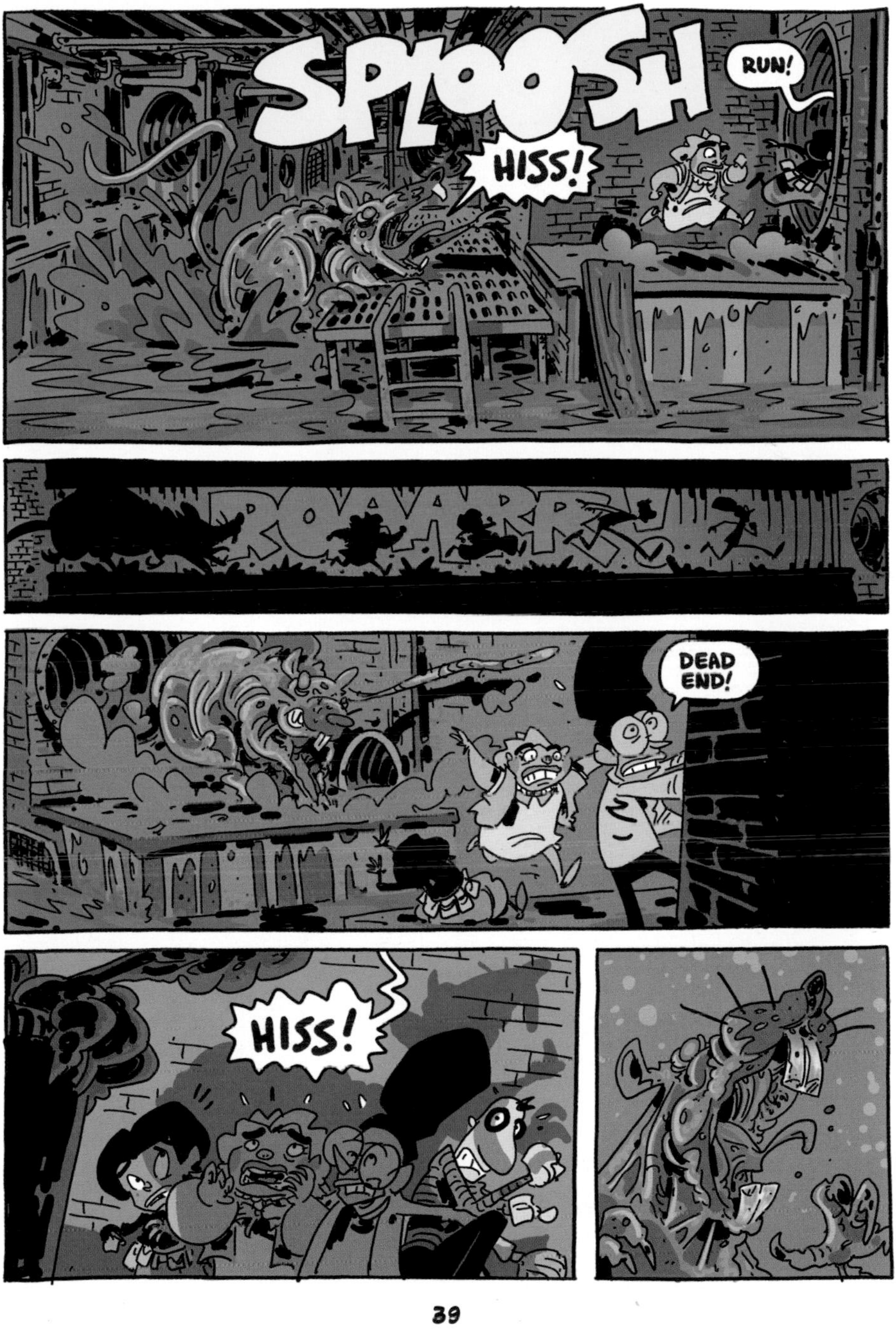
SPLOOSH
RUN!
HISS!
ROWRR!
DEAD END!
HISS!

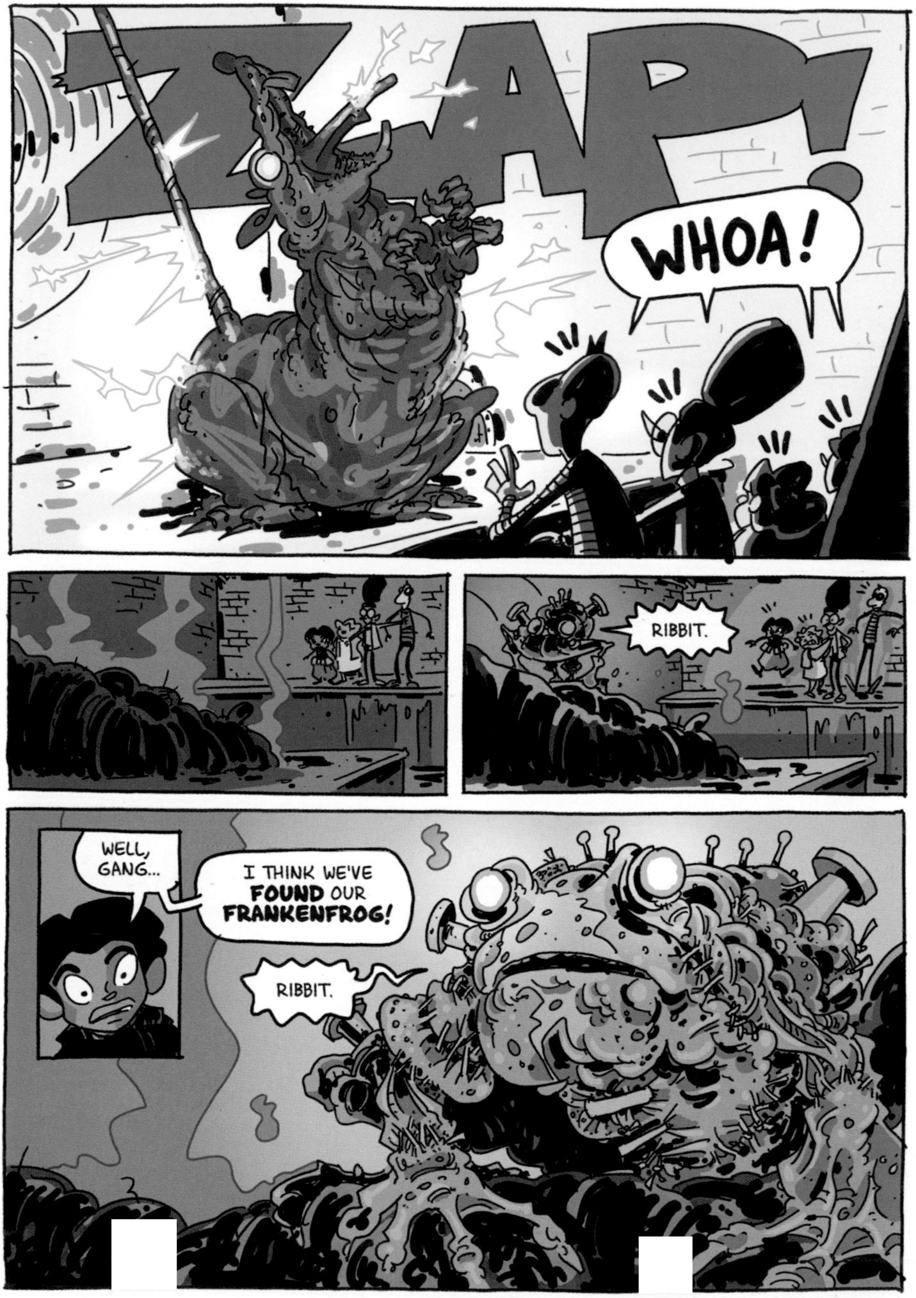
ZZAP!
WHOA!
RIBBIT.
WELL, GANG...
I THINK WE'VE **FOUND** OUR **FRANKENFROG!**
RIBBIT.

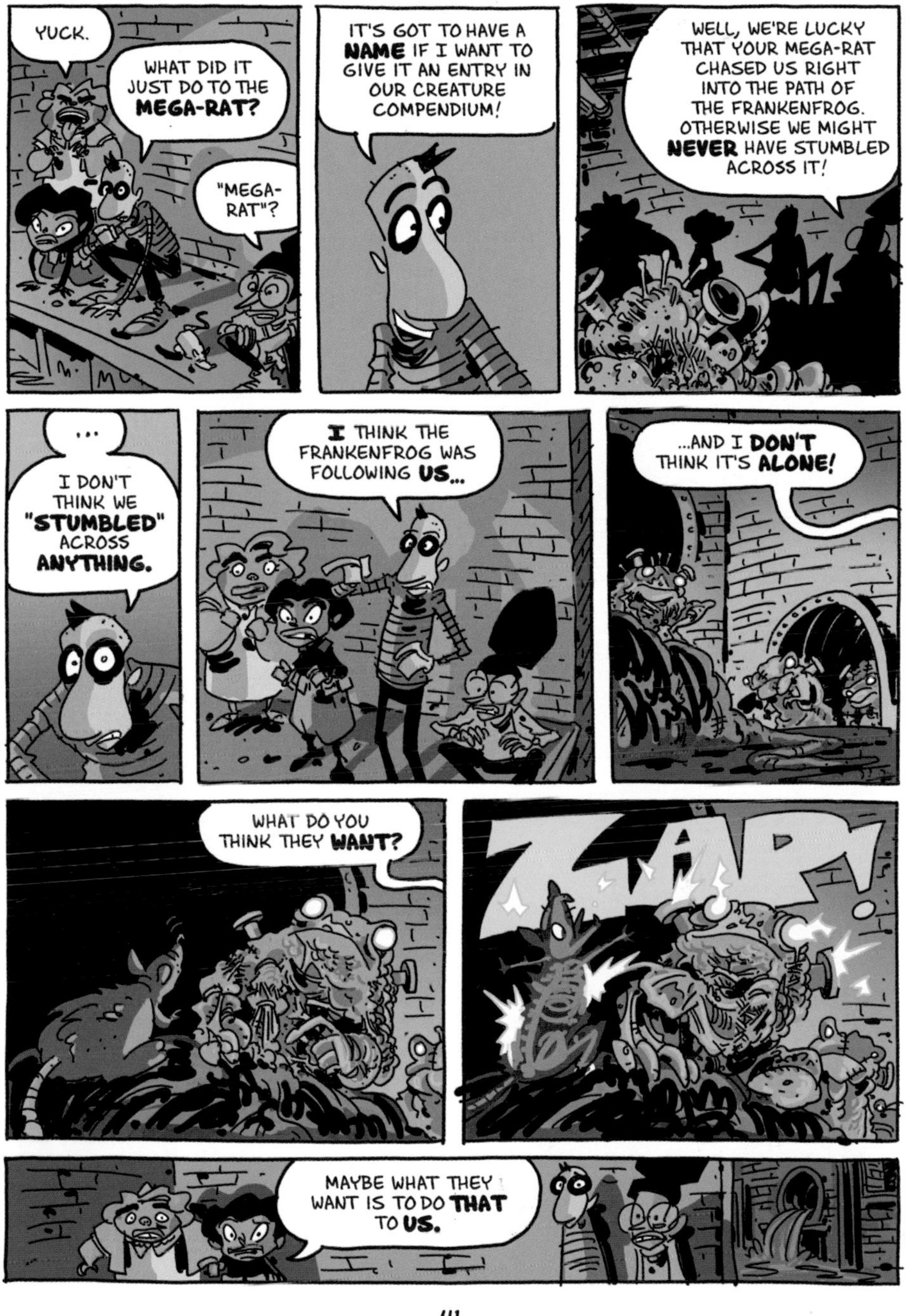
YUCK.
WHAT DID IT JUST DO TO THE MEGA-RAT?
"MEGA-RAT"?
IT'S GOT TO HAVE A NAME IF I WANT TO GIVE IT AN ENTRY IN OUR CREATURE COMPENDIUM!
WELL, WE'RE LUCKY THAT YOUR MEGA-RAT CHASED US RIGHT INTO THE PATH OF THE FRANKENFROG. OTHERWISE WE MIGHT NEVER HAVE STUMBLED ACROSS IT!
...
I DON'T THINK WE "STUMBLED" ACROSS ANYTHING.
I THINK THE FRANKENFROG WAS FOLLOWING US...
...AND I DON'T THINK IT'S ALONE!
WHAT DO YOU THINK THEY WANT?
ZAP!
MAYBE WHAT THEY WANT IS TO DO THAT TO US.

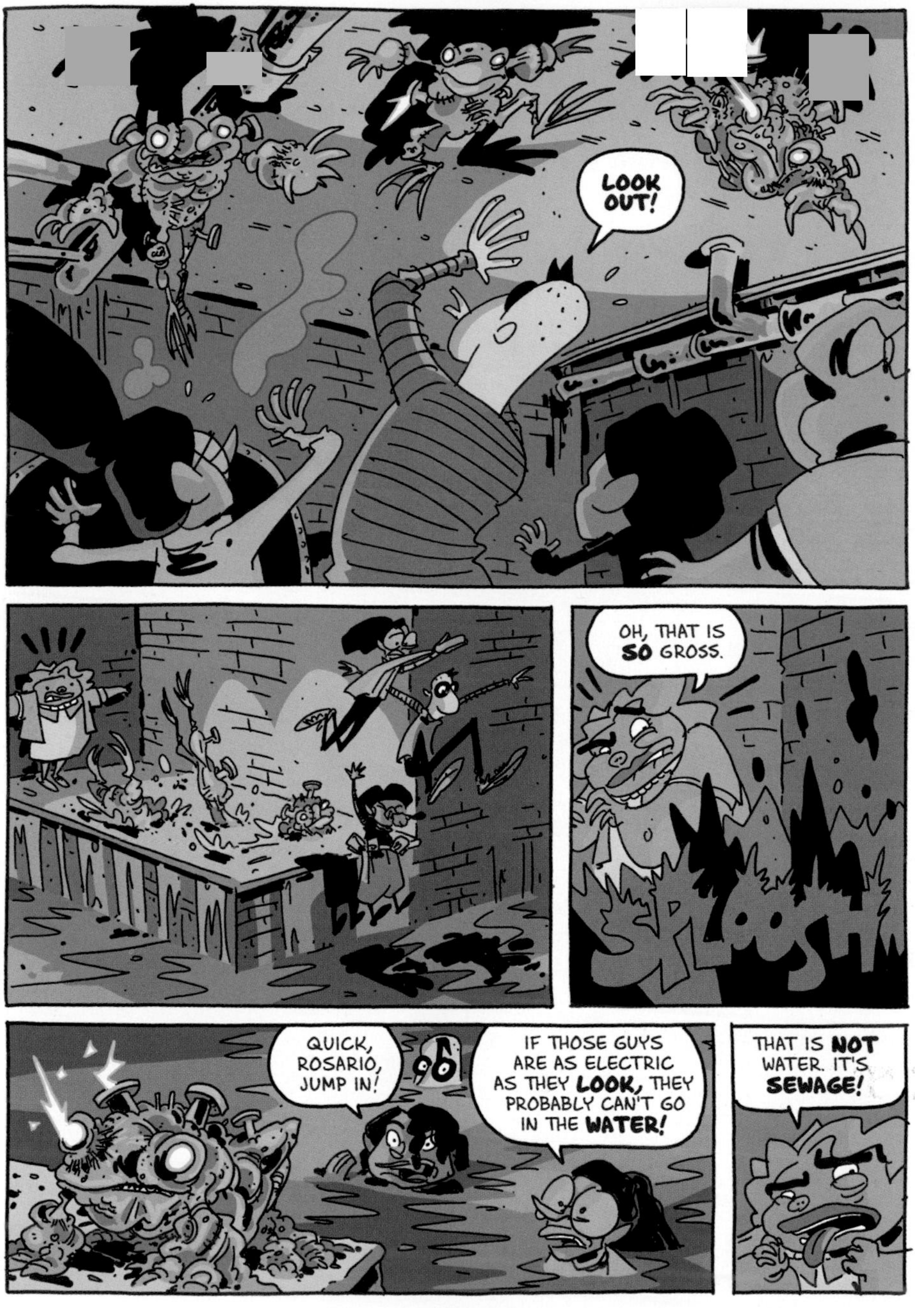
LOOK OUT!
OH, THAT IS SO GROSS.
SPLOOSH
QUICK, ROSARIO, JUMP IN!
IF THOSE GUYS ARE AS ELECTRIC AS THEY LOOK, THEY PROBABLY CAN'T GO IN THE WATER!
THAT IS NOT WATER. IT'S SEWAGE!

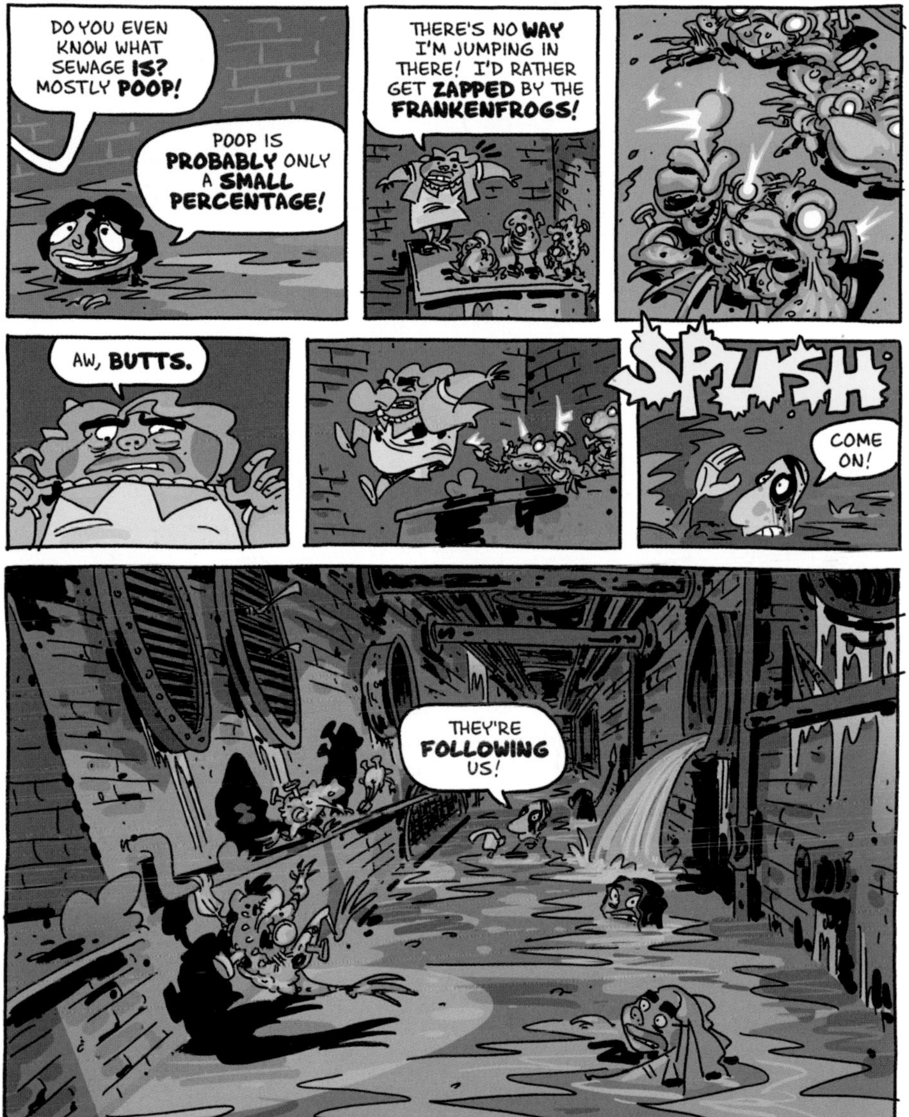
DO YOU EVEN KNOW WHAT SEWAGE IS? MOSTLY POOP!
POOP IS PROBABLY ONLY A SMALL PERCENTAGE!
THERE'S NO WAY I'M JUMPING IN THERE! I'D RATHER GET ZAPPED BY THE FRANKENFROGS!
AW, BUTTS.
SPLASH
COME ON!
THEY'RE FOLLOWING US!

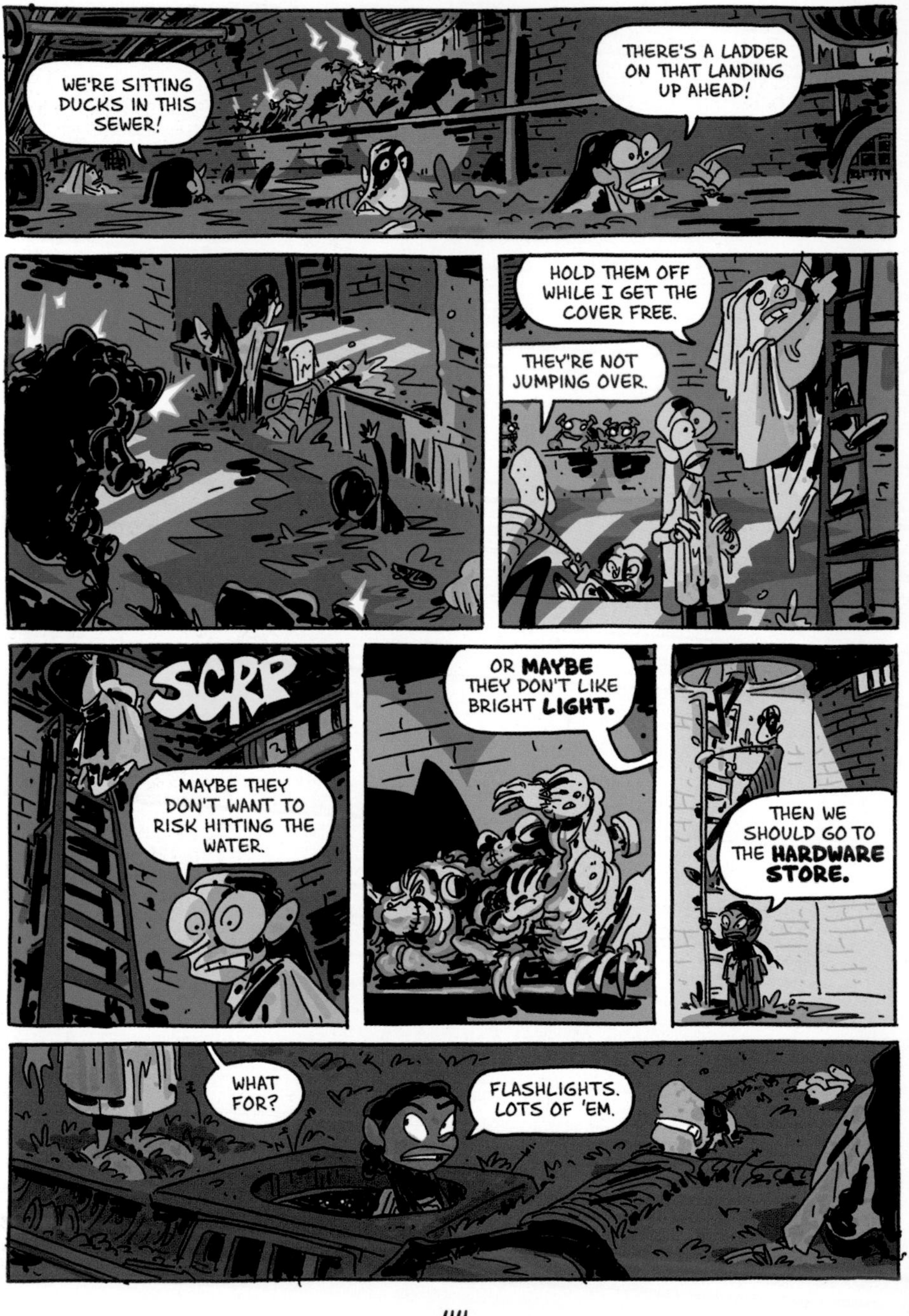

WE'RE SITTING DUCKS IN THIS SEWER!
THERE'S A LADDER ON THAT LANDING UP AHEAD!
HOLD THEM OFF WHILE I GET THE COVER FREE.
THEY'RE NOT JUMPING OVER.
SCRP
MAYBE THEY DON'T WANT TO RISK HITTING THE WATER.
OR MAYBE THEY DON'T LIKE BRIGHT LIGHT.
THEN WE SHOULD GO TO THE HARDWARE STORE.
WHAT FOR?
FLASHLIGHTS. LOTS OF 'EM.

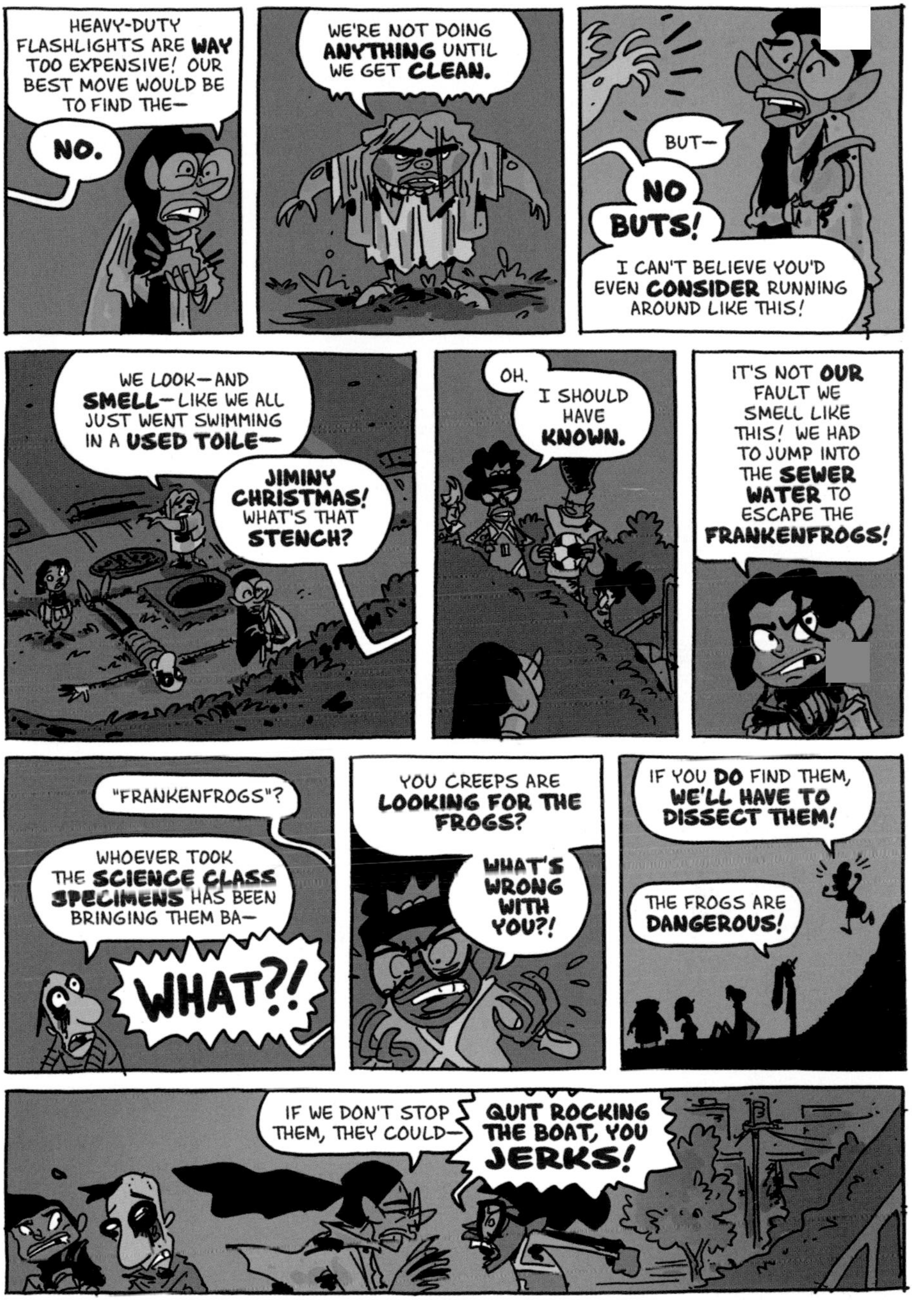
HEAVY-DUTY FLASHLIGHTS ARE WAY TOO EXPENSIVE! OUR BEST MOVE WOULD BE TO FIND THE—
NO.
WE'RE NOT DOING ANYTHING UNTIL WE GET CLEAN.
BUT—
NO BUTS!
I CAN'T BELIEVE YOU'D EVEN CONSIDER RUNNING AROUND LIKE THIS!
WE LOOK—AND SMELL—LIKE WE ALL JUST WENT SWIMMING IN A USED TOILE—
JIMINY CHRISTMAS! WHAT'S THAT STENCH?
OH.
I SHOULD HAVE KNOWN.
IT'S NOT OUR FAULT WE SMELL LIKE THIS! WE HAD TO JUMP INTO THE SEWER WATER TO ESCAPE THE FRANKENFROGS!
"FRANKENFROGS"?
WHOEVER TOOK THE SCIENCE CLASS SPECIMENS HAS BEEN BRINGING THEM BA—
WHAT?!
YOU CREEPS ARE LOOKING FOR THE FROGS?
WHAT'S WRONG WITH YOU?!
IF YOU DO FIND THEM, WE'LL HAVE TO DISSECT THEM!
THE FROGS ARE DANGEROUS!
IF WE DON'T STOP THEM, THEY COULD—
QUIT ROCKING THE BOAT, YOU JERKS!

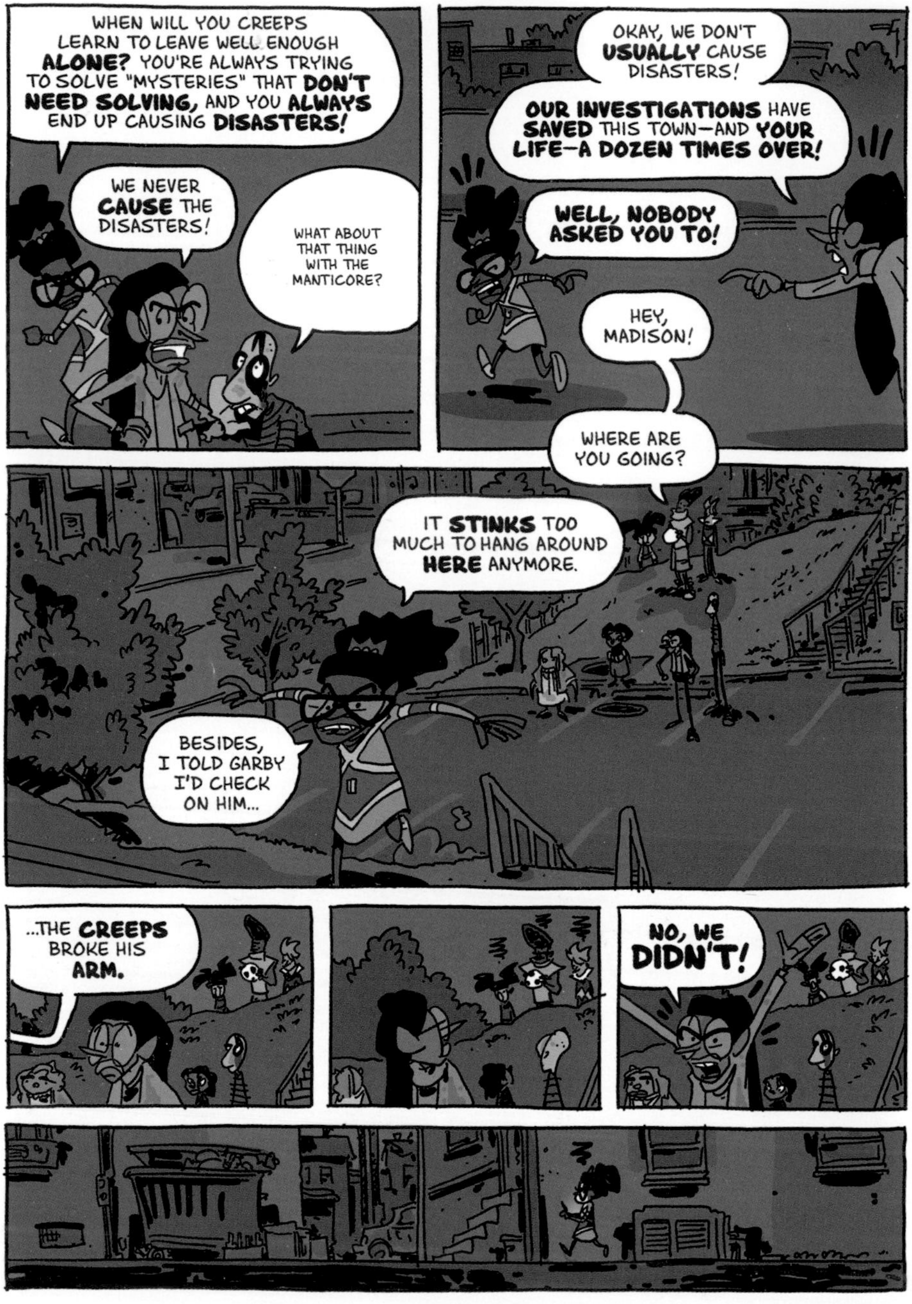

WHEN WILL YOU CREEPS LEARN TO LEAVE WELL ENOUGH ALONE? YOU'RE ALWAYS TRYING TO SOLVE "MYSTERIES" THAT DON'T NEED SOLVING, AND YOU ALWAYS END UP CAUSING DISASTERS!
WE NEVER CAUSE THE DISASTERS!
WHAT ABOUT THAT THING WITH THE MANTICORE?
OKAY, WE DON'T USUALLY CAUSE DISASTERS!
OUR INVESTIGATIONS HAVE SAVED THIS TOWN—AND YOUR LIFE—A DOZEN TIMES OVER!
WELL, NOBODY ASKED YOU TO!
HEY, MADISON!
WHERE ARE YOU GOING?
IT STINKS TOO MUCH TO HANG AROUND HERE ANYMORE.
BESIDES, I TOLD GARBY I'D CHECK ON HIM...
...THE CREEPS BROKE HIS ARM.
NO, WE DIDN'T!

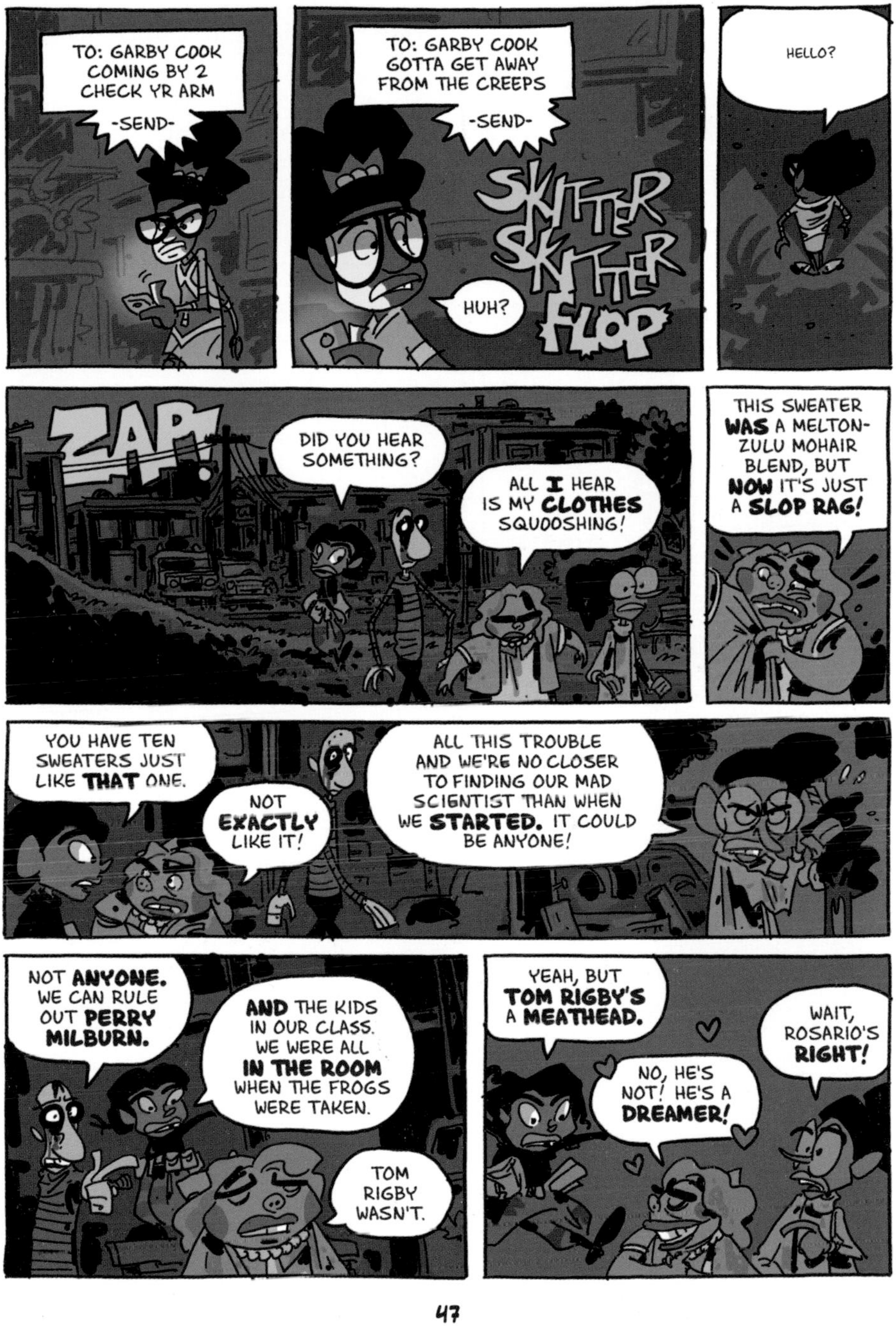
TO: GARBY COOK COMING BY 2 CHECK YR ARM
-SEND-
TO: GARBY COOK GOTTA GET AWAY FROM THE CREEPS
-SEND-
SKITTER SKITTER FLOP
HUH?
HELLO?
ZAP
DID YOU HEAR SOMETHING?
ALL I HEAR IS MY CLOTHES SQUOOSHING!
THIS SWEATER WAS A MELTON-ZULU MOHAIR BLEND, BUT NOW IT'S JUST A SLOP RAG!
YOU HAVE TEN SWEATERS JUST LIKE THAT ONE.
NOT EXACTLY LIKE IT!
ALL THIS TROUBLE AND WE'RE NO CLOSER TO FINDING OUR MAD SCIENTIST THAN WHEN WE STARTED. IT COULD BE ANYONE!
NOT ANYONE. WE CAN RULE OUT PERRY MILBURN.
AND THE KIDS IN OUR CLASS. WE WERE ALL IN THE ROOM WHEN THE FROGS WERE TAKEN.
TOM RIGBY WASN'T.
YEAH, BUT TOM RIGBY'S A MEATHEAD.
NO, HE'S NOT! HE'S A DREAMER!
WAIT, ROSARIO'S RIGHT!

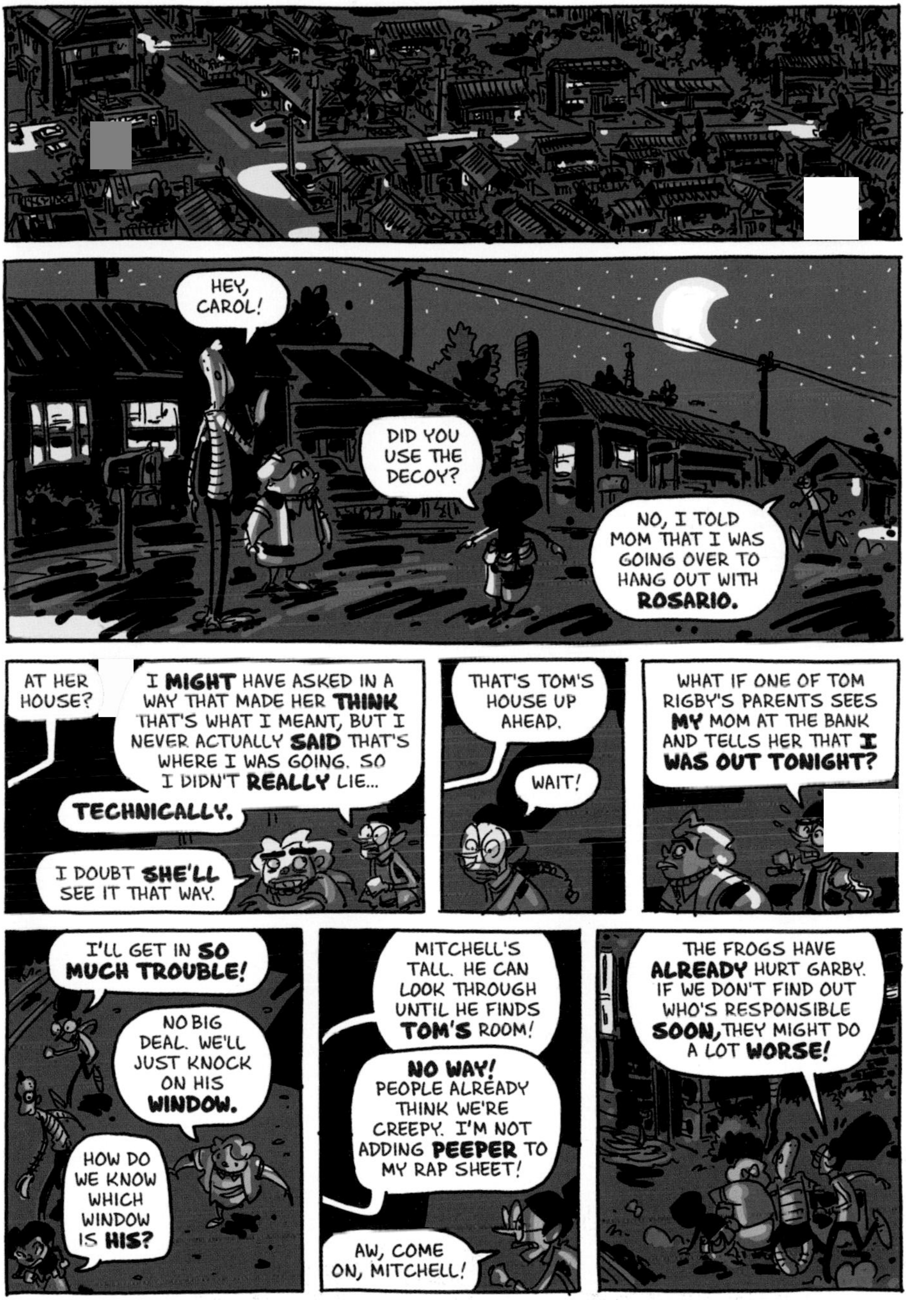
HEY, CAROL!
DID YOU USE THE DECOY?
NO, I TOLD MOM THAT I WAS GOING OVER TO HANG OUT WITH **ROSARIO.**
AT HER HOUSE?
I **MIGHT** HAVE ASKED IN A WAY THAT MADE HER **THINK** THAT'S WHAT I MEANT, BUT I NEVER ACTUALLY **SAID** THAT'S WHERE I WAS GOING. SO I DIDN'T **REALLY** LIE...
TECHNICALLY.
I DOUBT **SHE'LL** SEE IT THAT WAY.
THAT'S TOM'S HOUSE UP AHEAD.
WAIT!
WHAT IF ONE OF TOM RIGBY'S PARENTS SEES **MY** MOM AT THE BANK AND TELLS HER THAT **I WAS OUT TONIGHT?**
I'LL GET IN **SO MUCH TROUBLE!**
NO BIG DEAL. WE'LL JUST KNOCK ON HIS **WINDOW.**
HOW DO WE KNOW WHICH WINDOW IS **HIS?**
MITCHELL'S TALL. HE CAN LOOK THROUGH UNTIL HE FINDS **TOM'S** ROOM!
NO WAY! PEOPLE ALREADY THINK WE'RE CREEPY. I'M NOT ADDING **PEEPER** TO MY RAP SHEET!
AW, COME ON, MITCHELL!
THE FROGS HAVE **ALREADY** HURT GARBY. IF WE DON'T FIND OUT WHO'S RESPONSIBLE **SOON,** THEY MIGHT DO A LOT **WORSE!**

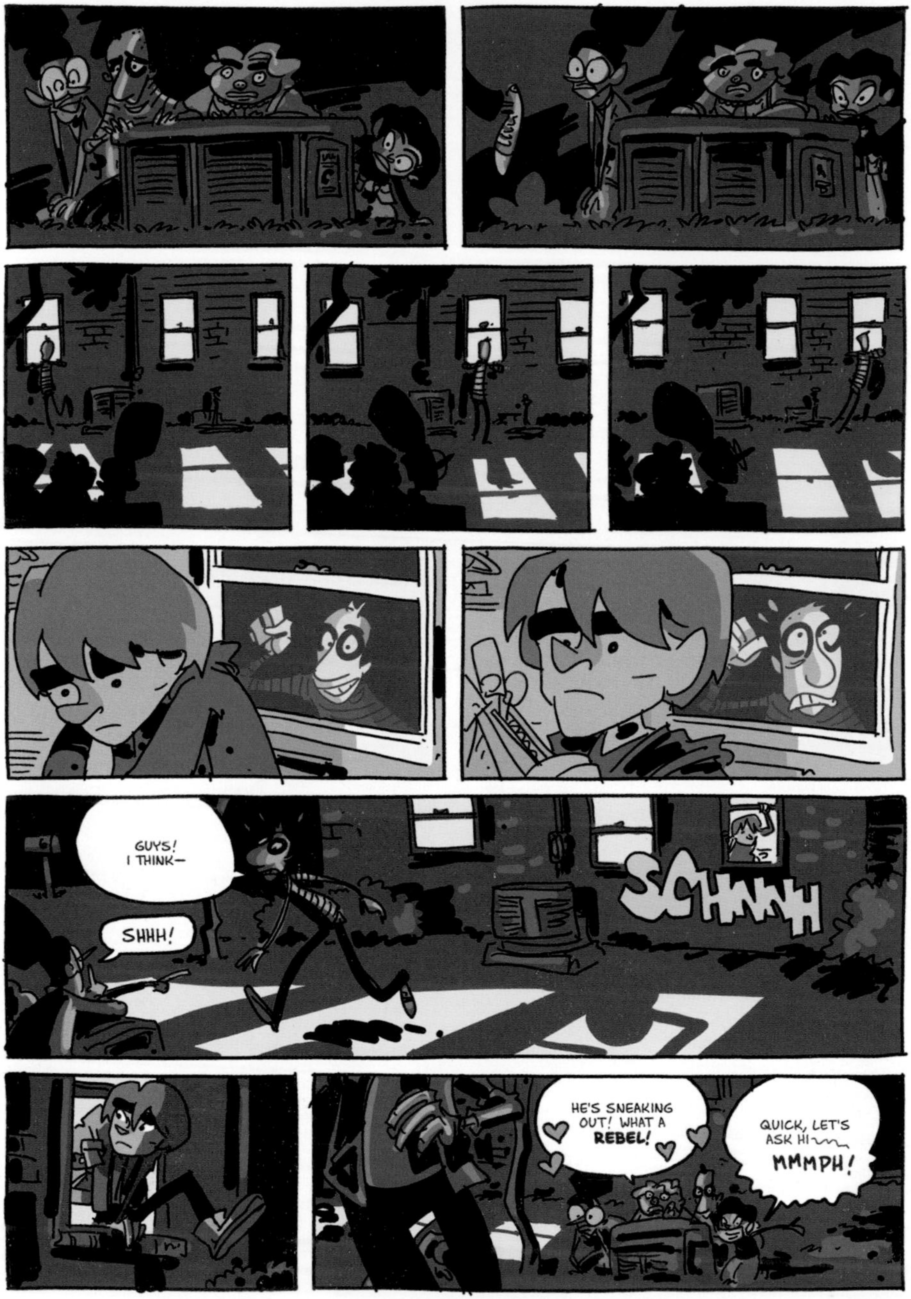
GUYS! I THINK—
SHHH!
SCHNNNH
HE'S SNEAKING OUT! WHAT A REBEL!
QUICK, LET'S ASK HI— MMMPH!

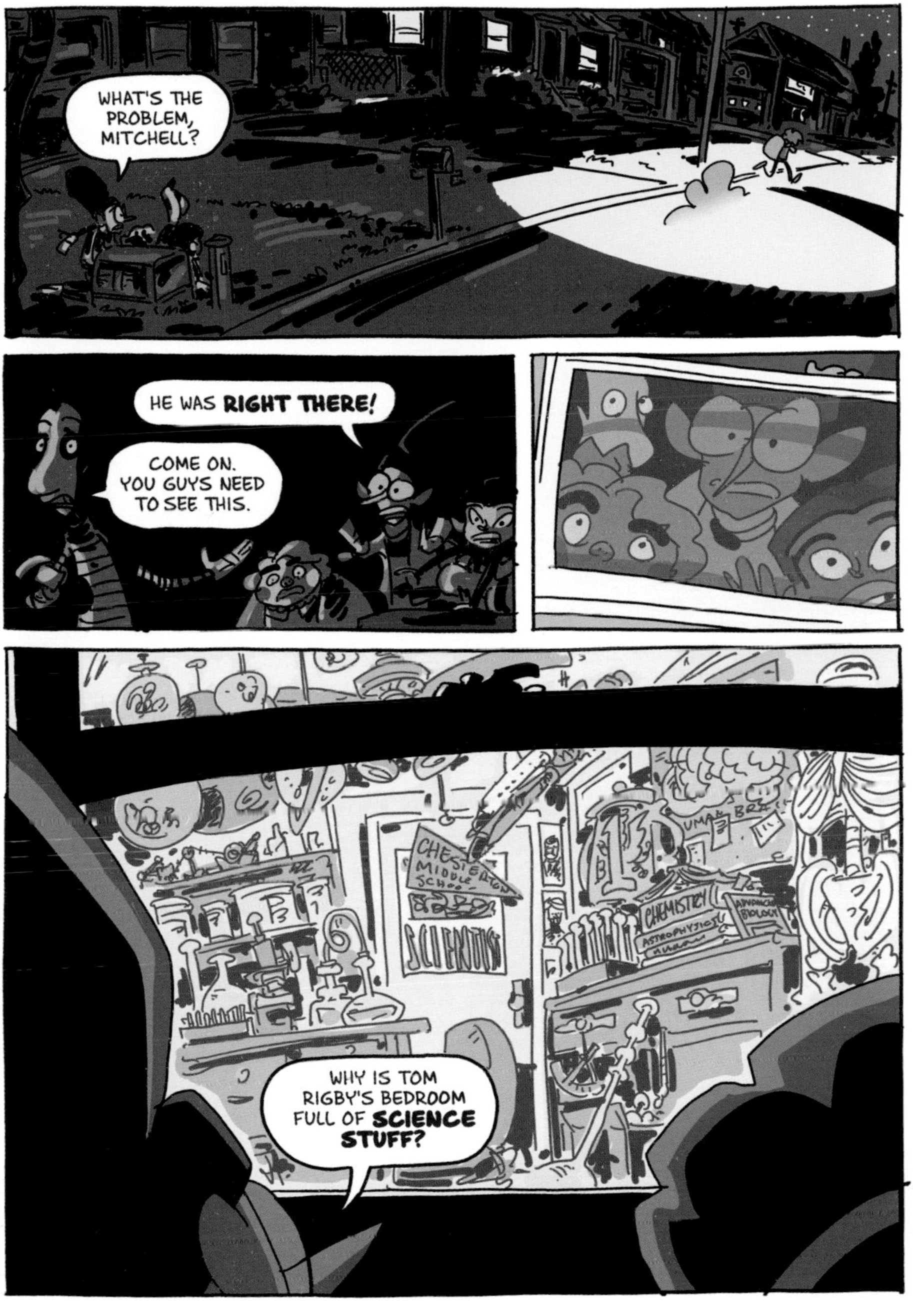
WHAT'S THE PROBLEM, MITCHELL?
HE WAS **RIGHT THERE!**
COME ON. YOU GUYS NEED TO SEE THIS.
CHEMISTRY
WHY IS TOM RIGBY'S BEDROOM FULL OF **SCIENCE STUFF?**

CREAK

I THOUGHT **WE** WERE THE ONLY KIDS WHO SNEAK INTO THE SCHOOL AFTER DARK!

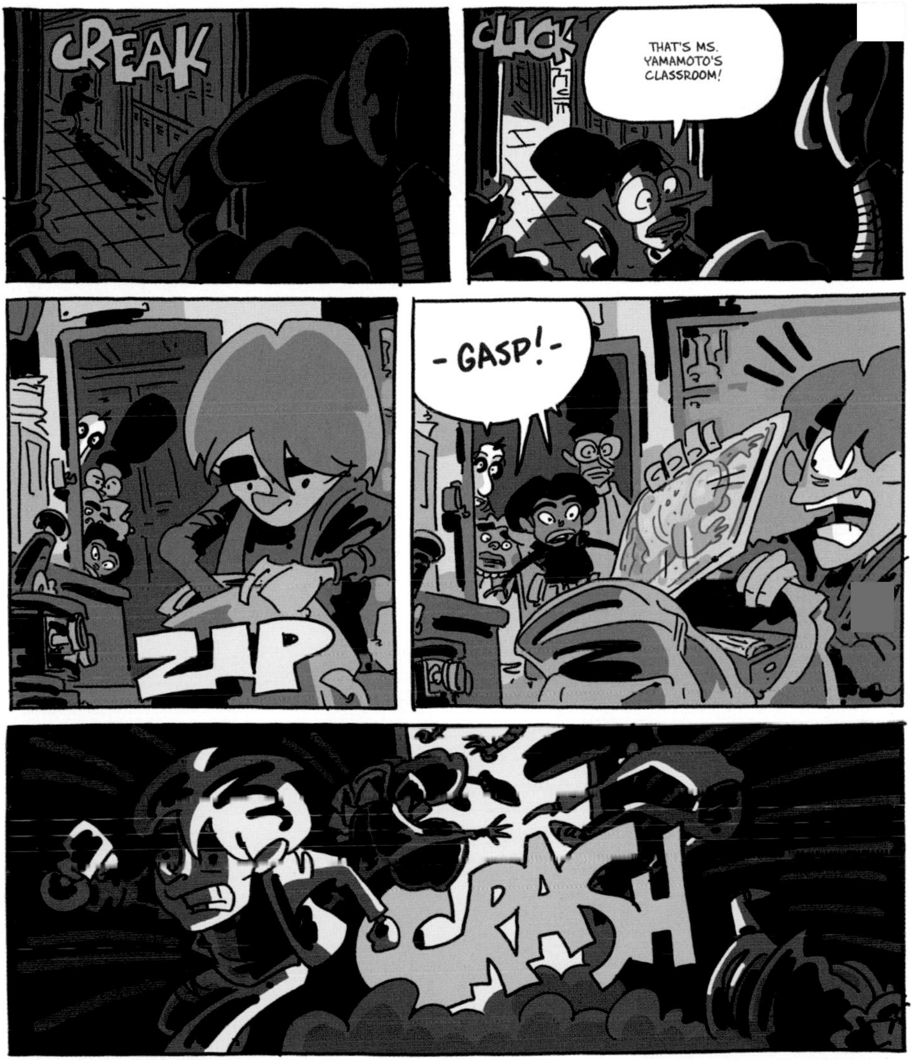
CREAK
CLICK
THAT'S MS. YAMAMOTO'S CLASSROOM!
ZIP
- GASP! -
CRASH
WELL, **HE** LEFT IN A HURRY!
LOOK, HE HAD A **FROG SPECIMEN!**
I GUESS WE'VE FOUND OUR **MAD SCIENTIST.**
MEATHEAD TOM RIGBY. DIDN'T SEE **THAT** COMING.
GUYS...

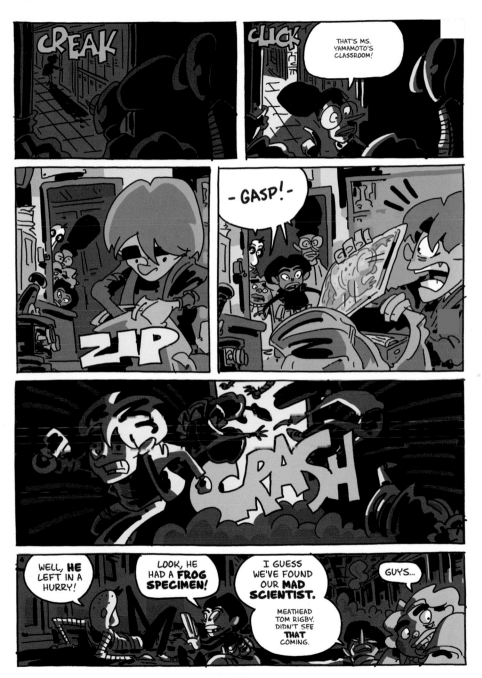

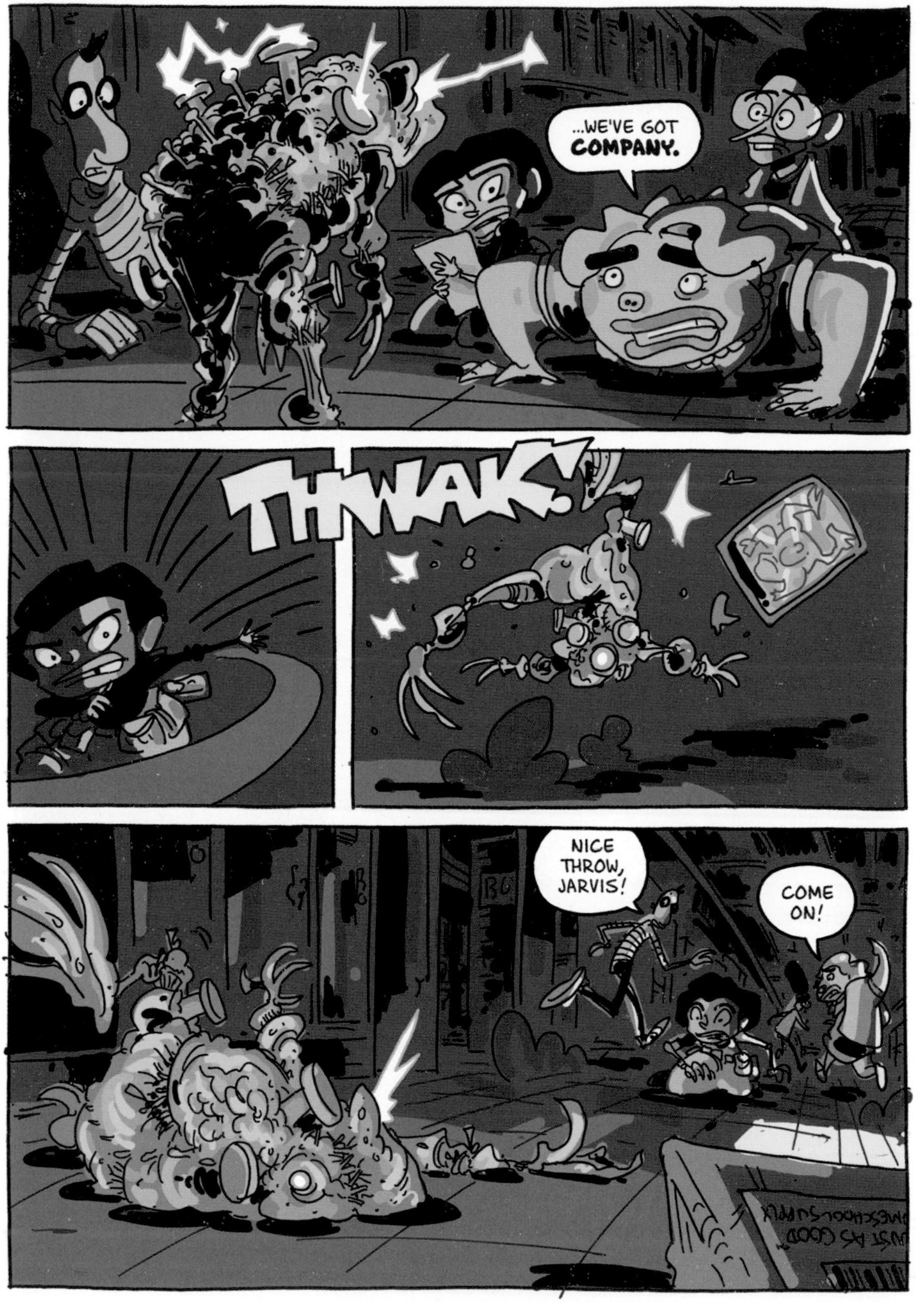
...WE'VE GOT COMPANY.
THWAK!
NICE THROW, JARVIS!
COME ON!

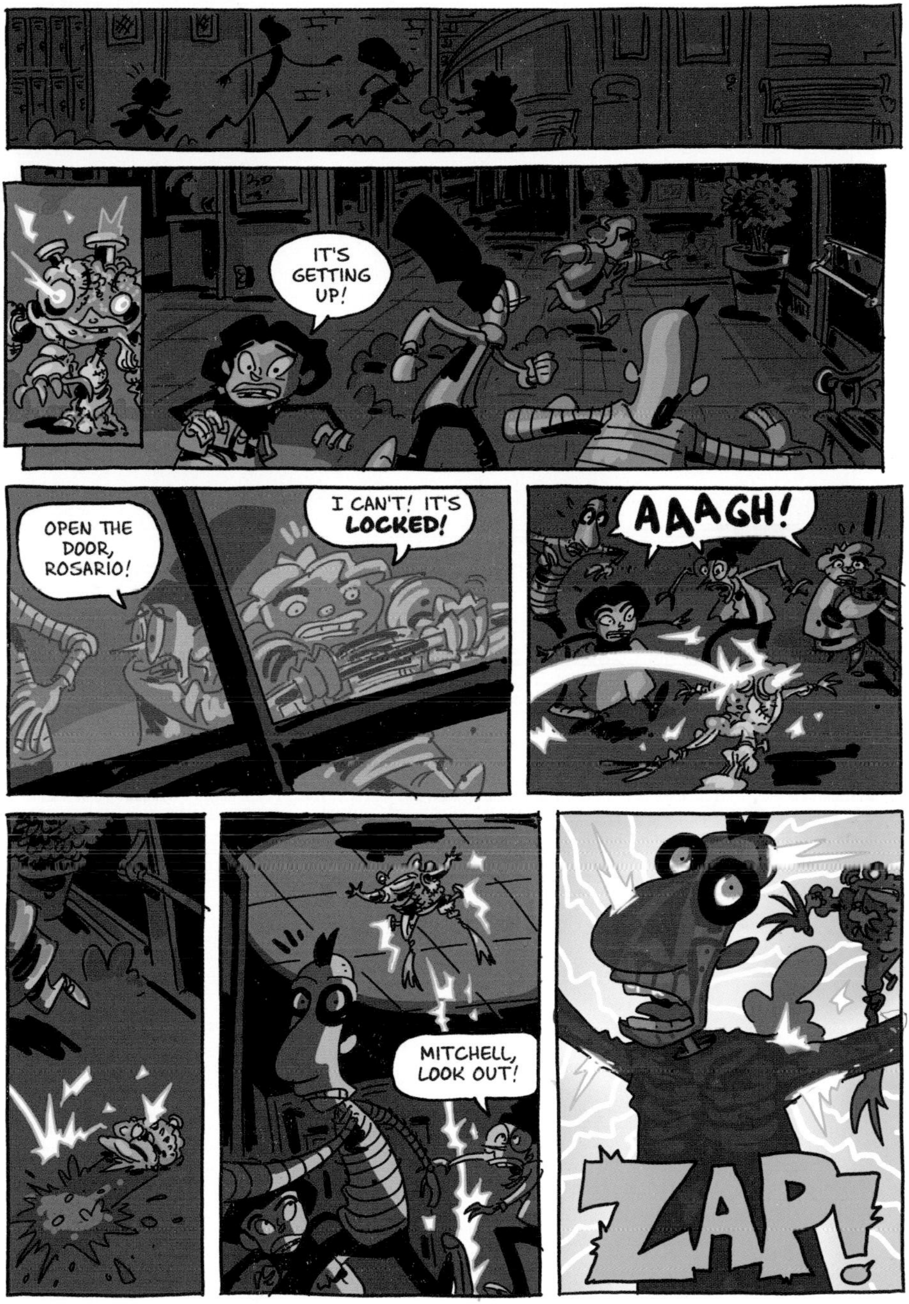
IT'S GETTING UP!
OPEN THE DOOR, ROSARIO!
I CAN'T! IT'S LOCKED!
AAAGH!
MITCHELL, LOOK OUT!
ZAP!

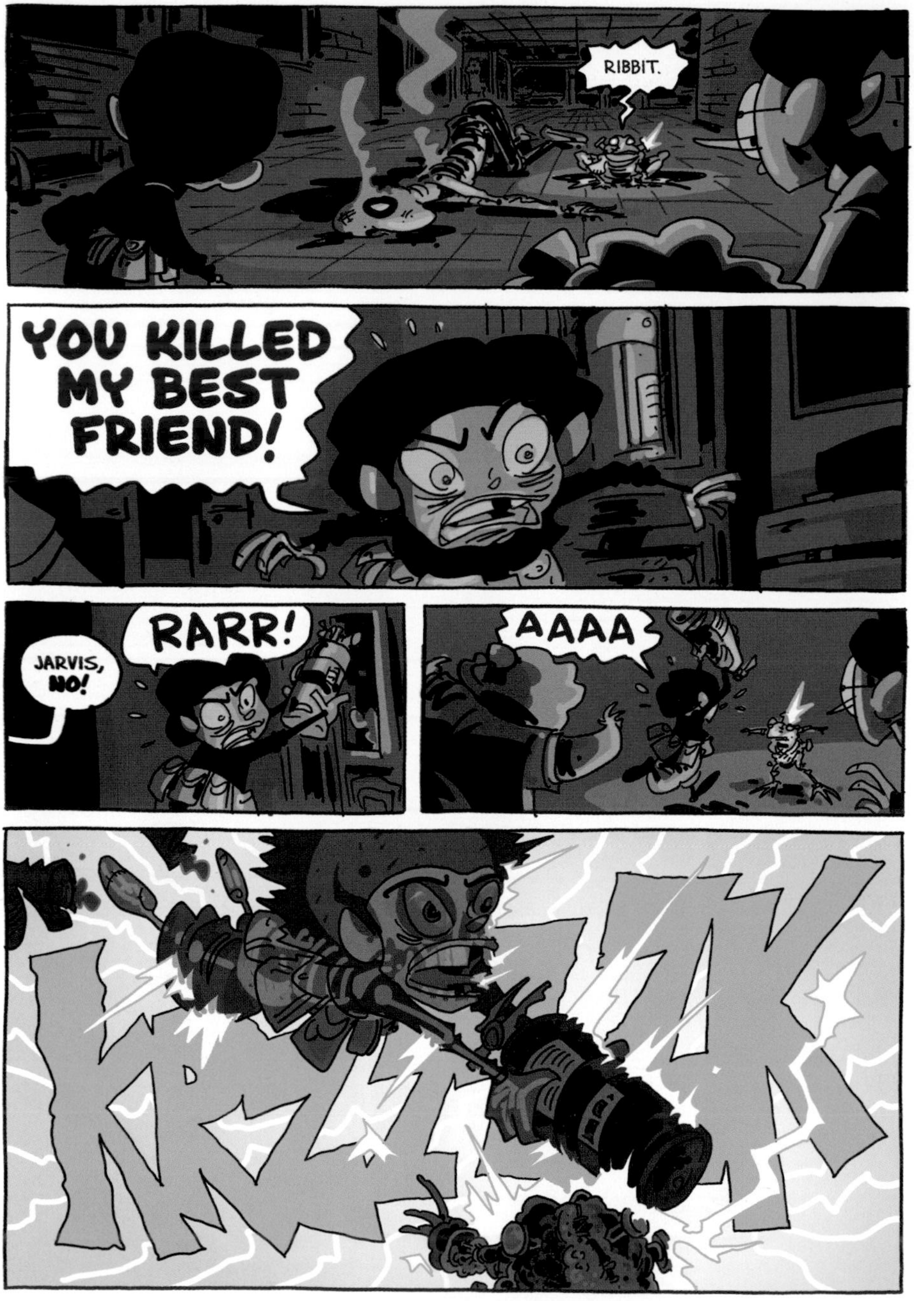
RIBBIT.
YOU KILLED MY BEST FRIEND!
JARVIS, NO!
RARR!
AAAA

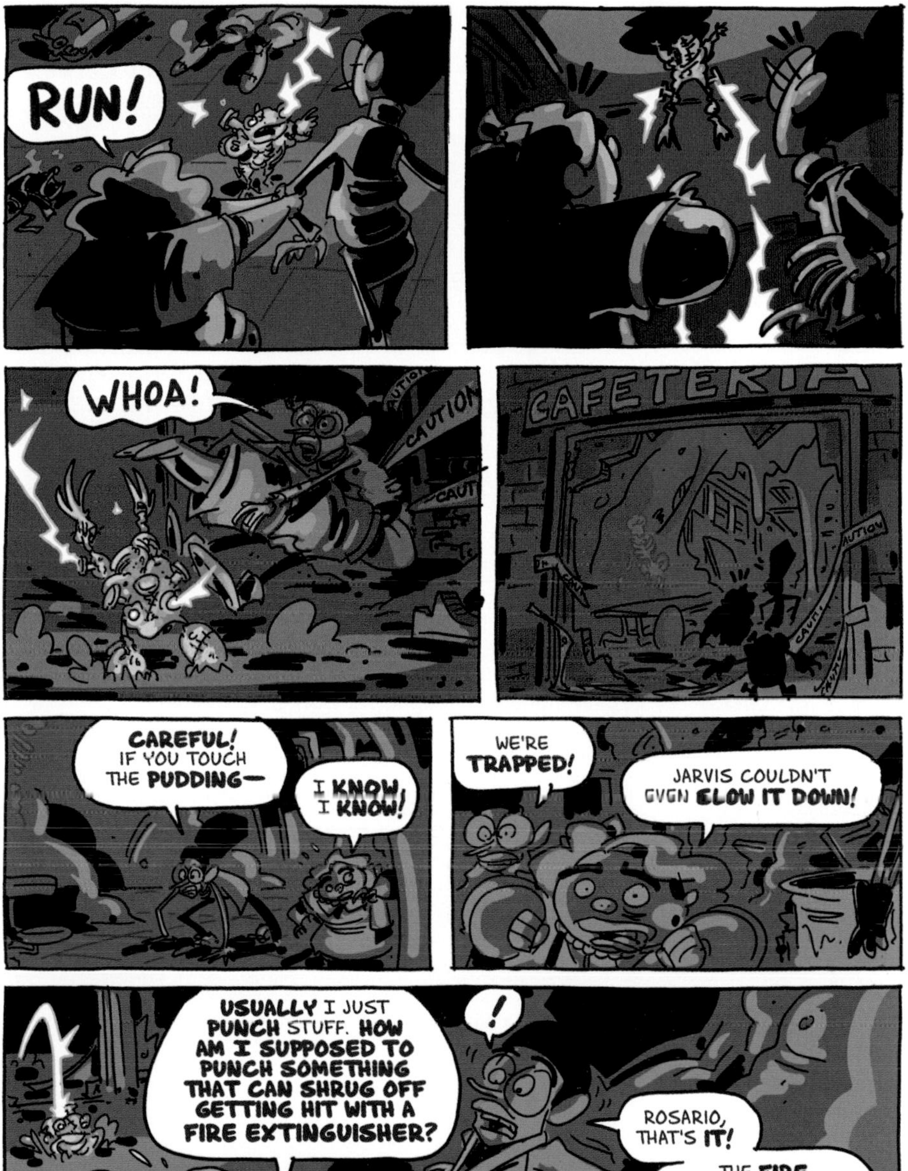
RUN!
WHOA!
CAUTION
CAFETERIA
CAREFUL! IF YOU TOUCH THE PUDDING—
I KNOW, I KNOW!
WE'RE TRAPPED!
JARVIS COULDN'T EVEN SLOW IT DOWN!
USUALLY I JUST PUNCH STUFF. HOW AM I SUPPOSED TO PUNCH SOMETHING THAT CAN SHRUG OFF GETTING HIT WITH A FIRE EXTINGUISHER?
FLOP
!
ROSARIO, THAT'S IT!
THE FIRE EXTINGUISHER WAS MADE OF METAL...IT CONDUCTED THE ELECTRICITY!

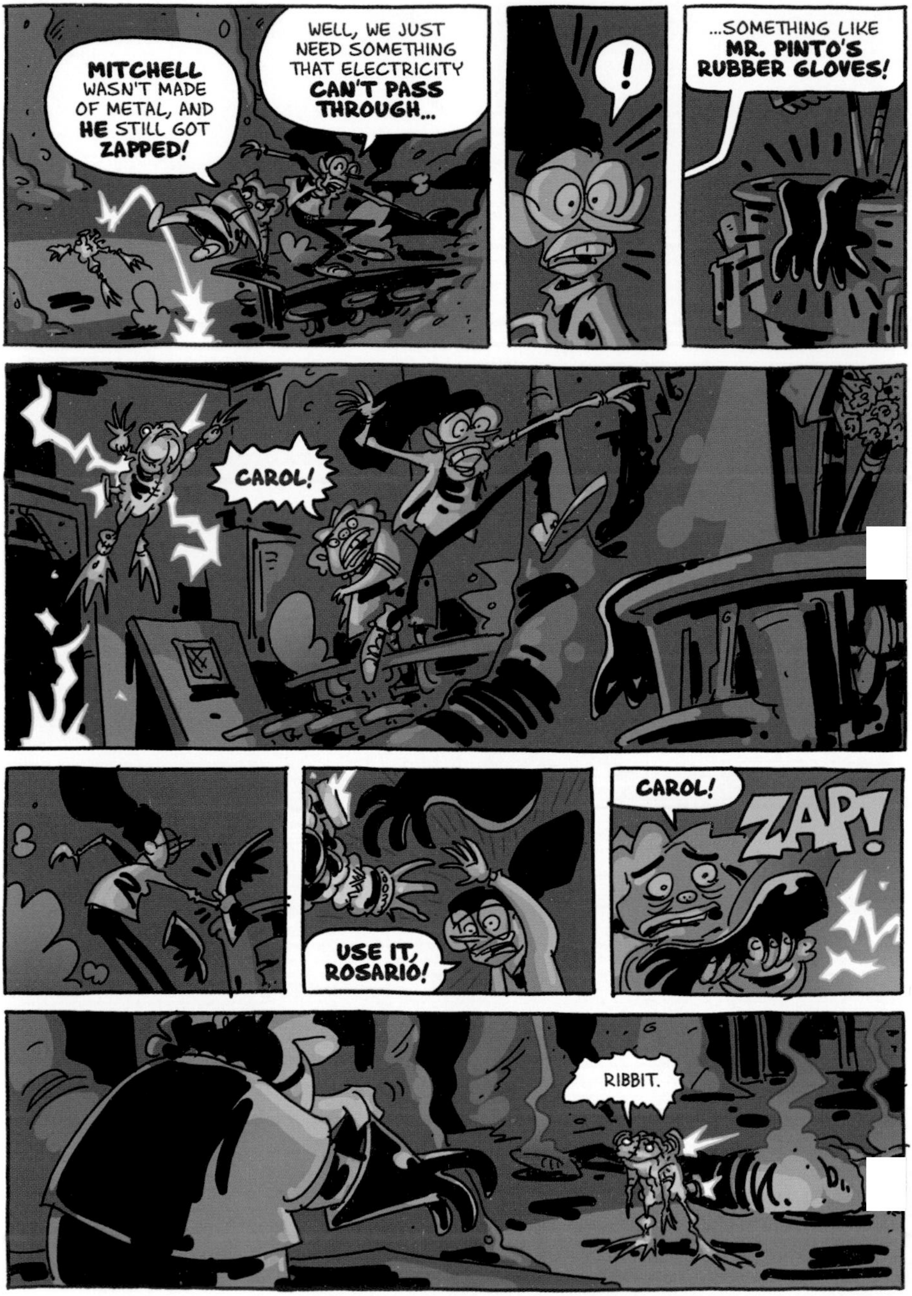
MITCHELL WASN'T MADE OF METAL, AND HE STILL GOT ZAPPED!
WELL, WE JUST NEED SOMETHING THAT ELECTRICITY CAN'T PASS THROUGH...
!
...SOMETHING LIKE MR. PINTO'S RUBBER GLOVES!
CAROL!
USE IT, ROSARIO!
CAROL!
ZAP!
RIBBIT.

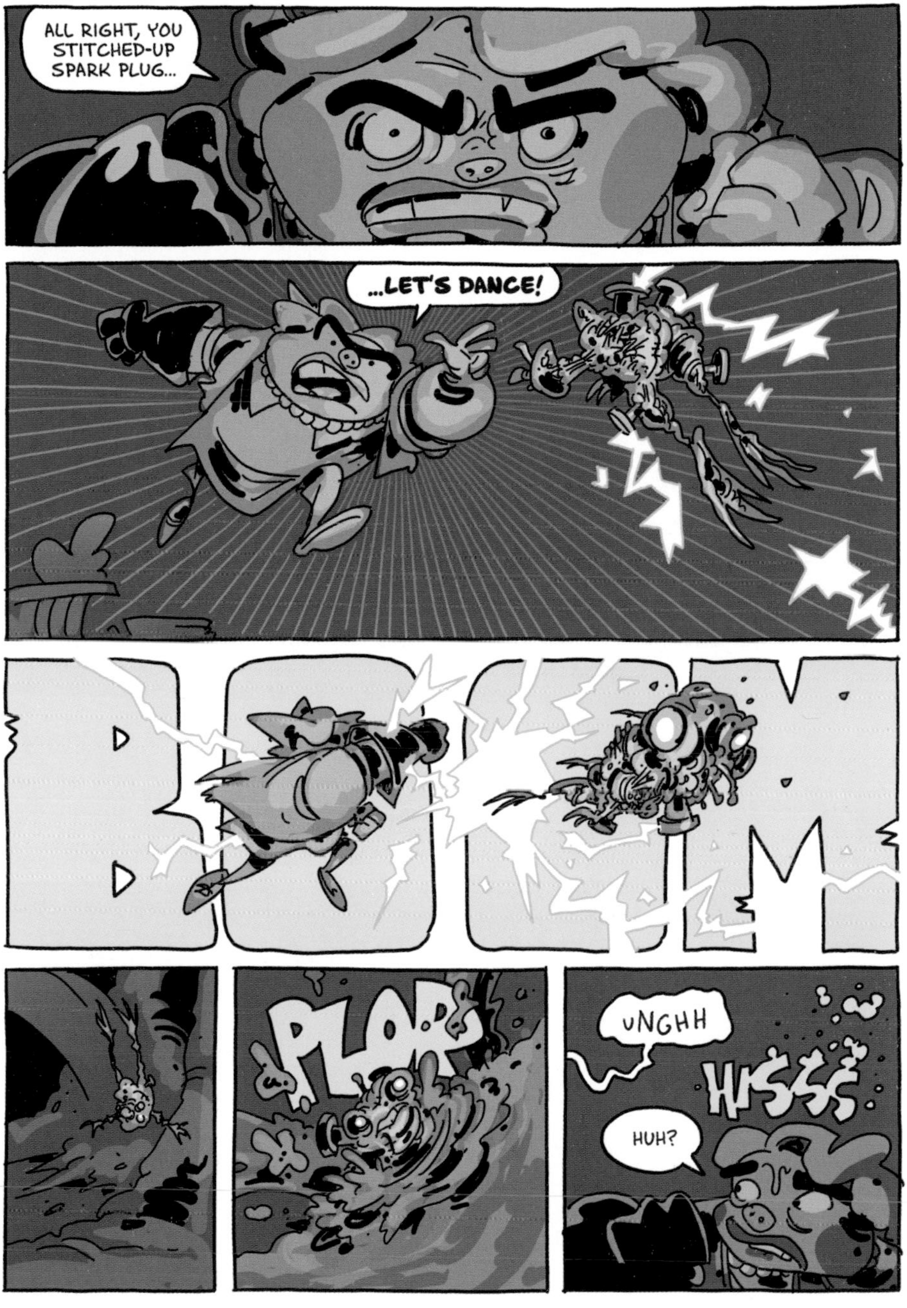
ALL RIGHT, YOU STITCHED-UP SPARK PLUG...
...LET'S DANCE!
BOOM
PLOP
UNGHH
HISSS
HUH?

66

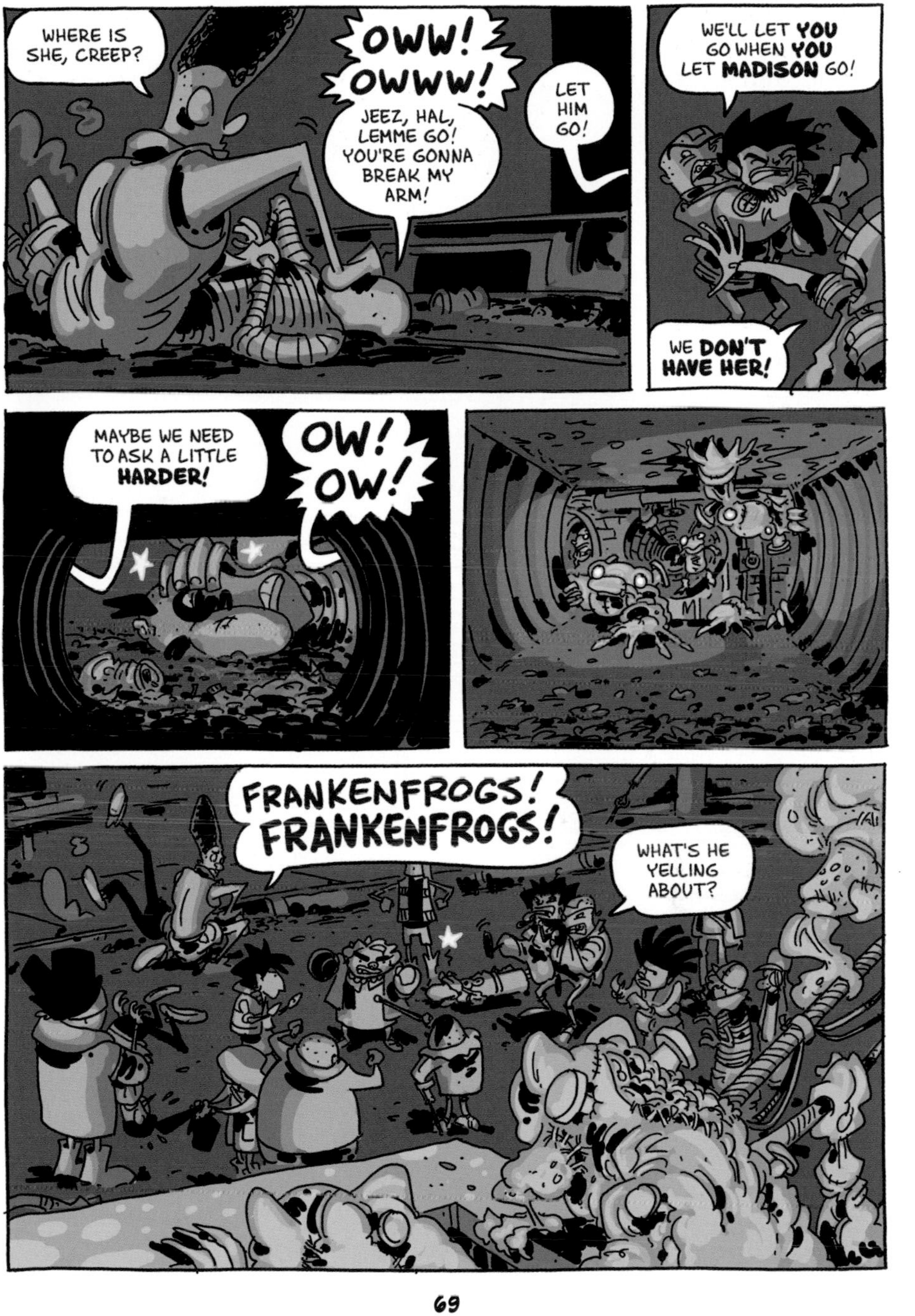
WHERE IS SHE, CREEP?
OWW! OWWW!
JEEZ, HAL, LEMME GO! YOU'RE GONNA BREAK MY ARM!
LET HIM GO!
WE'LL LET **YOU** GO WHEN **YOU** LET **MADISON** GO!
WE **DON'T HAVE HER!**
MAYBE WE NEED TO ASK A LITTLE **HARDER!**
OW! OW!
FRANKENFROGS! FRANKENFROGS!
WHAT'S HE YELLING ABOUT?

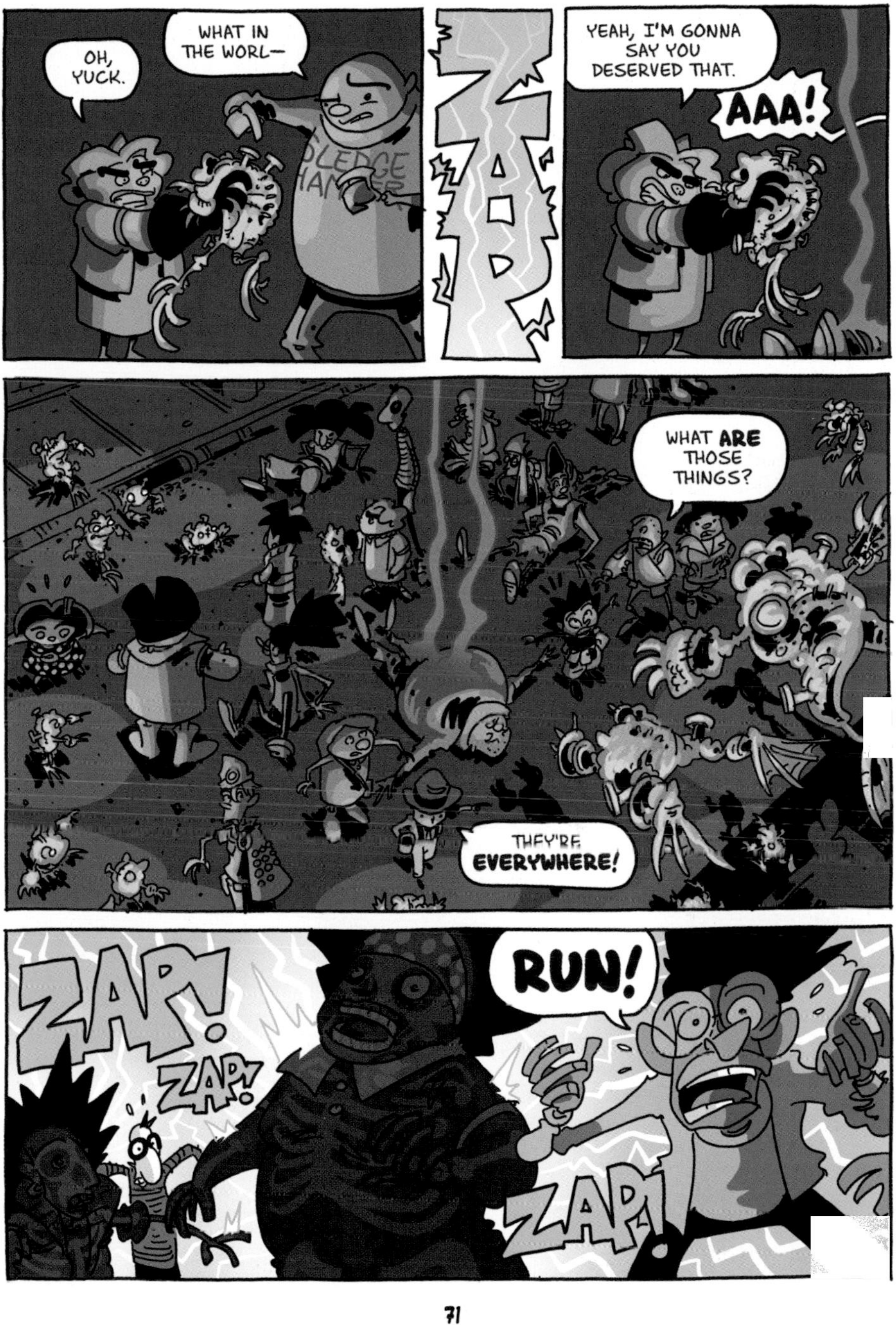

OH, YUCK.
WHAT IN THE WORL—
SLEDGE HAMMER
ZAP!
YEAH, I'M GONNA SAY YOU DESERVED THAT.
AAA!
WHAT **ARE** THOSE THINGS?
THEY'RE **EVERYWHERE!**
ZAP!
ZAP!
RUN!
ZAP!

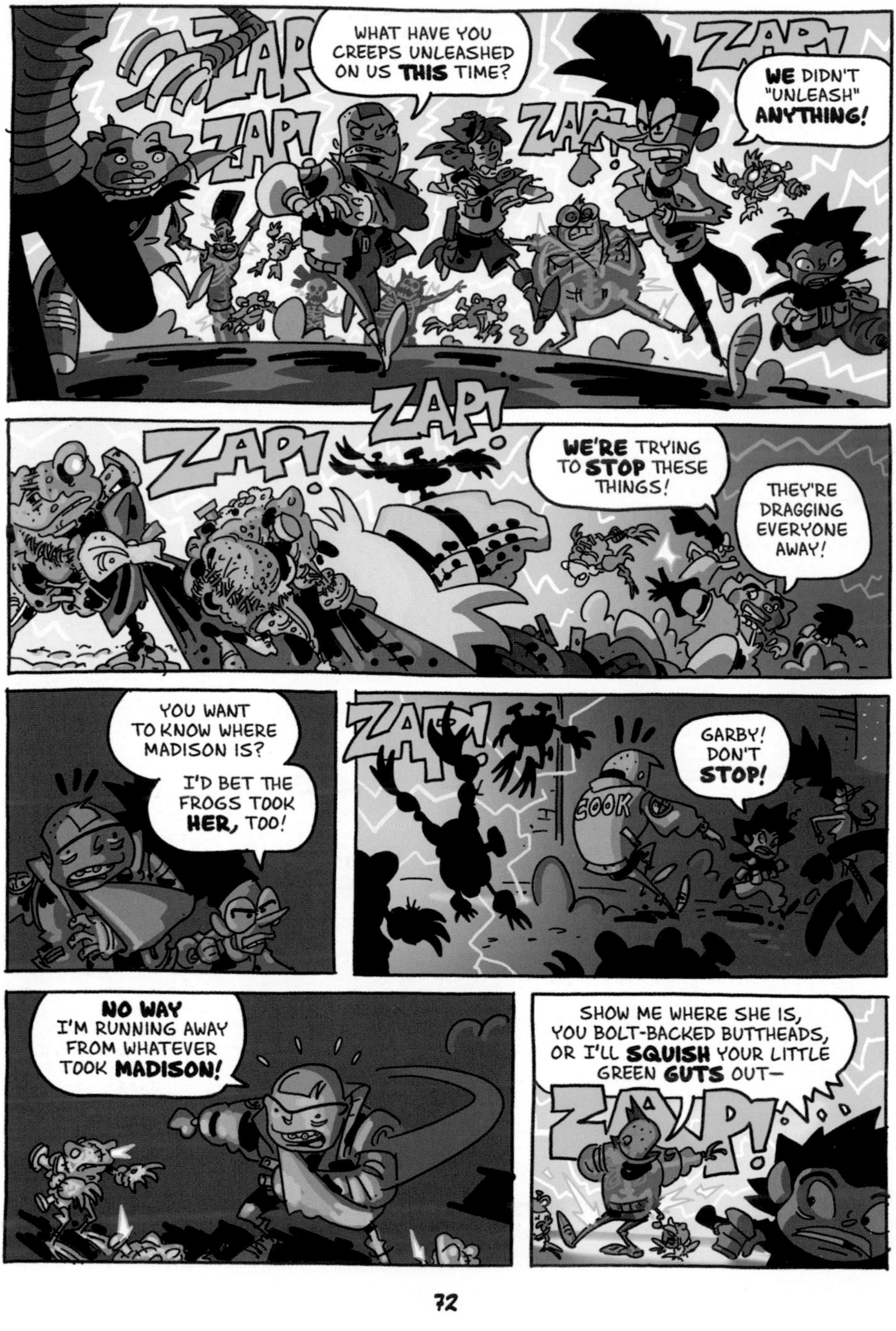
ZAP!
ZAP!
WHAT HAVE YOU CREEPS UNLEASHED ON US **THIS** TIME?
ZAP!
ZAP!
WE DIDN'T "UNLEASH" **ANYTHING!**
ZAP!
ZAP!
WE'RE TRYING TO **STOP** THESE THINGS!
THEY'RE DRAGGING EVERYONE AWAY!
YOU WANT TO KNOW WHERE MADISON IS?
I'D BET THE FROGS TOOK **HER,** TOO!
ZAP!
GARBY! DON'T **STOP!**
COOK
NO WAY I'M RUNNING AWAY FROM WHATEVER TOOK **MADISON!**
SHOW ME WHERE SHE IS, YOU BOLT-BACKED BUTTHEADS, OR I'LL **SQUISH** YOUR LITTLE GREEN **GUTS** OUT—
ZAP!

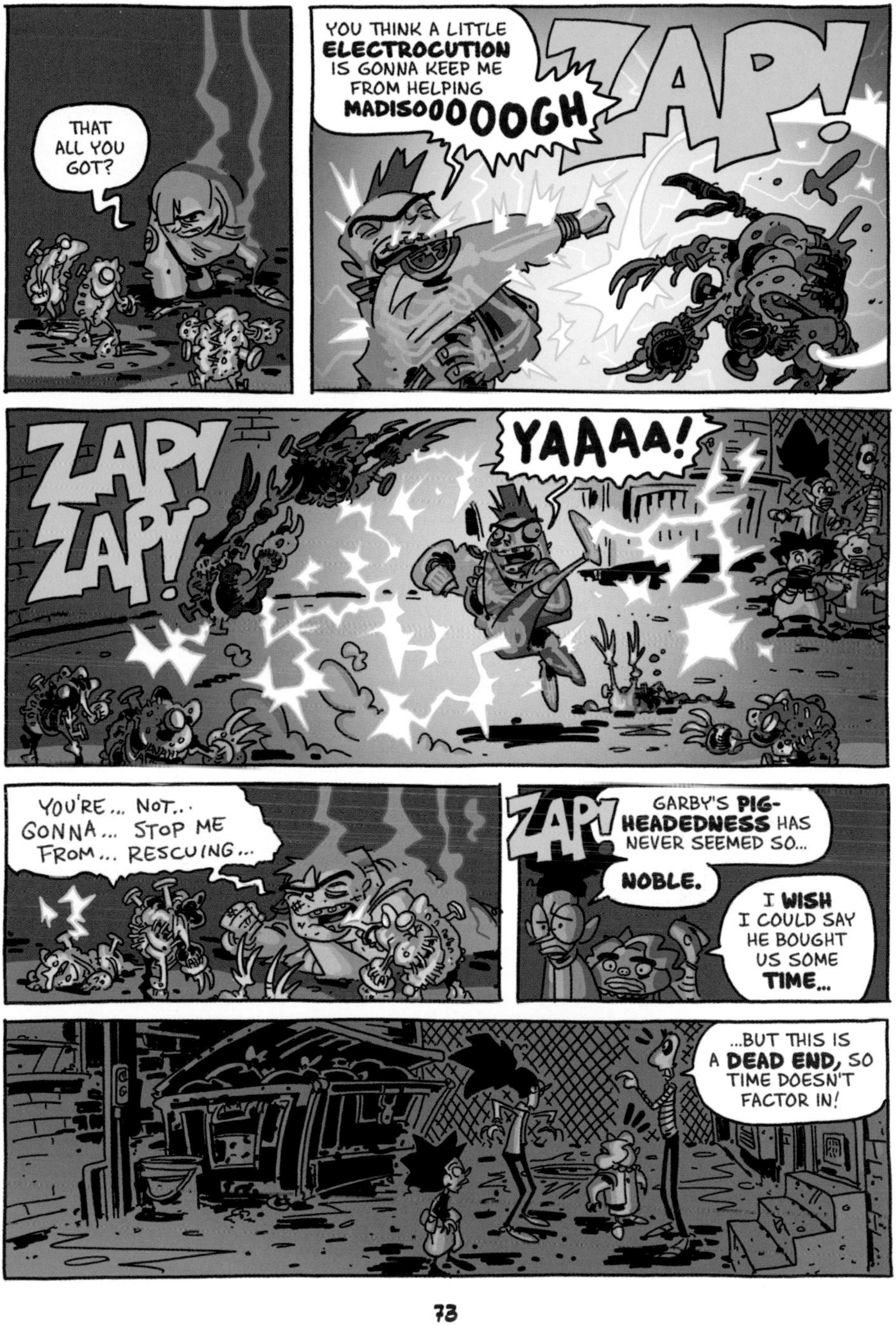
THAT ALL YOU GOT?
YOU THINK A LITTLE **ELECTROCUTION** IS GONNA KEEP ME FROM HELPING MADISOOOOOGH
ZAP!
ZAP! ZAP!
YAAAA!
YOU'RE... NOT... GONNA... STOP ME FROM... RESCUING...
ZAP!
GARBY'S **PIG-HEADEDNESS** HAS NEVER SEEMED SO...
NOBLE.
I **WISH** I COULD SAY HE BOUGHT US SOME **TIME...**
...BUT THIS IS A **DEAD END,** SO TIME DOESN'T FACTOR IN!

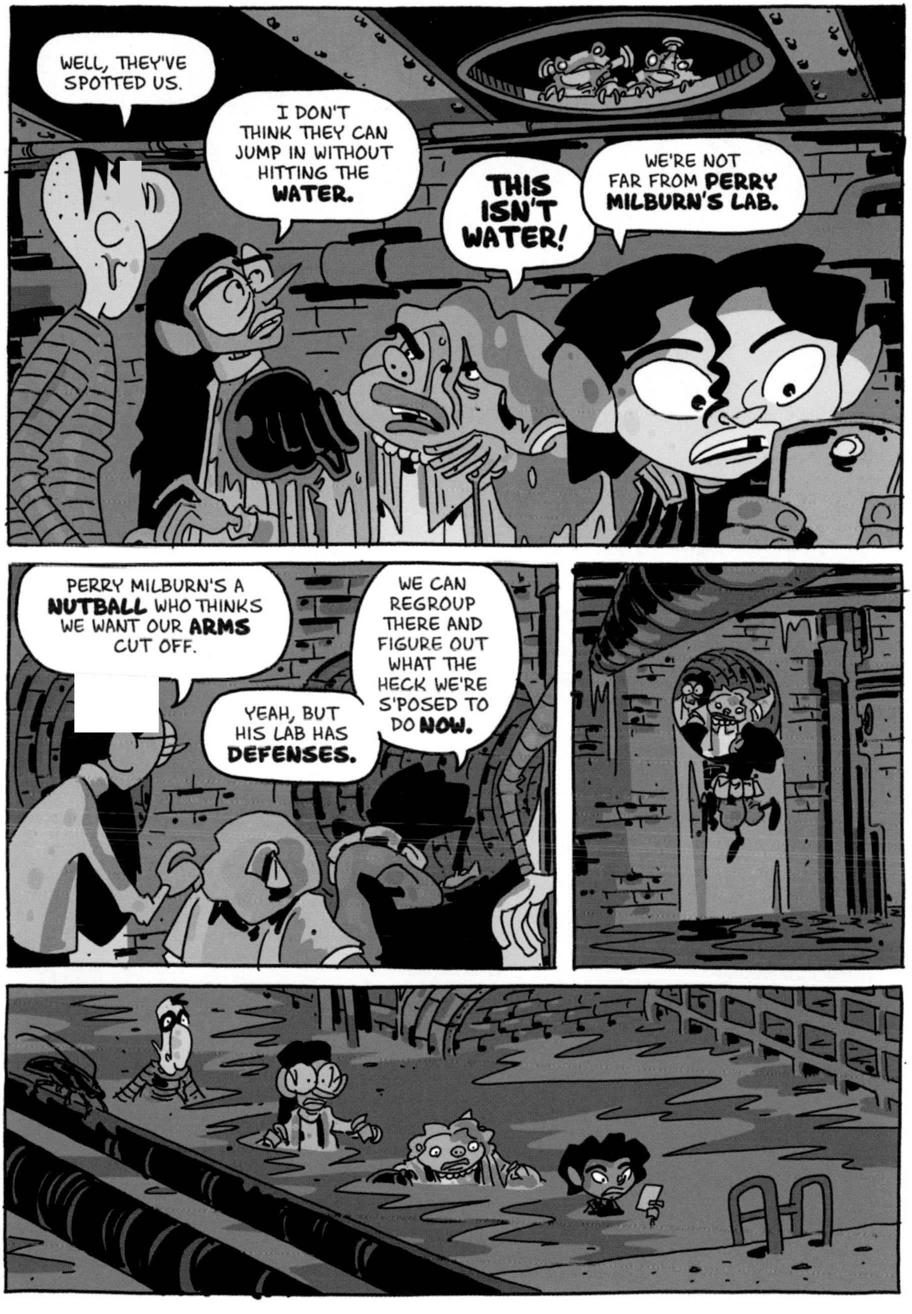
WELL, THEY'VE SPOTTED US.
I DON'T THINK THEY CAN JUMP IN WITHOUT HITTING THE **WATER.**
THIS ISN'T WATER!
WE'RE NOT FAR FROM **PERRY MILBURN'S LAB.**
PERRY MILBURN'S A **NUTBALL** WHO THINKS WE WANT OUR **ARMS** CUT OFF.
YEAH, BUT HIS LAB HAS **DEFENSES.**
WE CAN REGROUP THERE AND FIGURE OUT WHAT THE HECK WE'RE S'POSED TO DO **NOW.**

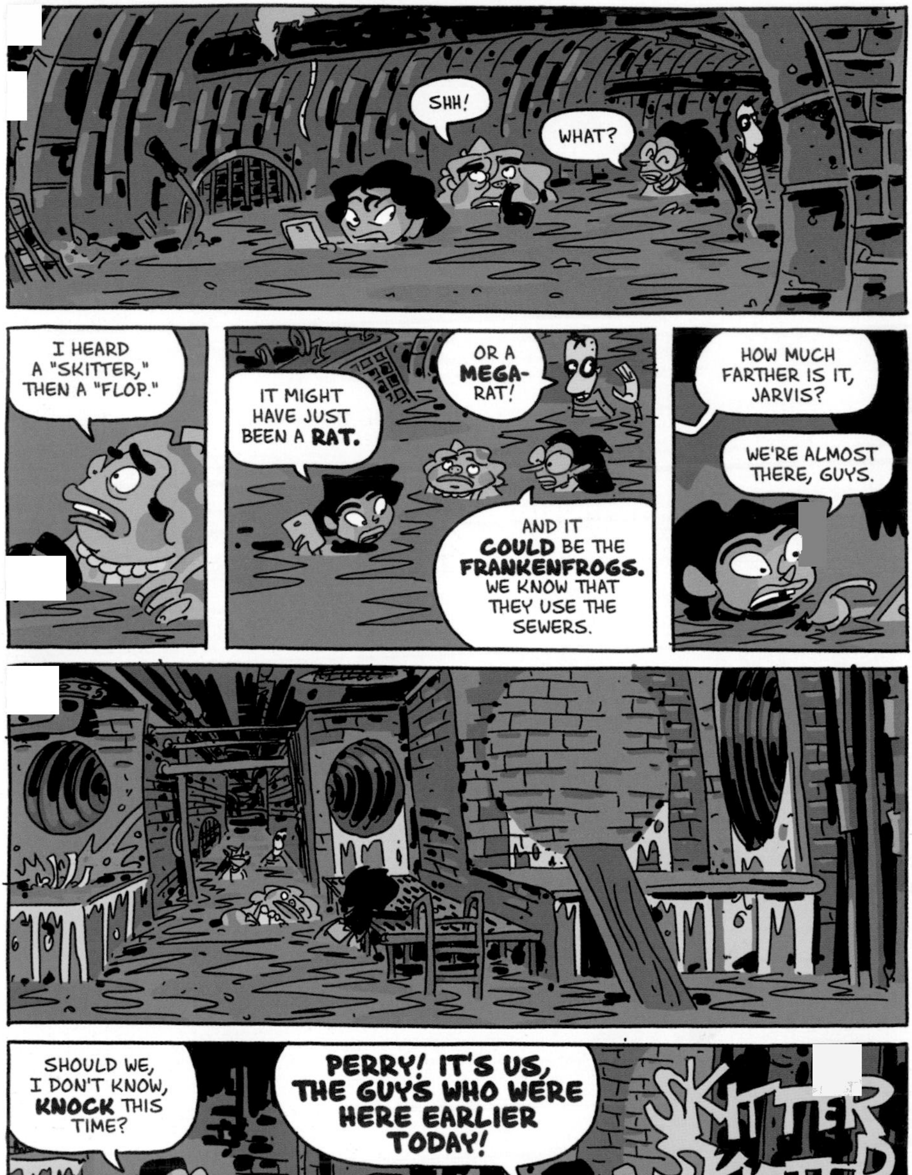

SHH!
WHAT?
I HEARD A "SKITTER," THEN A "FLOP."
IT MIGHT HAVE JUST BEEN A RAT.
OR A MEGA-RAT!
AND IT COULD BE THE FRANKENFROGS. WE KNOW THAT THEY USE THE SEWERS.
HOW MUCH FARTHER IS IT, JARVIS?
WE'RE ALMOST THERE, GUYS.
SHOULD WE, I DON'T KNOW, KNOCK THIS TIME?
PERRY! IT'S US, THE GUYS WHO WERE HERE EARLIER TODAY!
SKITTER SKITTER FLOP

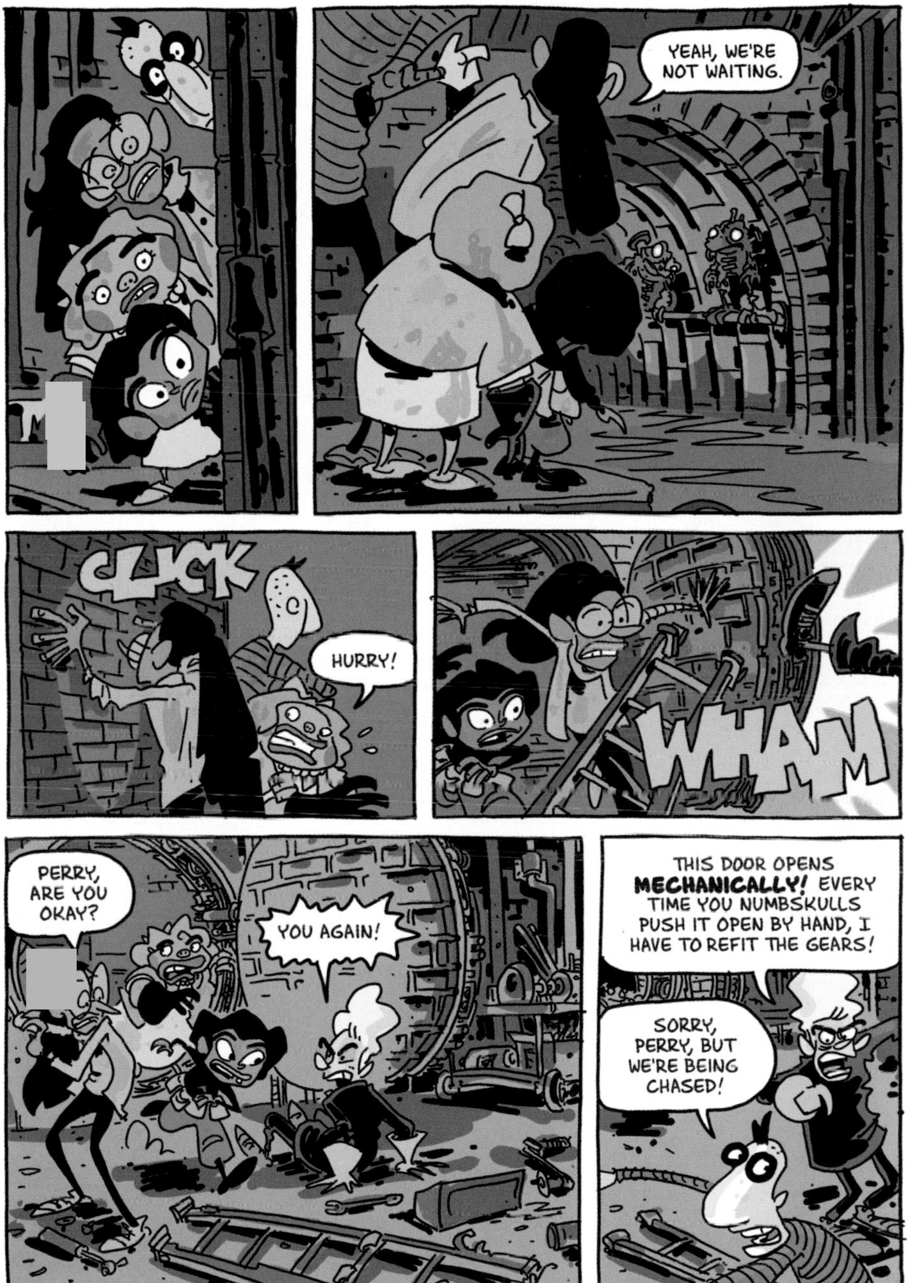

YEAH, WE'RE NOT WAITING.
CLICK
HURRY!
WHAM
PERRY, ARE YOU OKAY?
YOU AGAIN!
THIS DOOR OPENS MECHANICALLY! EVERY TIME YOU NUMBSKULLS PUSH IT OPEN BY HAND, I HAVE TO REFIT THE GEARS!
SORRY, PERRY, BUT WE'RE BEING CHASED!

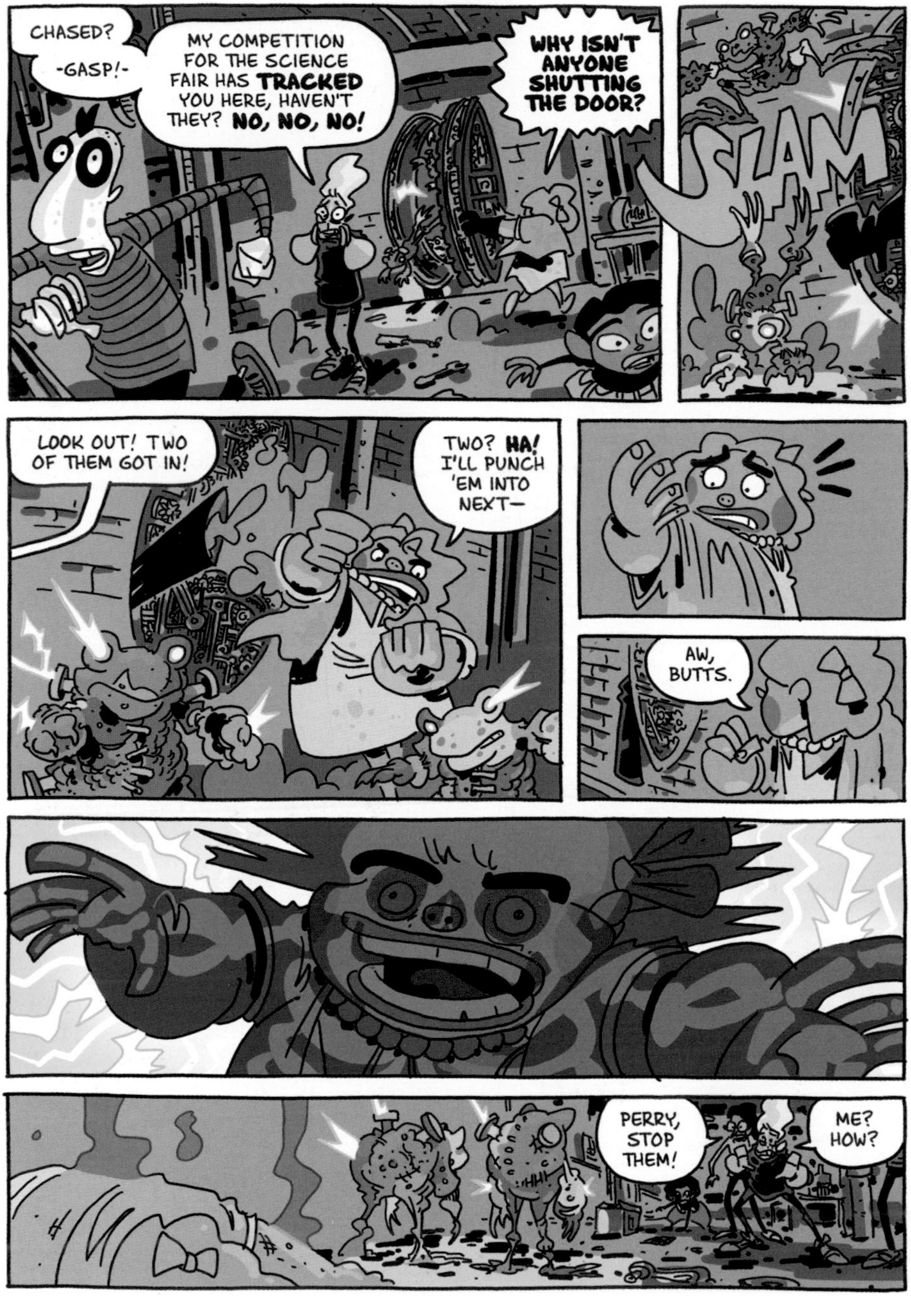
CHASED?
-GASP!-
MY COMPETITION FOR THE SCIENCE FAIR HAS **TRACKED** YOU HERE, HAVEN'T THEY? **NO, NO, NO!**
WHY ISN'T ANYONE SHUTTING THE DOOR?
SLAM
LOOK OUT! TWO OF THEM GOT IN!
TWO? **HA!** I'LL PUNCH 'EM INTO NEXT—
AW, BUTTS.
PERRY, STOP THEM!
ME? HOW?

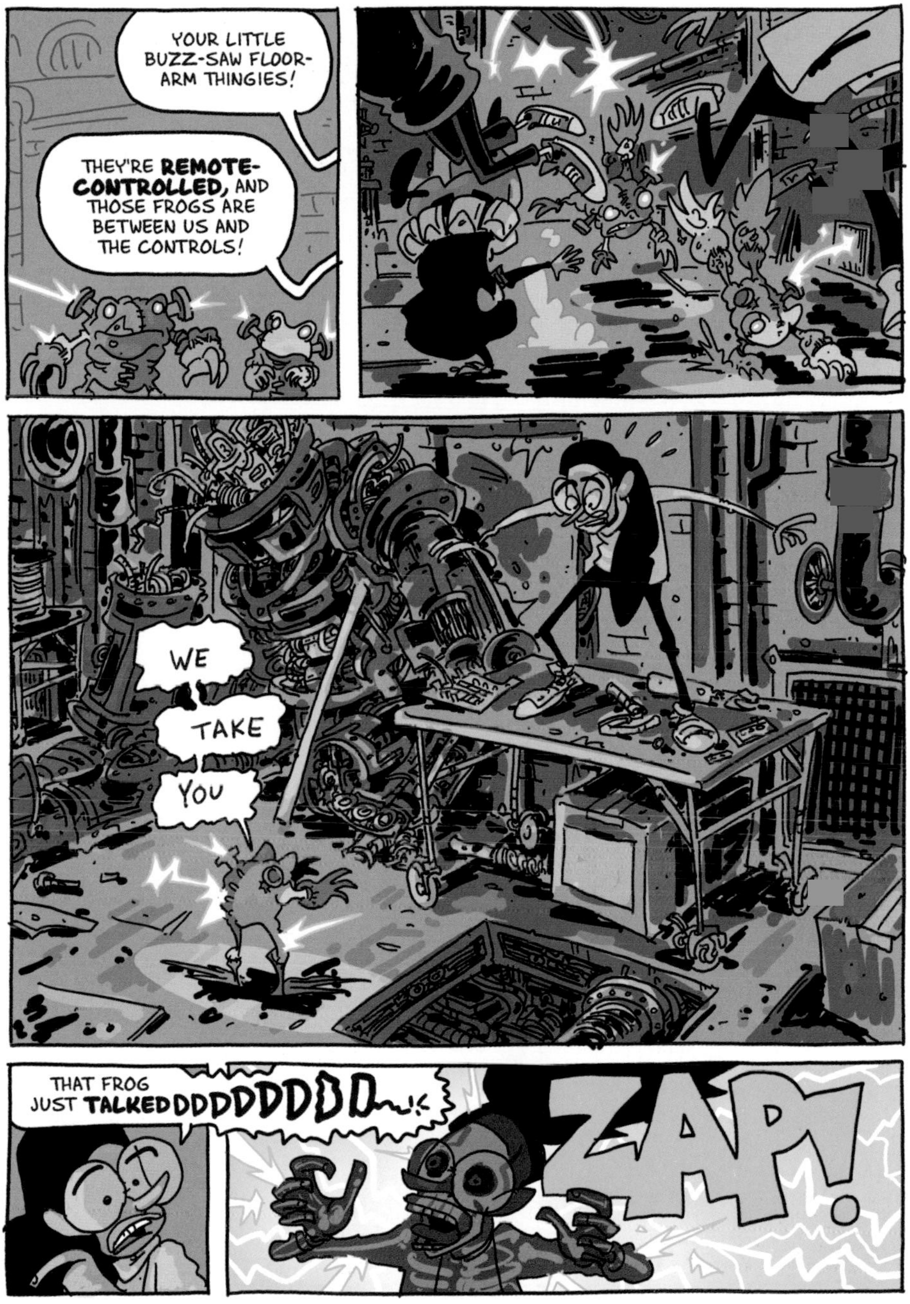

YOUR LITTLE BUZZ-SAW FLOOR-ARM THINGIES!
THEY'RE **REMOTE-CONTROLLED,** AND THOSE FROGS ARE BETWEEN US AND THE CONTROLS!
WE
TAKE
YOU
THAT FROG JUST **TALKEDDDDDDDDD**
ZAP!

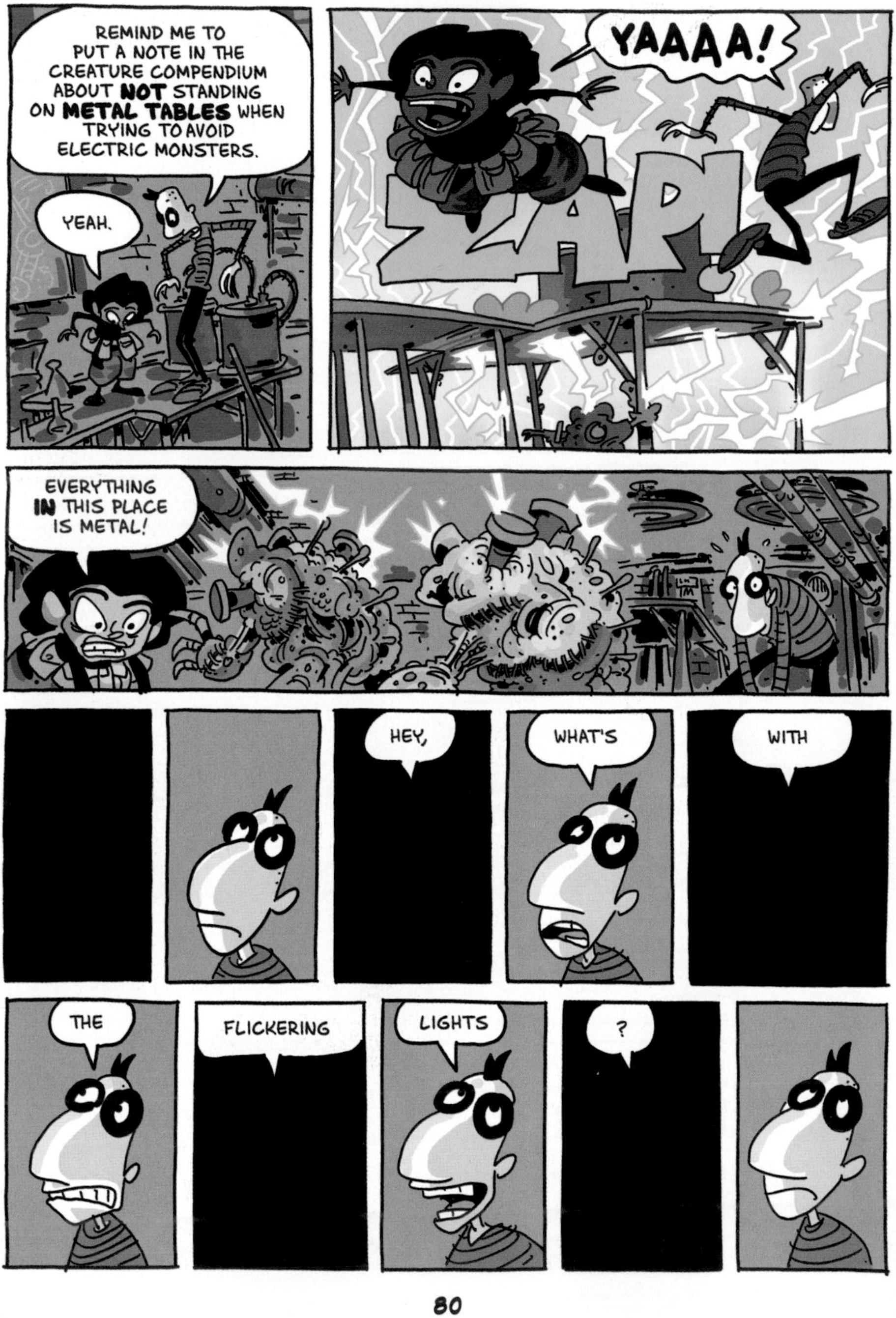
REMIND ME TO PUT A NOTE IN THE CREATURE COMPENDIUM ABOUT NOT STANDING ON METAL TABLES WHEN TRYING TO AVOID ELECTRIC MONSTERS.
YEAH.
YAAAA!
ZAP!
EVERYTHING IN THIS PLACE IS METAL!
HEY,
WHAT'S
WITH
THE
FLICKERING
LIGHTS
?

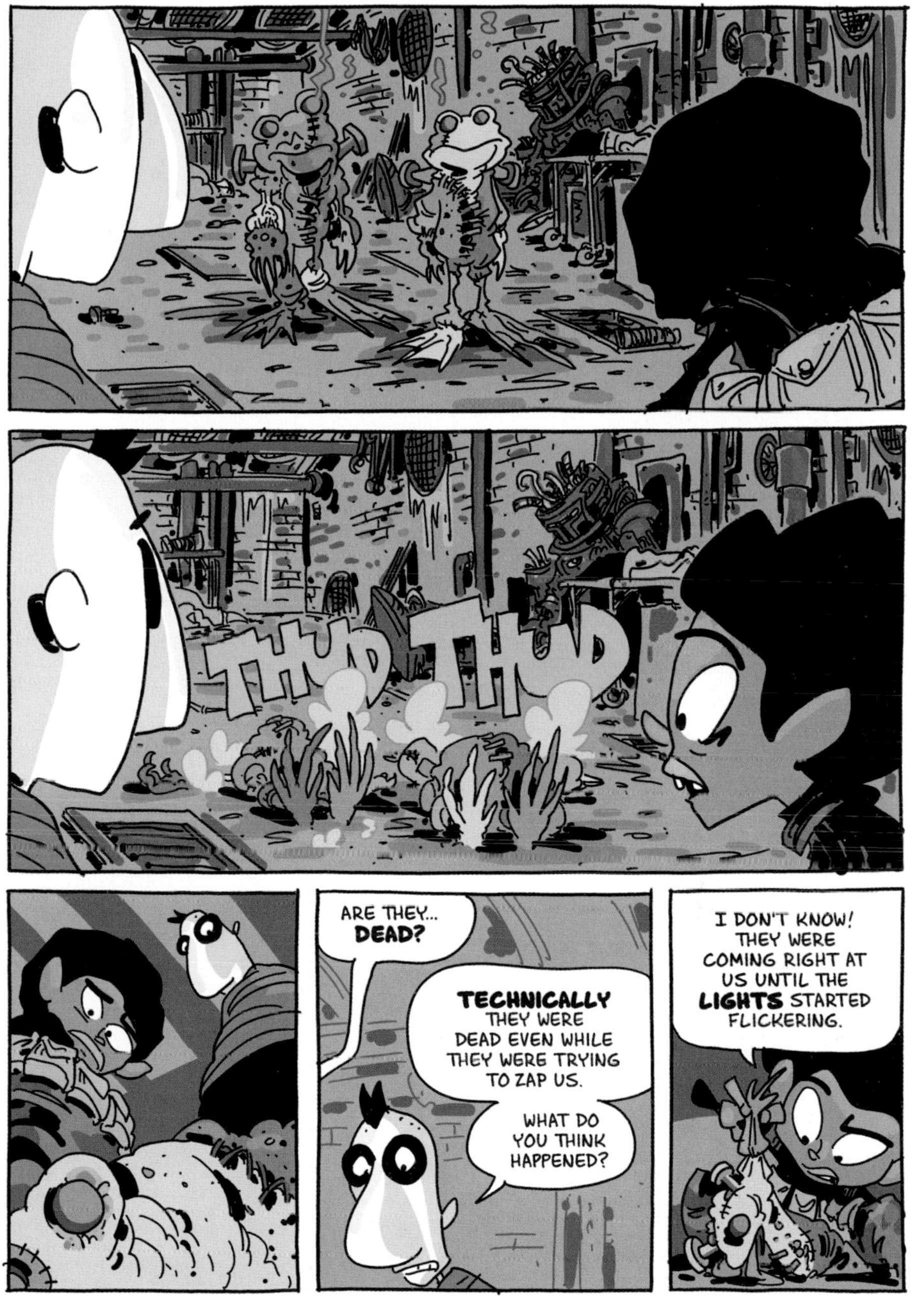
THUD THUD
ARE THEY... DEAD?
TECHNICALLY THEY WERE DEAD EVEN WHILE THEY WERE TRYING TO ZAP US.
WHAT DO YOU THINK HAPPENED?
I DON'T KNOW! THEY WERE COMING RIGHT AT US UNTIL THE LIGHTS STARTED FLICKERING.

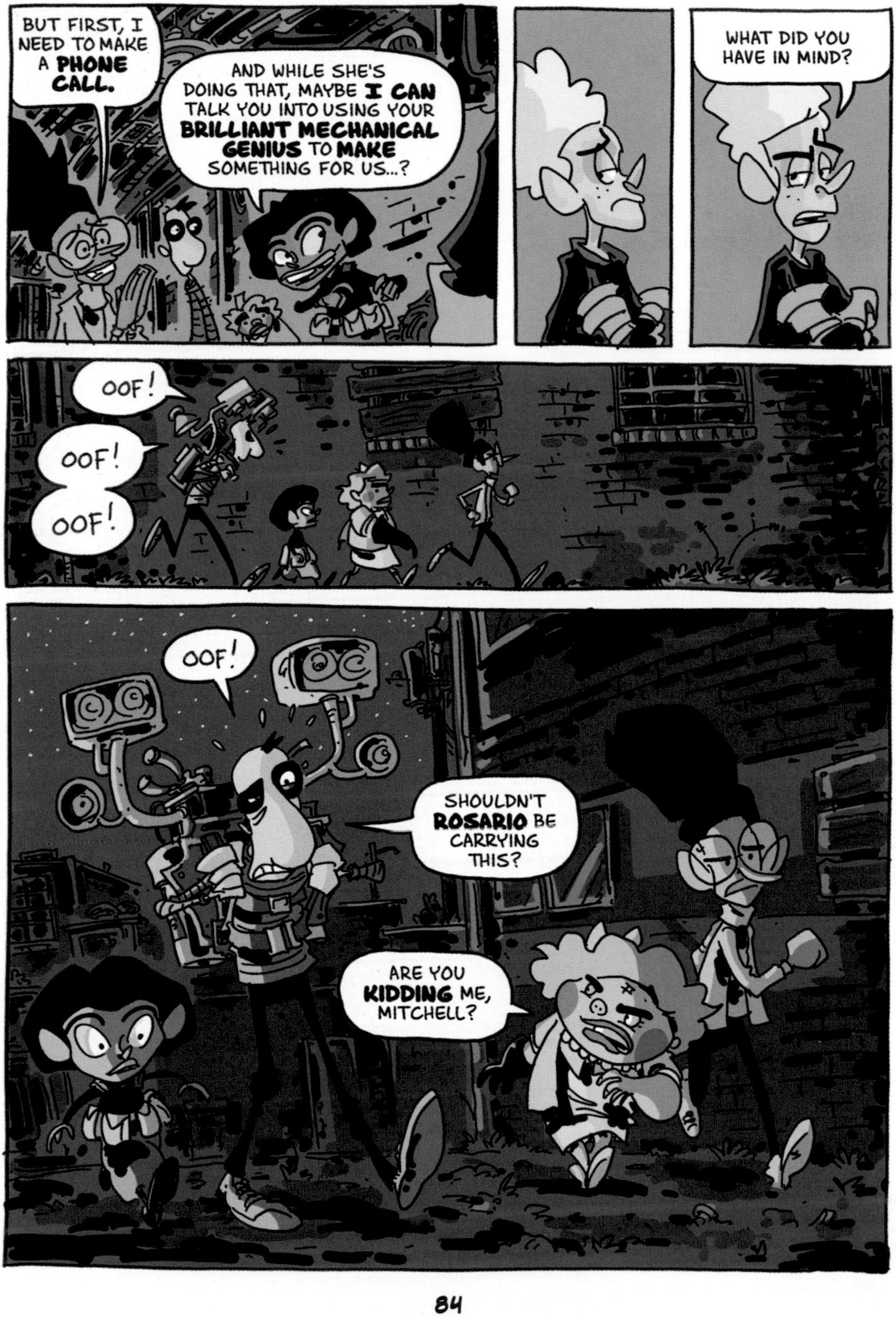
BUT FIRST, I NEED TO MAKE A PHONE CALL.
AND WHILE SHE'S DOING THAT, MAYBE I CAN TALK YOU INTO USING YOUR BRILLIANT MECHANICAL GENIUS TO MAKE SOMETHING FOR US...?
WHAT DID YOU HAVE IN MIND?
OOF!
OOF!
OOF!
OOF!
SHOULDN'T ROSARIO BE CARRYING THIS?
ARE YOU KIDDING ME, MITCHELL?

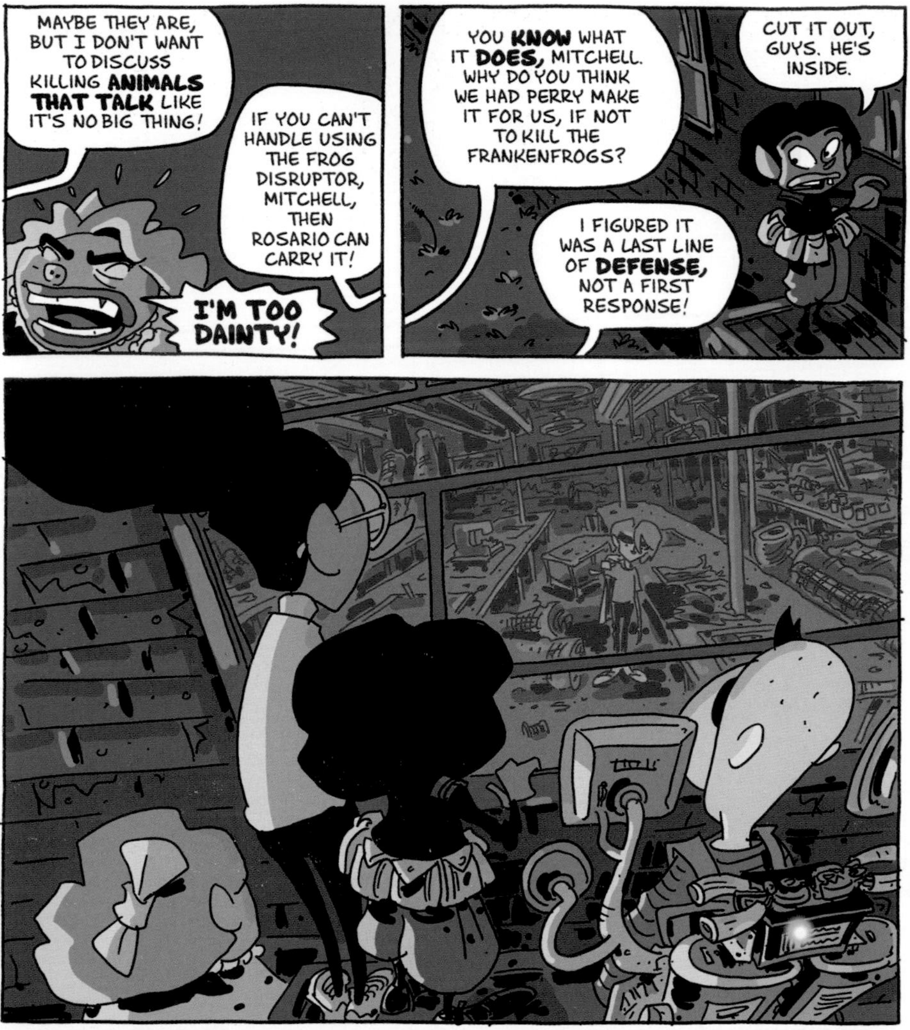

MAYBE THEY ARE, BUT I DON'T WANT TO DISCUSS KILLING **ANIMALS THAT TALK** LIKE IT'S NO BIG THING!
IF YOU CAN'T HANDLE USING THE FROG DISRUPTOR, MITCHELL, THEN ROSARIO CAN CARRY IT!
I'M TOO DAINTY!
YOU **KNOW** WHAT IT **DOES,** MITCHELL. WHY DO YOU THINK WE HAD PERRY MAKE IT FOR US, IF NOT TO KILL THE FRANKENFROGS?
I FIGURED IT WAS A LAST LINE OF **DEFENSE,** NOT A FIRST RESPONSE!
CUT IT OUT, GUYS. HE'S INSIDE.
YOU COMIN' IN, OR WHAT?

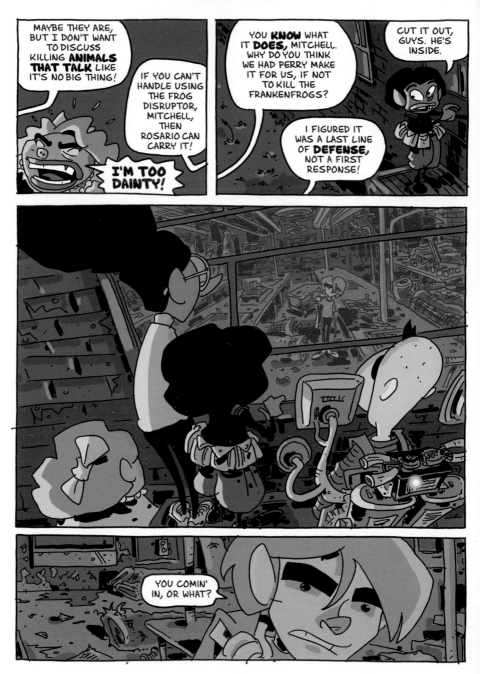

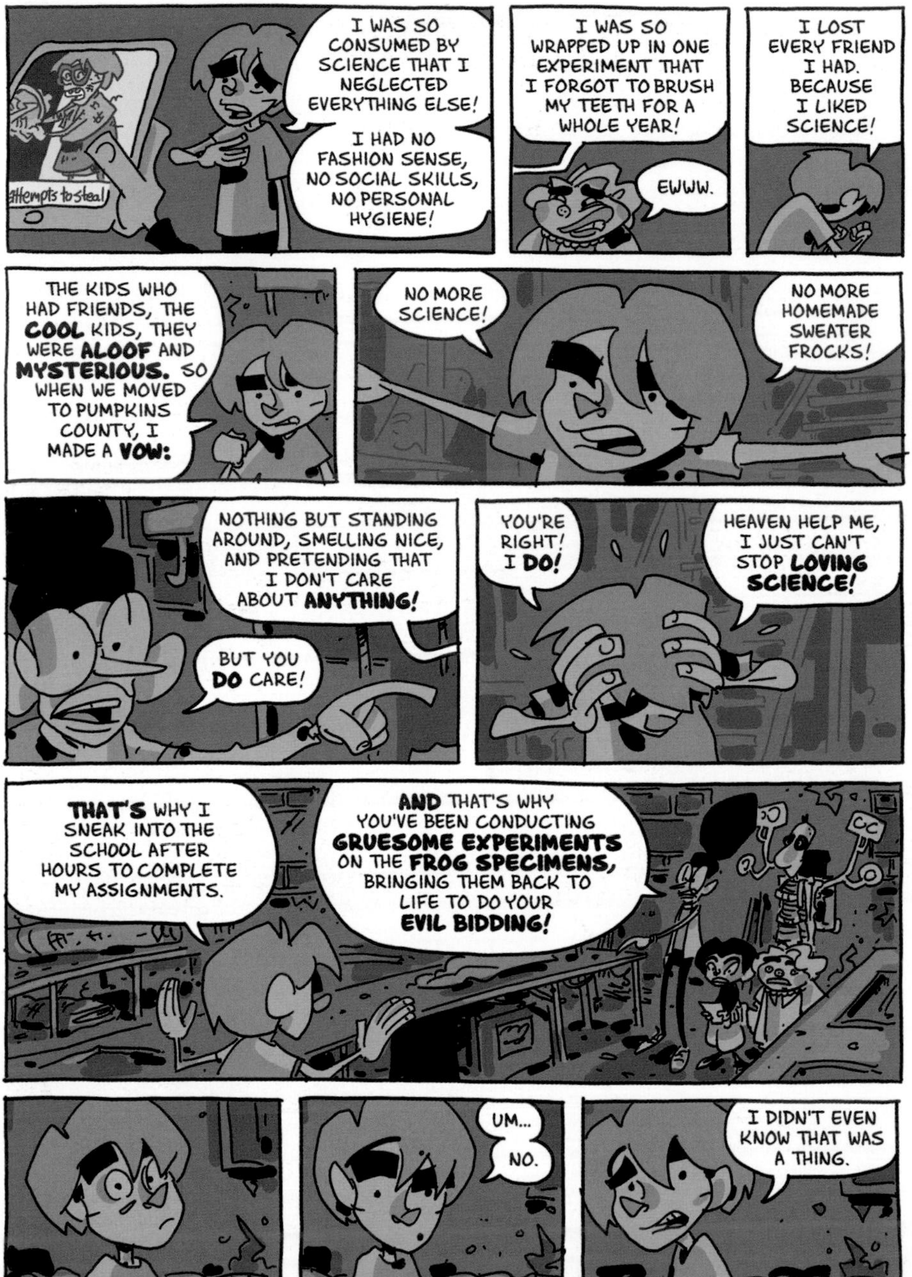
attempts to steal
I WAS SO CONSUMED BY SCIENCE THAT I NEGLECTED EVERYTHING ELSE!
I HAD NO FASHION SENSE, NO SOCIAL SKILLS, NO PERSONAL HYGIENE!
I WAS SO WRAPPED UP IN ONE EXPERIMENT THAT I FORGOT TO BRUSH MY TEETH FOR A WHOLE YEAR!
EWWW.
I LOST EVERY FRIEND I HAD. BECAUSE I LIKED SCIENCE!
THE KIDS WHO HAD FRIENDS, THE **COOL** KIDS, THEY WERE **ALOOF** AND **MYSTERIOUS.** SO WHEN WE MOVED TO PUMPKINS COUNTY, I MADE A **VOW:**
NO MORE SCIENCE!
NO MORE HOMEMADE SWEATER FROCKS!
NOTHING BUT STANDING AROUND, SMELLING NICE, AND PRETENDING THAT I DON'T CARE ABOUT **ANYTHING!**
BUT YOU **DO** CARE!
YOU'RE RIGHT! I **DO!**
HEAVEN HELP ME, I JUST CAN'T STOP **LOVING SCIENCE!**
THAT'S WHY I SNEAK INTO THE SCHOOL AFTER HOURS TO COMPLETE MY ASSIGNMENTS.
AND THAT'S WHY YOU'VE BEEN CONDUCTING **GRUESOME EXPERIMENTS** ON THE **FROG SPECIMENS,** BRINGING THEM BACK TO LIFE TO DO YOUR **EVIL BIDDING!**
UM...
NO.
I DIDN'T EVEN KNOW THAT WAS A THING.

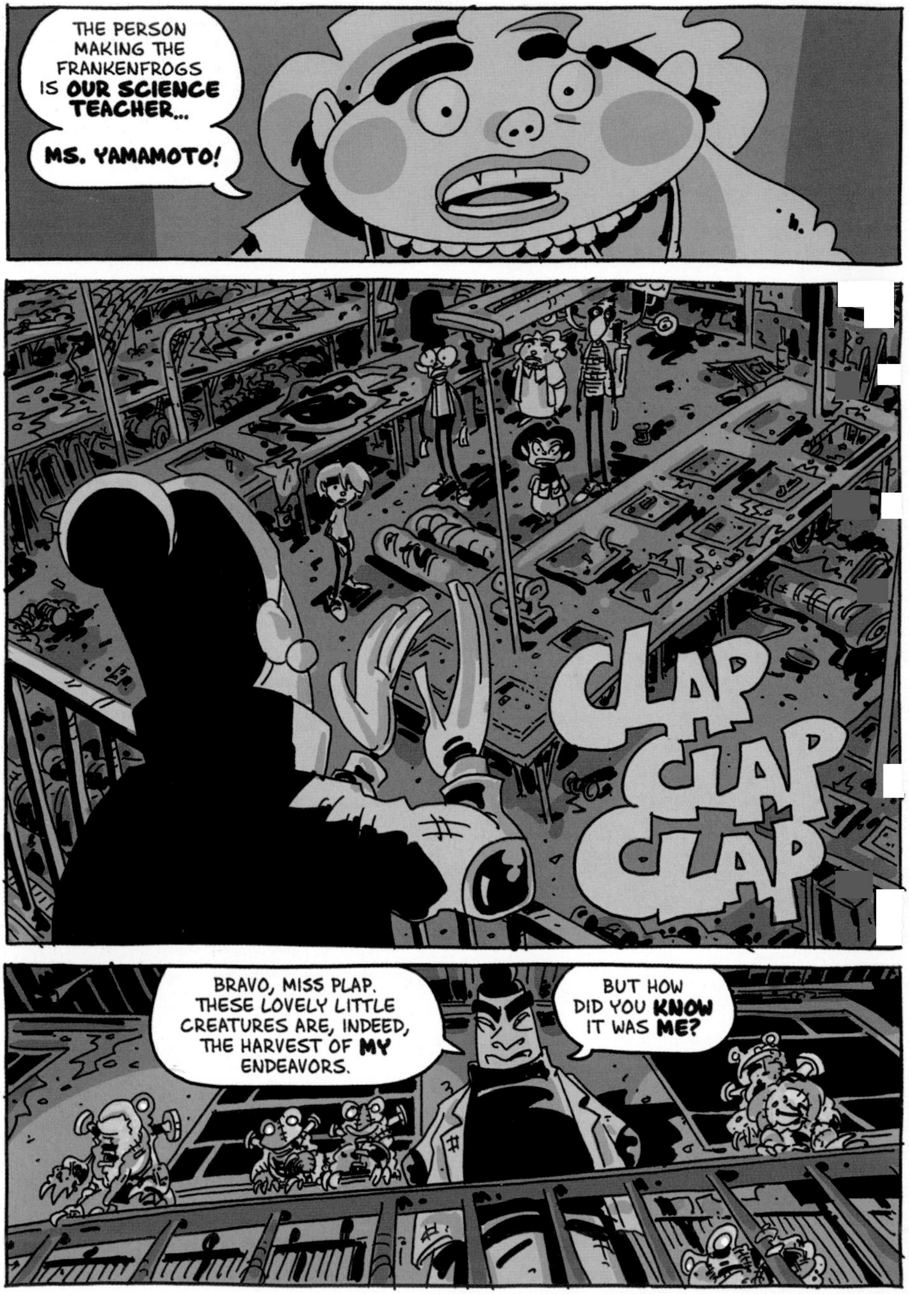
THE PERSON MAKING THE FRANKENFROGS IS OUR SCIENCE TEACHER...
MS. YAMAMOTO!
CLAP CLAP CLAP
BRAVO, MISS PLAP. THESE LOVELY LITTLE CREATURES ARE, INDEED, THE HARVEST OF MY ENDEAVORS.
BUT HOW DID YOU KNOW IT WAS ME?

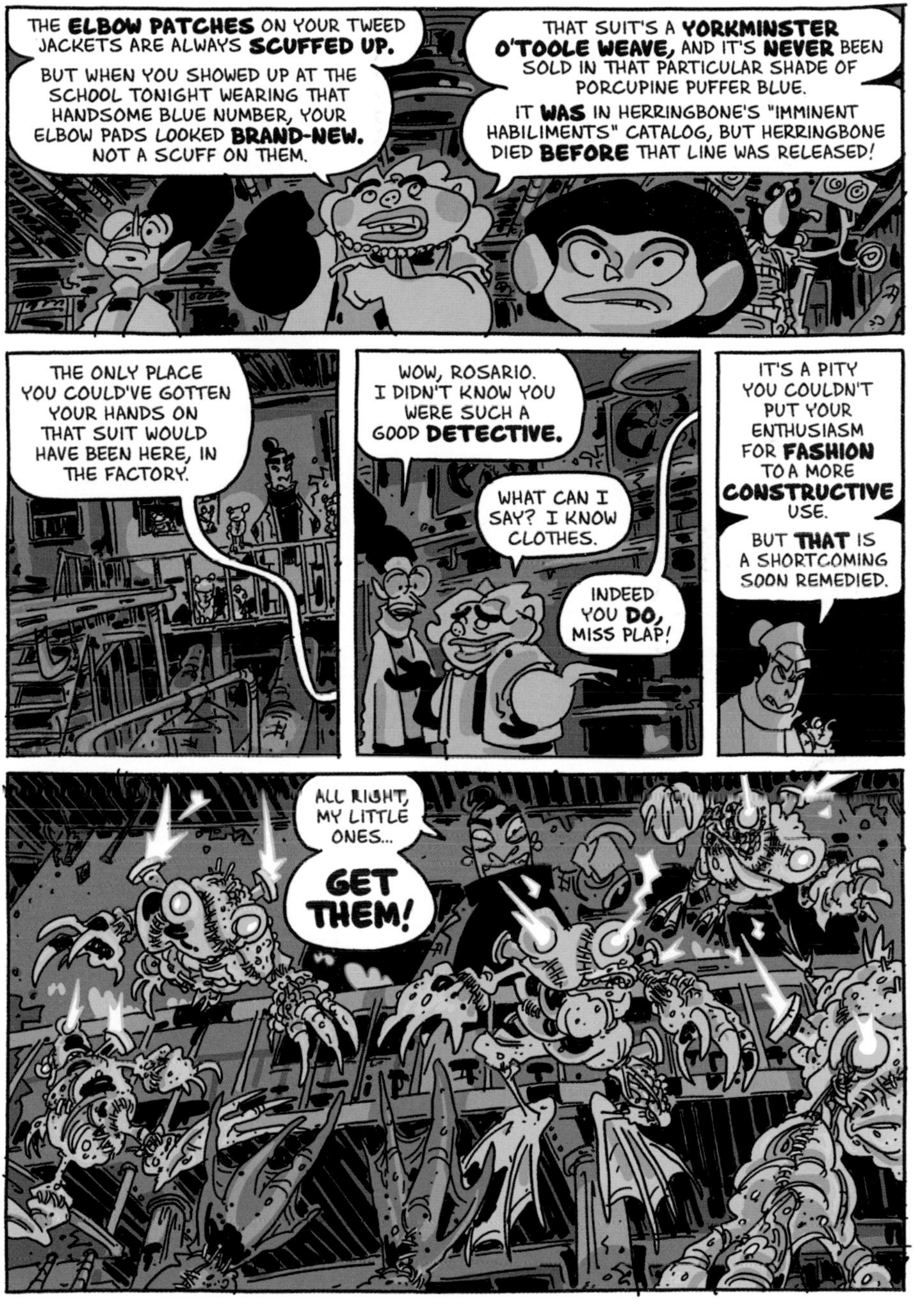

THE **ELBOW PATCHES** ON YOUR TWEED JACKETS ARE ALWAYS **SCUFFED UP.**
BUT WHEN YOU SHOWED UP AT THE SCHOOL TONIGHT WEARING THAT HANDSOME BLUE NUMBER, YOUR ELBOW PADS LOOKED **BRAND-NEW.** NOT A SCUFF ON THEM.
THAT SUIT'S A **YORKMINSTER O'TOOLE WEAVE,** AND IT'S **NEVER** BEEN SOLD IN THAT PARTICULAR SHADE OF PORCUPINE PUFFER BLUE.
IT **WAS** IN HERRINGBONE'S "IMMINENT HABILIMENTS" CATALOG, BUT HERRINGBONE DIED **BEFORE** THAT LINE WAS RELEASED!
THE ONLY PLACE YOU COULD'VE GOTTEN YOUR HANDS ON THAT SUIT WOULD HAVE BEEN HERE, IN THE FACTORY.
WOW, ROSARIO. I DIDN'T KNOW YOU WERE SUCH A GOOD **DETECTIVE.**
WHAT CAN I SAY? I KNOW CLOTHES.
INDEED YOU **DO,** MISS PLAP!
IT'S A PITY YOU COULDN'T PUT YOUR ENTHUSIASM FOR **FASHION** TO A MORE **CONSTRUCTIVE** USE.
BUT **THAT** IS A SHORTCOMING SOON REMEDIED.
ALL RIGHT, MY LITTLE ONES...
GET THEM!

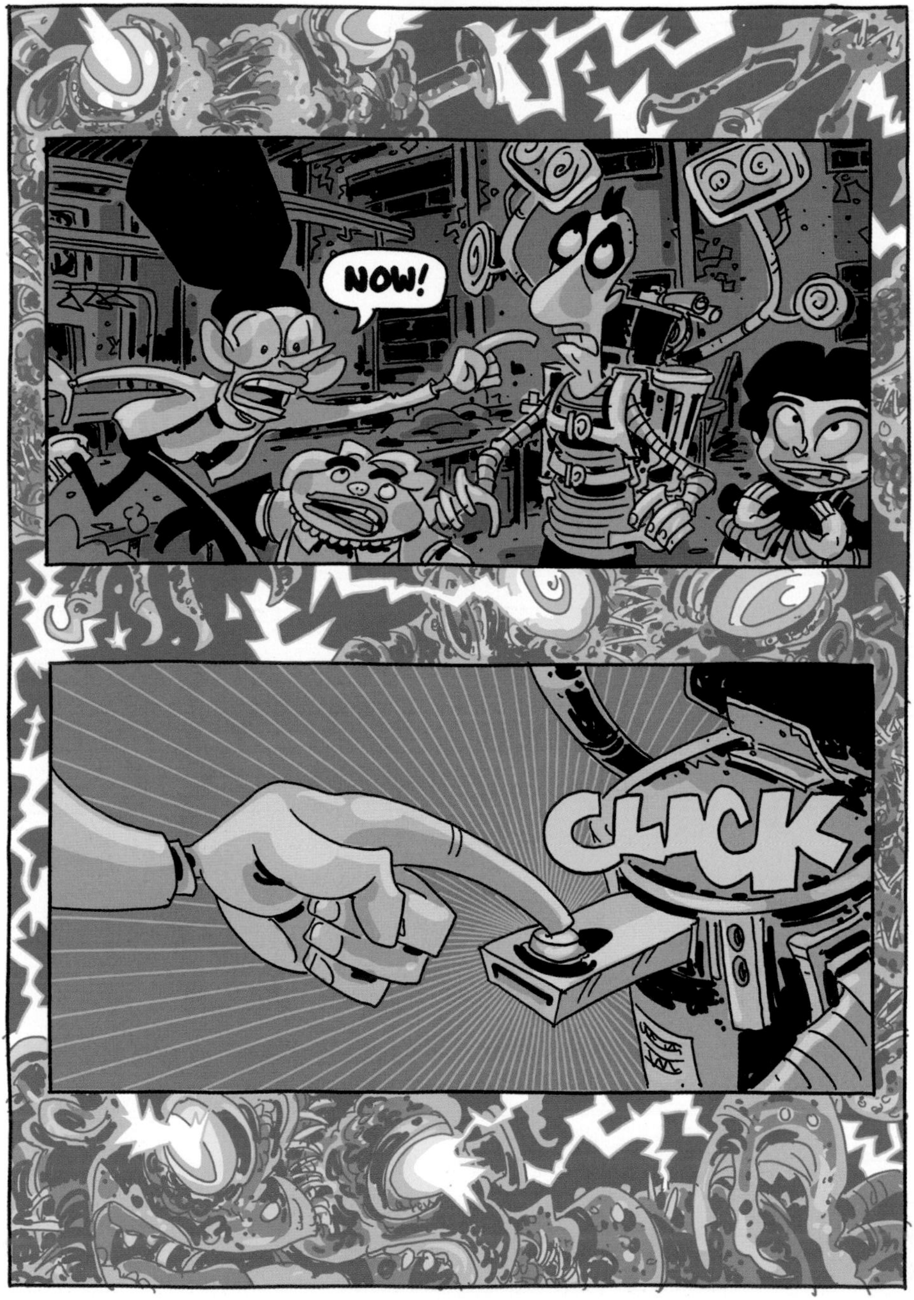
NOW!
CLICK

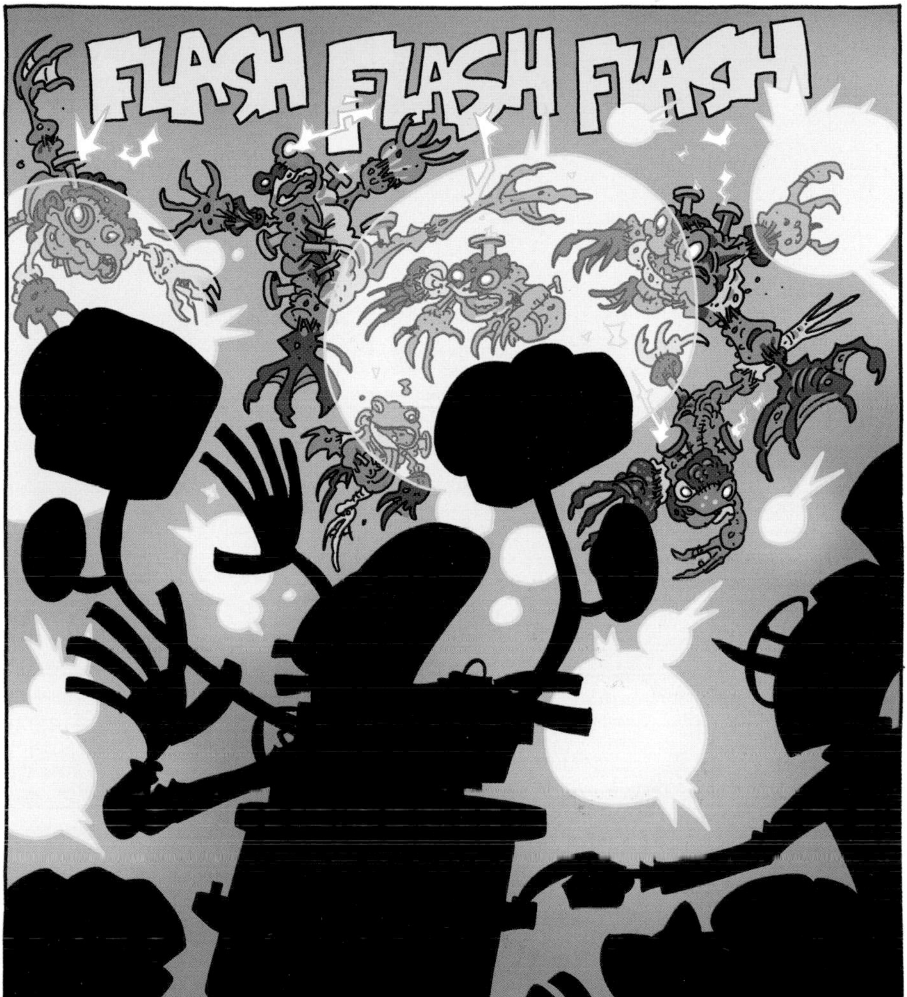
FLASH FLASH FLASH

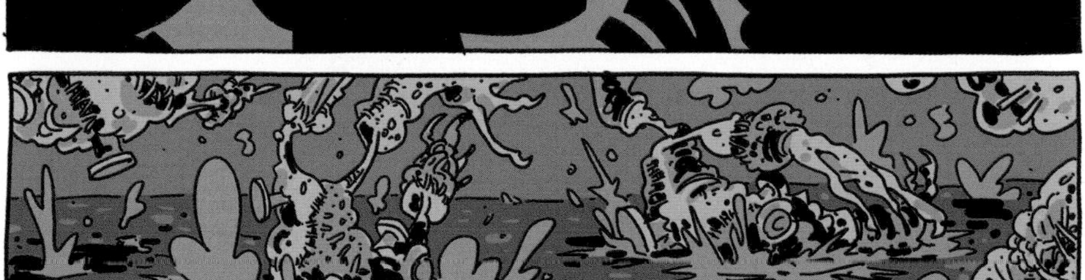

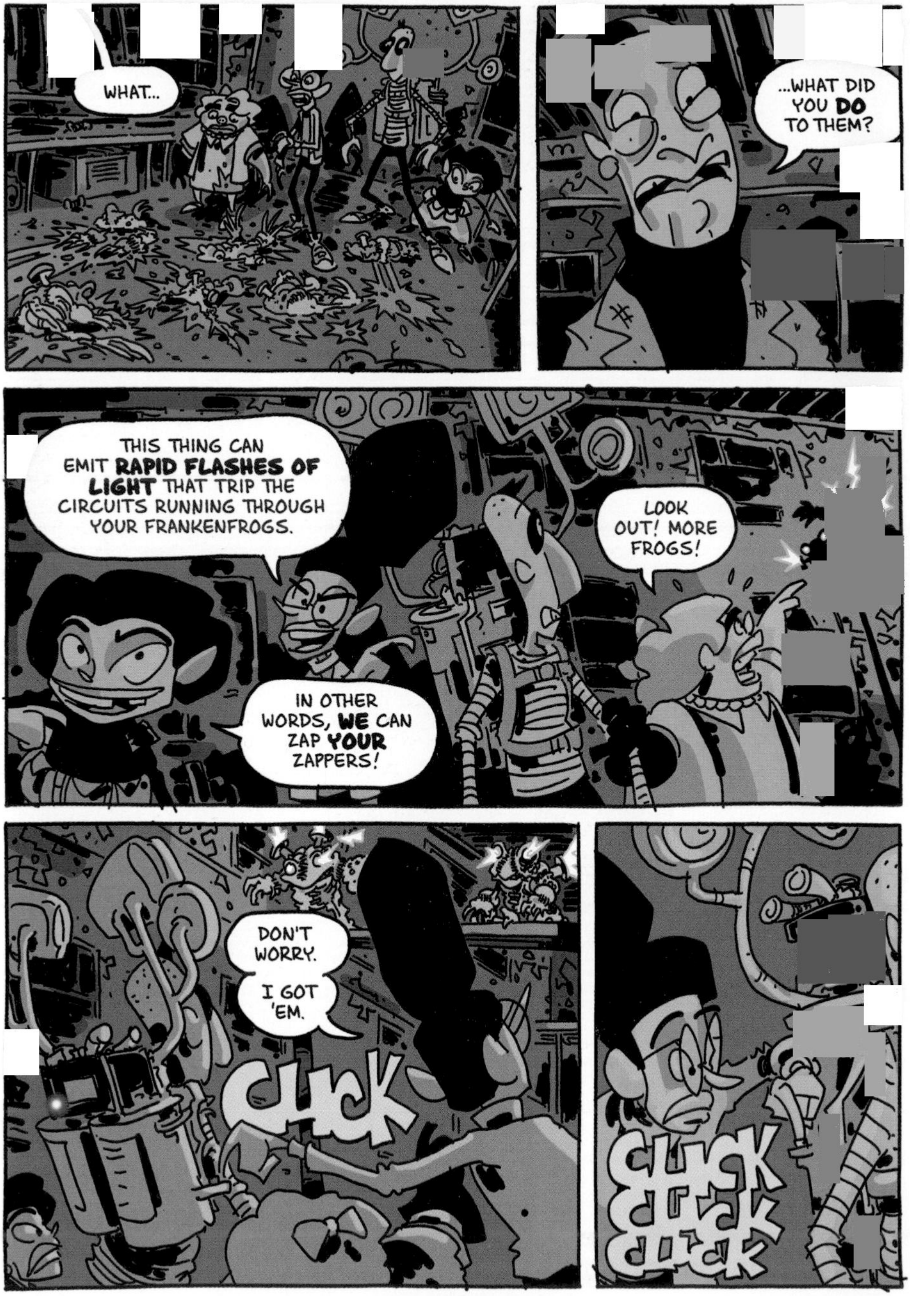
WHAT...
...WHAT DID YOU DO TO THEM?
THIS THING CAN EMIT RAPID FLASHES OF LIGHT THAT TRIP THE CIRCUITS RUNNING THROUGH YOUR FRANKENFROGS.
LOOK OUT! MORE FROGS!
IN OTHER WORDS, WE CAN ZAP YOUR ZAPPERS!
DON'T WORRY.
I GOT 'EM.
CLICK
CLICK CLICK CLICK

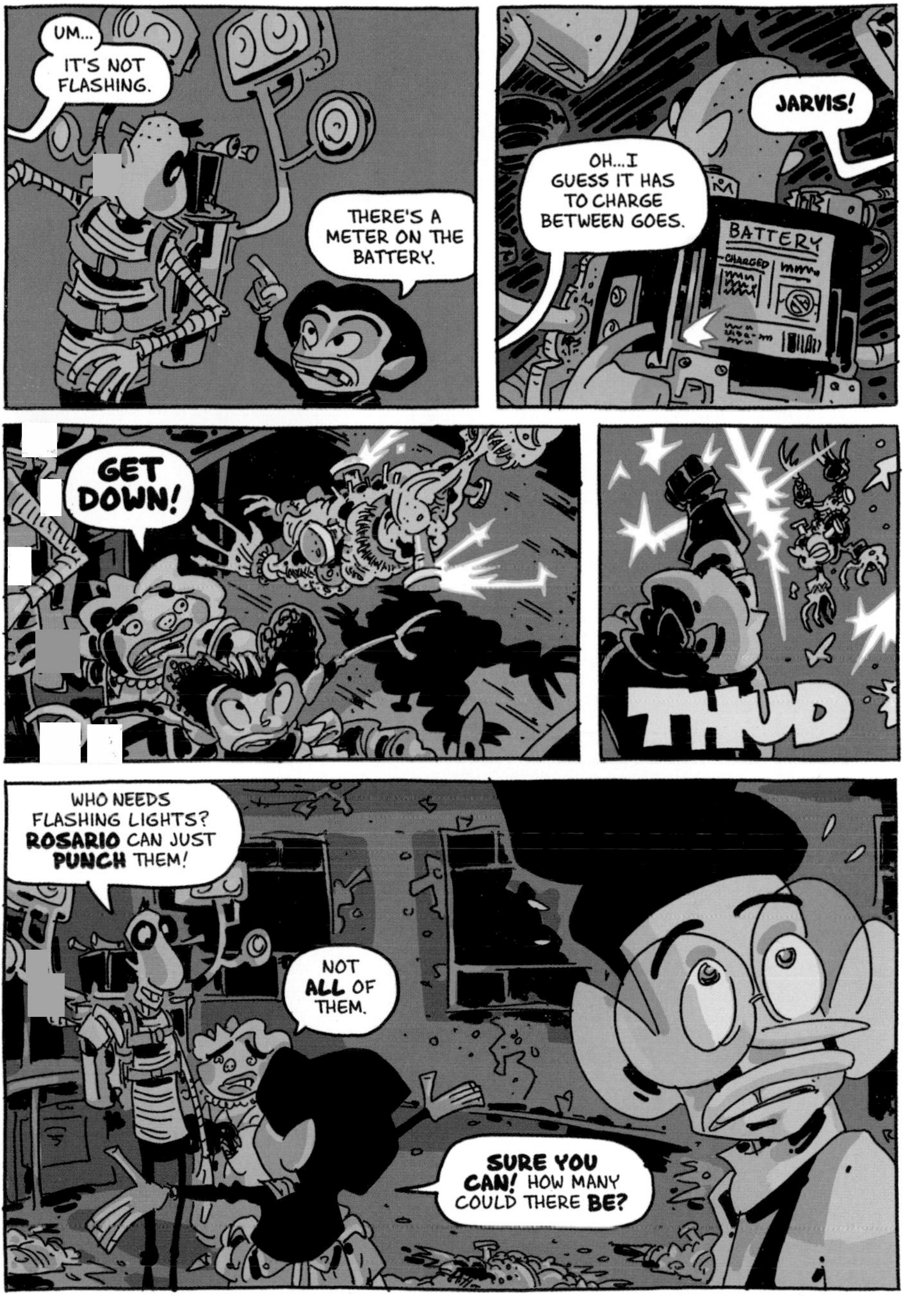
UM...
IT'S NOT FLASHING.
THERE'S A METER ON THE BATTERY.
JARVIS!
OH...I GUESS IT HAS TO CHARGE BETWEEN GOES.
BATTERY
CHARGED
GET DOWN!
THUD
WHO NEEDS FLASHING LIGHTS? ROSARIO CAN JUST PUNCH THEM!
NOT ALL OF THEM.
SURE YOU CAN! HOW MANY COULD THERE BE?

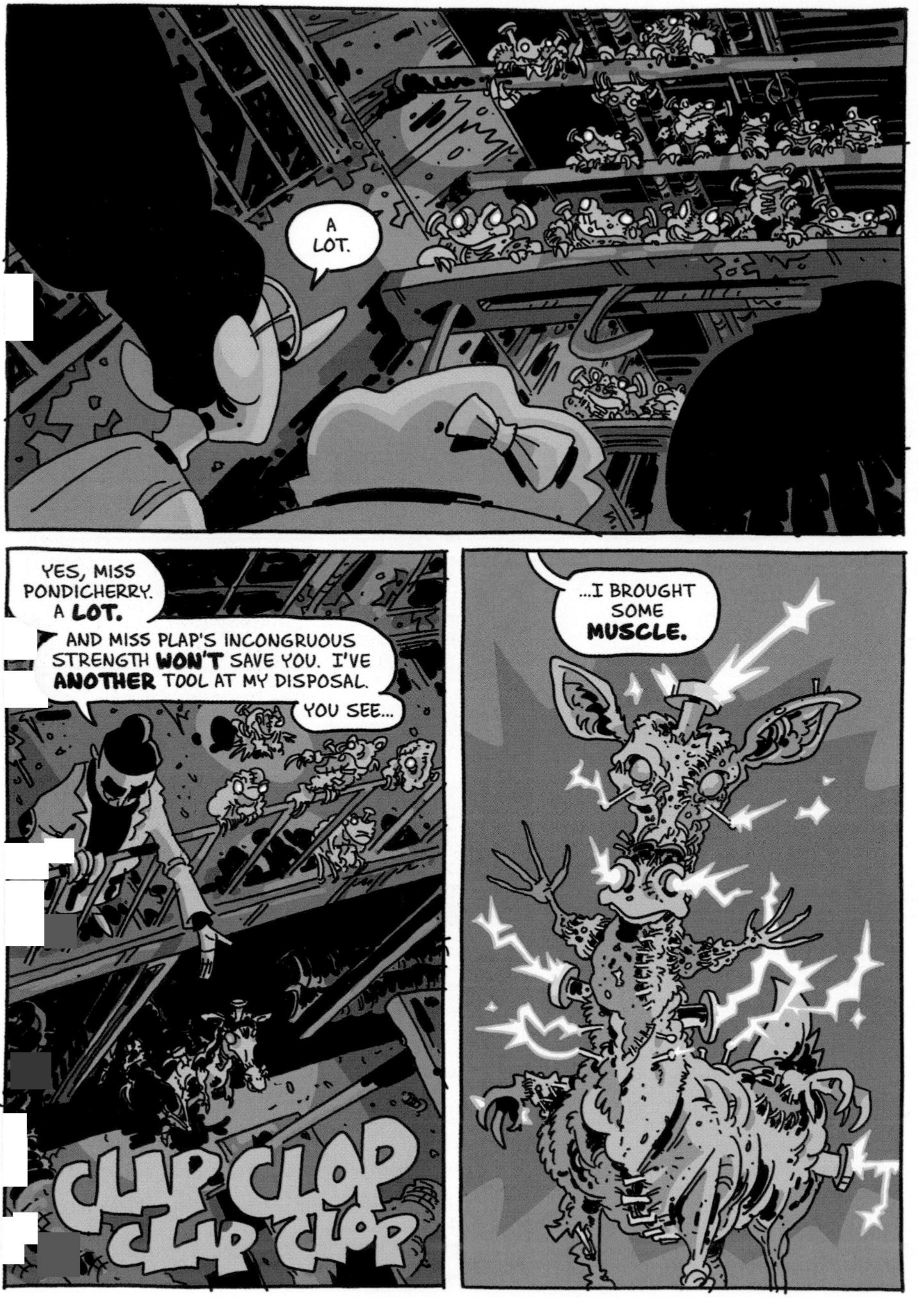
A LOT.
YES, MISS PONDICHERRY. A **LOT.**
AND MISS PLAP'S INCONGRUOUS STRENGTH **WON'T** SAVE YOU. I'VE **ANOTHER** TOOL AT MY DISPOSAL.
YOU SEE...
CLIP CLOP CLIP CLOP
...I BROUGHT SOME **MUSCLE.**

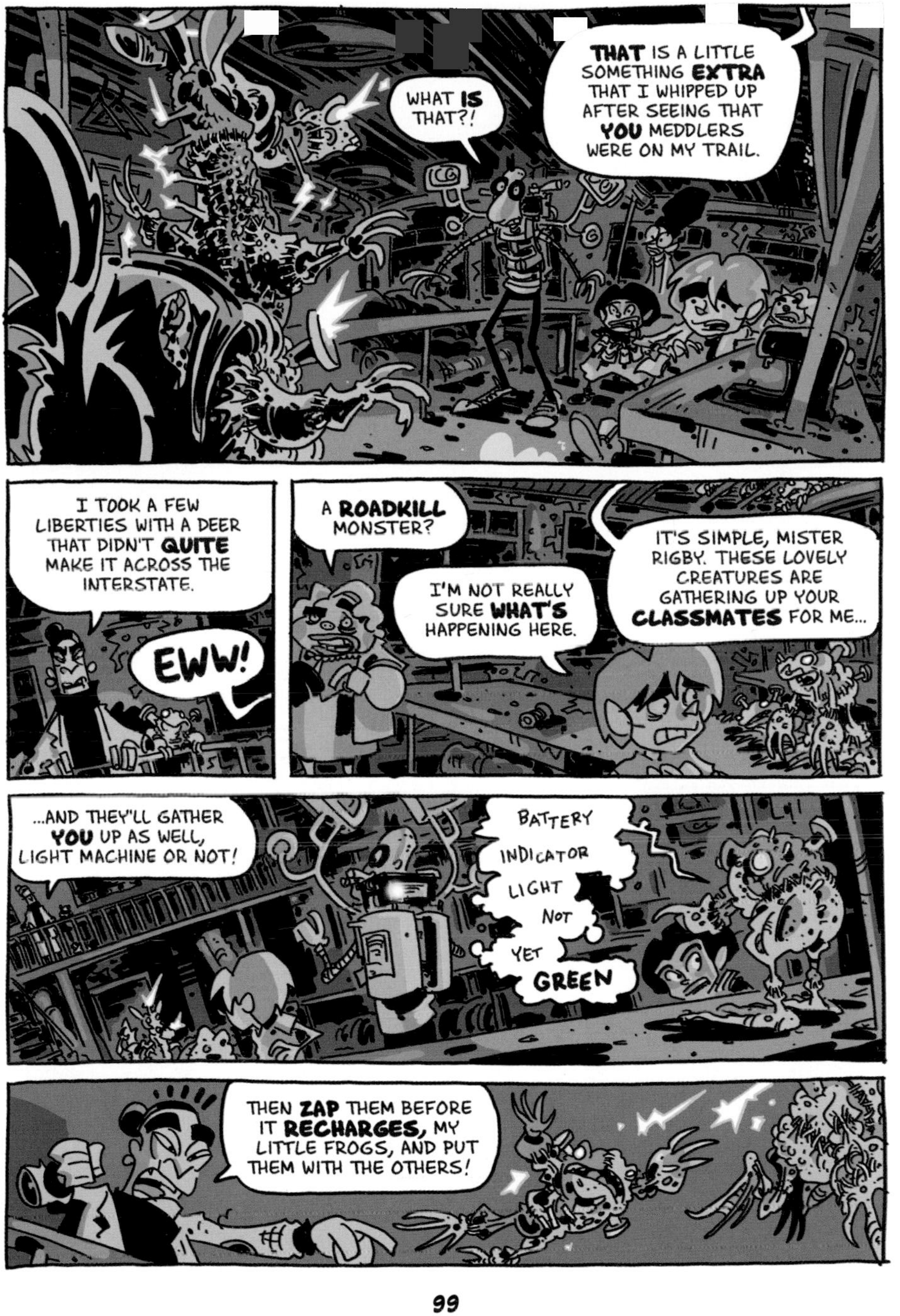

WHAT IS THAT?!
THAT IS A LITTLE SOMETHING EXTRA THAT I WHIPPED UP AFTER SEEING THAT YOU MEDDLERS WERE ON MY TRAIL.
I TOOK A FEW LIBERTIES WITH A DEER THAT DIDN'T QUITE MAKE IT ACROSS THE INTERSTATE.
EWW!
A ROADKILL MONSTER?
I'M NOT REALLY SURE WHAT'S HAPPENING HERE.
IT'S SIMPLE, MISTER RIGBY. THESE LOVELY CREATURES ARE GATHERING UP YOUR CLASSMATES FOR ME...
...AND THEY'LL GATHER YOU UP AS WELL, LIGHT MACHINE OR NOT!
BATTERY INDICATOR LIGHT NOT YET GREEN
THEN ZAP THEM BEFORE IT RECHARGES, MY LITTLE FROGS, AND PUT THEM WITH THE OTHERS!

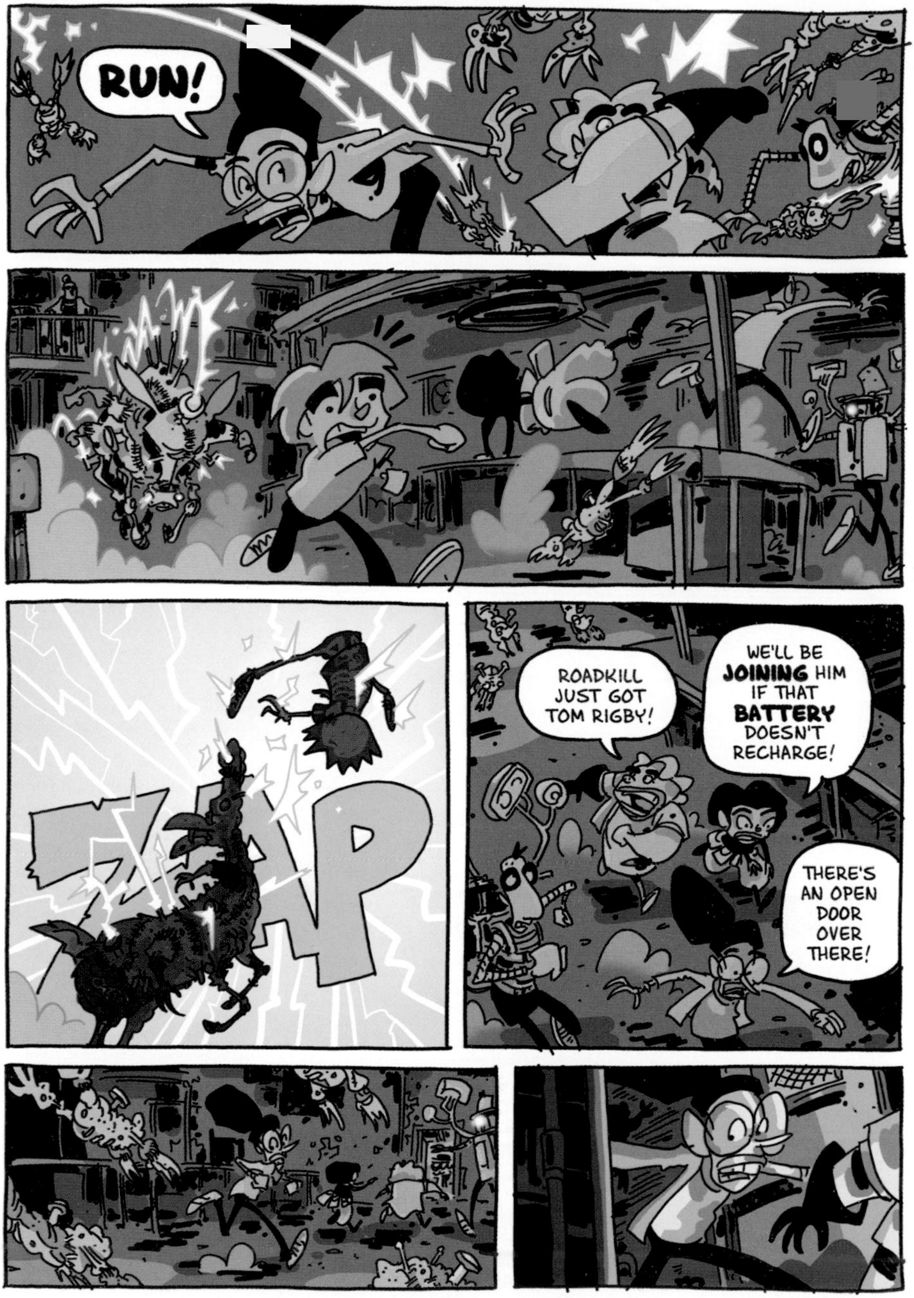
RUN!
ZAP
ROADKILL JUST GOT TOM RIGBY!
WE'LL BE **JOINING** HIM IF THAT **BATTERY** DOESN'T RECHARGE!
THERE'S AN OPEN DOOR OVER THERE!

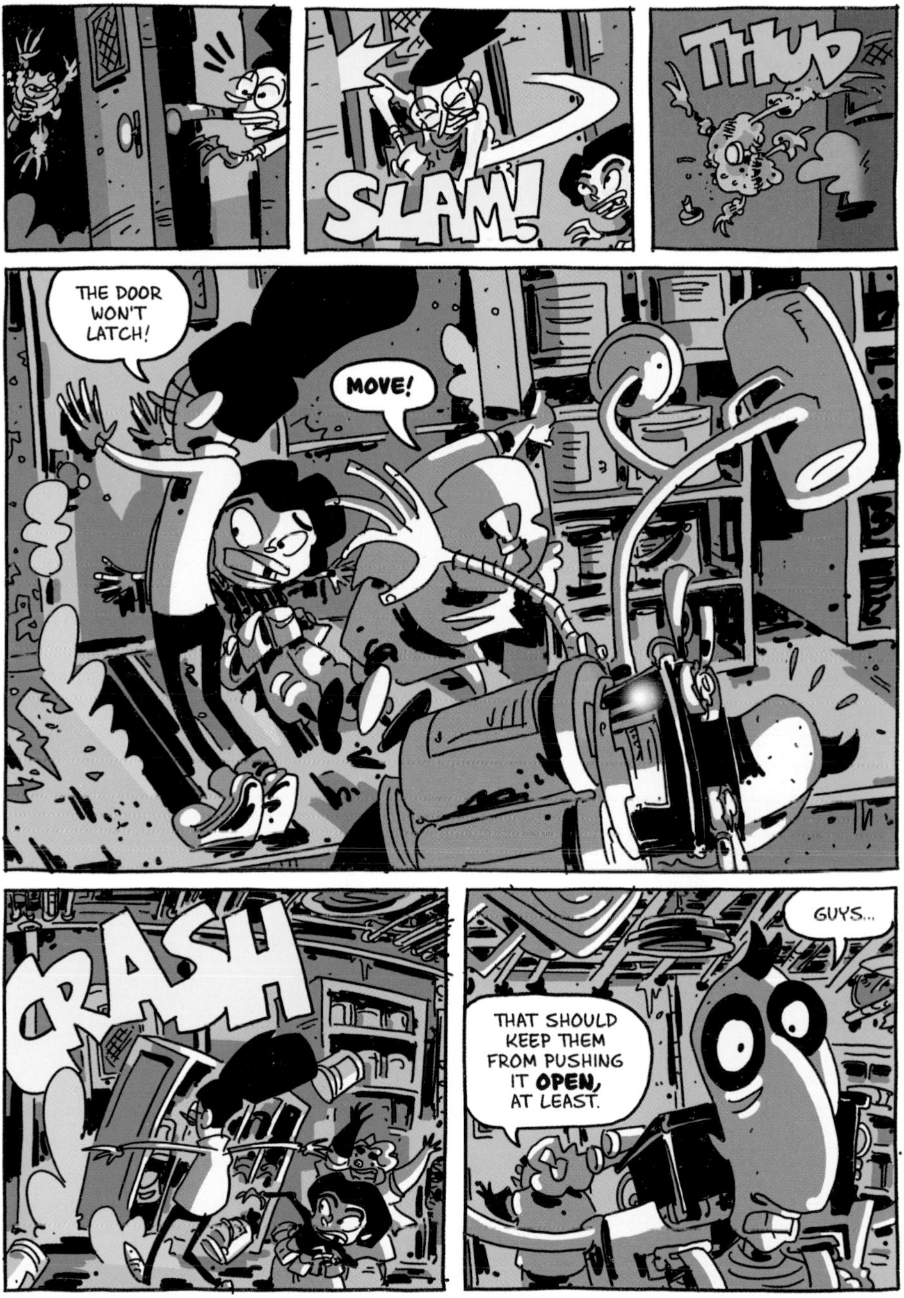
THUD
SLAM!
THE DOOR WON'T LATCH!
MOVE!
CRASH
GUYS...
THAT SHOULD KEEP THEM FROM PUSHING IT **OPEN,** AT LEAST.

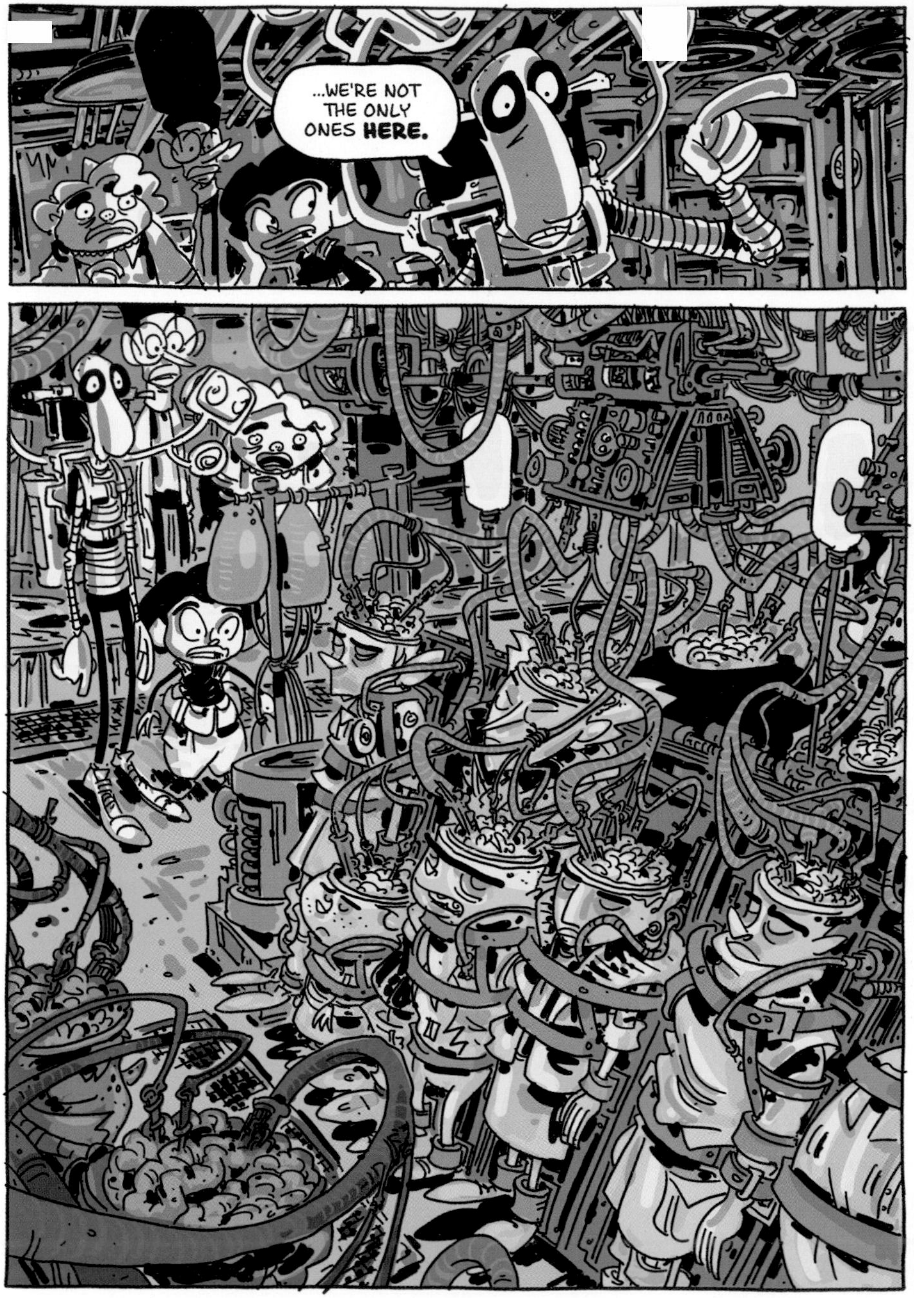
...WE'RE NOT THE ONLY ONES HERE.

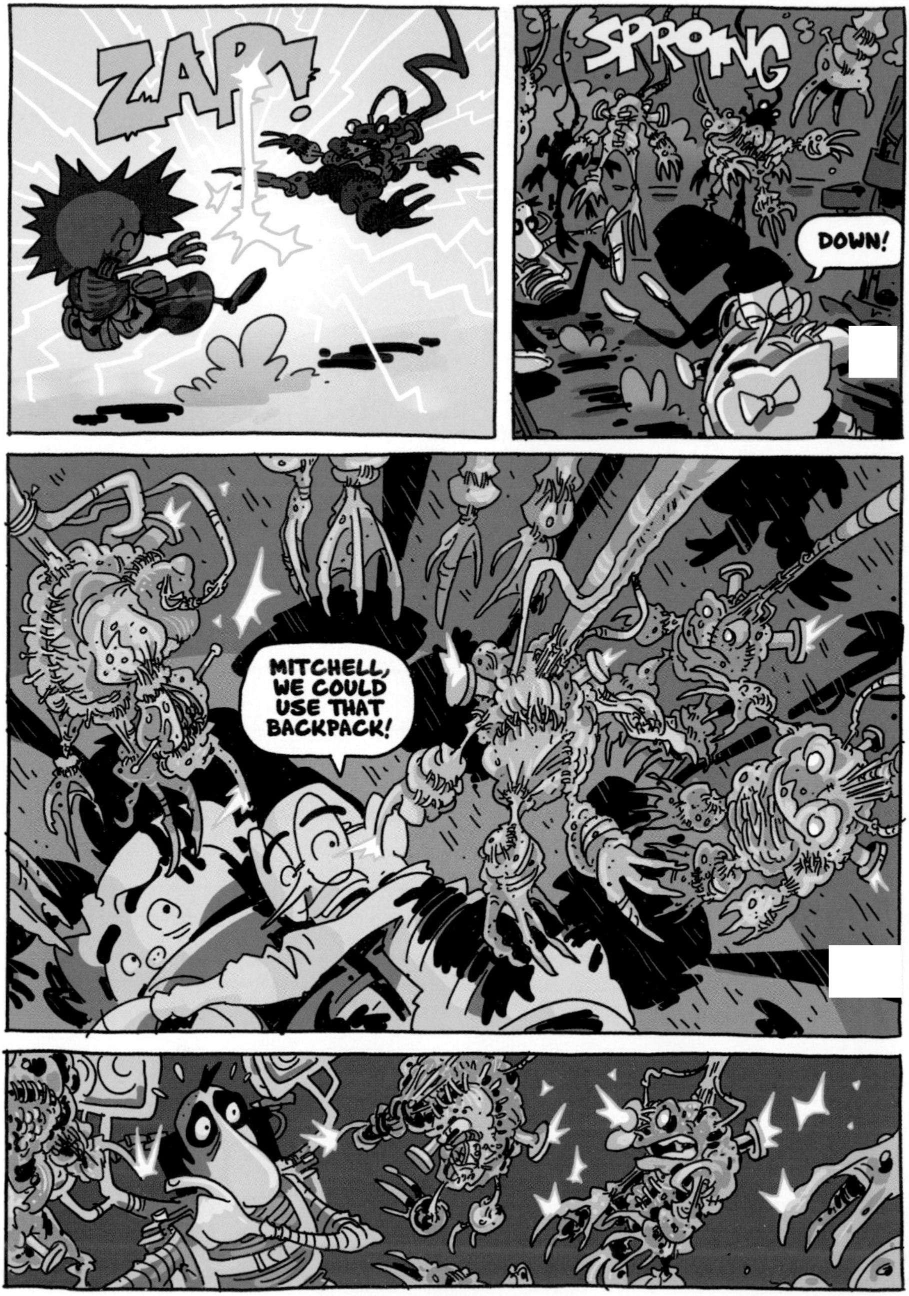
ZAP!
SPRONG
DOWN!
MITCHELL, WE COULD USE THAT BACKPACK!

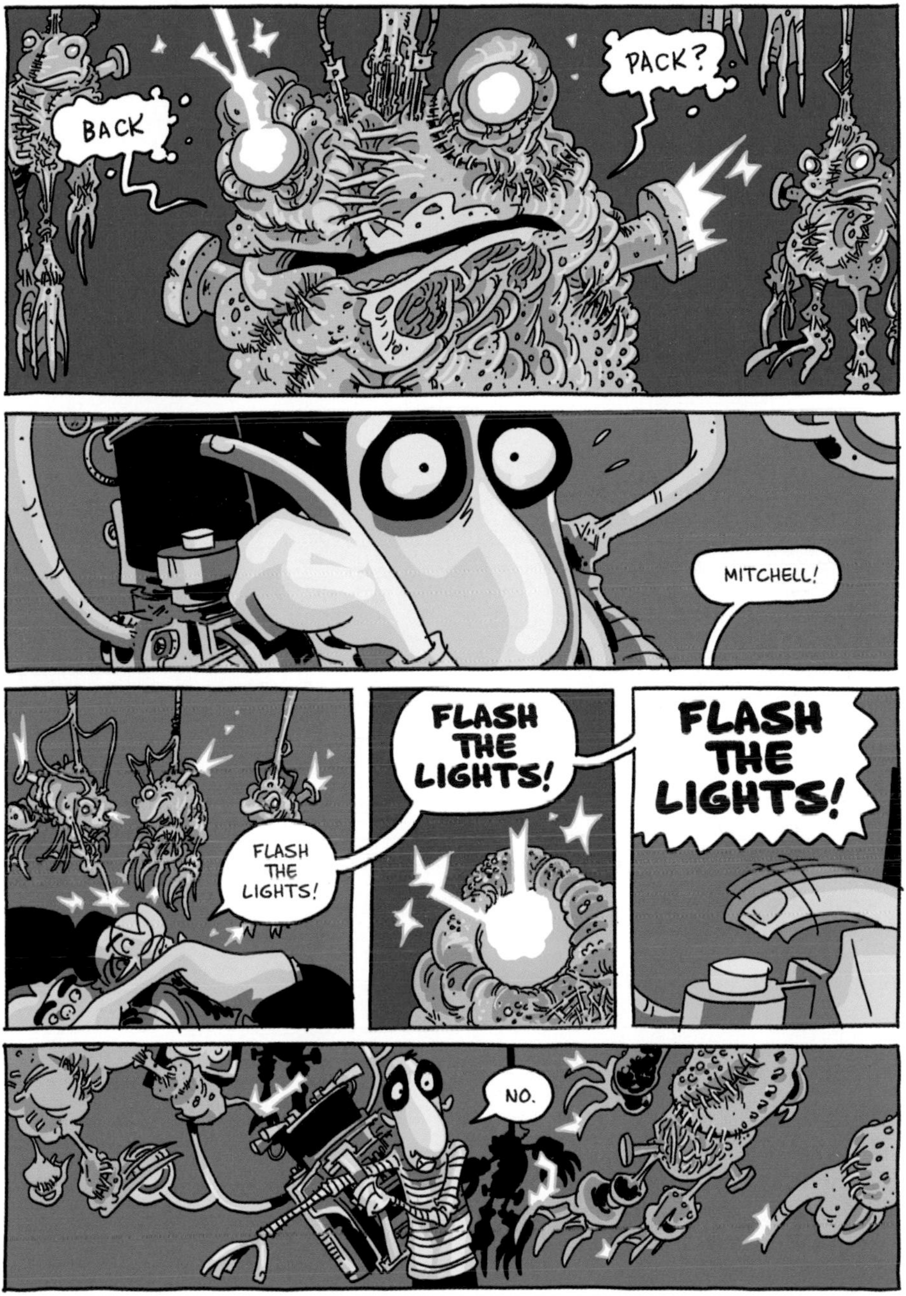
BACK
PACK?
MITCHELL!
FLASH THE LIGHTS!
FLASH THE LIGHTS!
FLASH THE LIGHTS!
NO.

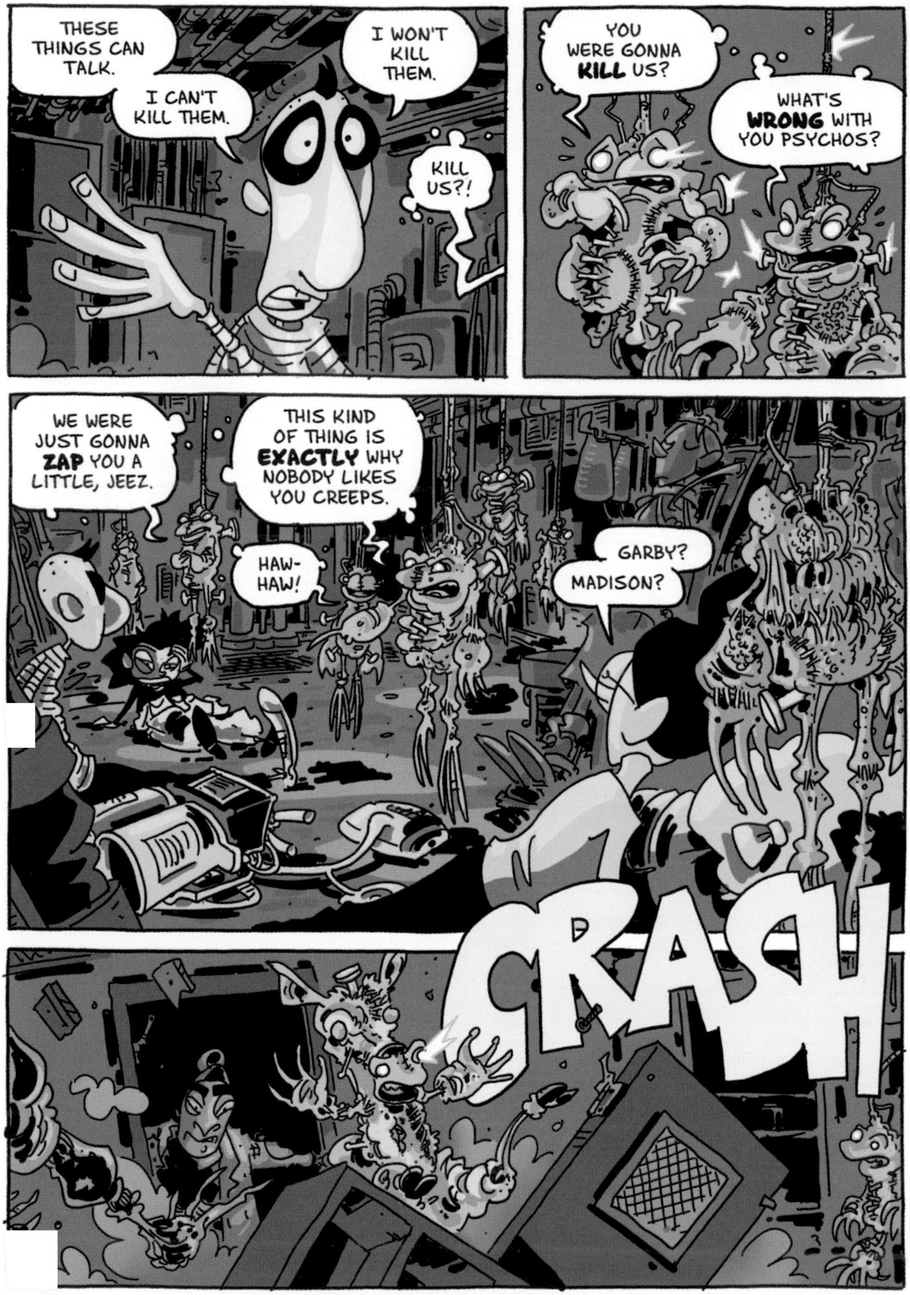

THESE THINGS CAN TALK.
I CAN'T KILL THEM.
I WON'T KILL THEM.
KILL US?!
YOU WERE GONNA **KILL** US?
WHAT'S **WRONG** WITH YOU PSYCHOS?
WE WERE JUST GONNA **ZAP** YOU A LITTLE, JEEZ.
THIS KIND OF THING IS **EXACTLY** WHY NOBODY LIKES YOU CREEPS.
HAW-HAW!
GARBY?
MADISON?
CRASH

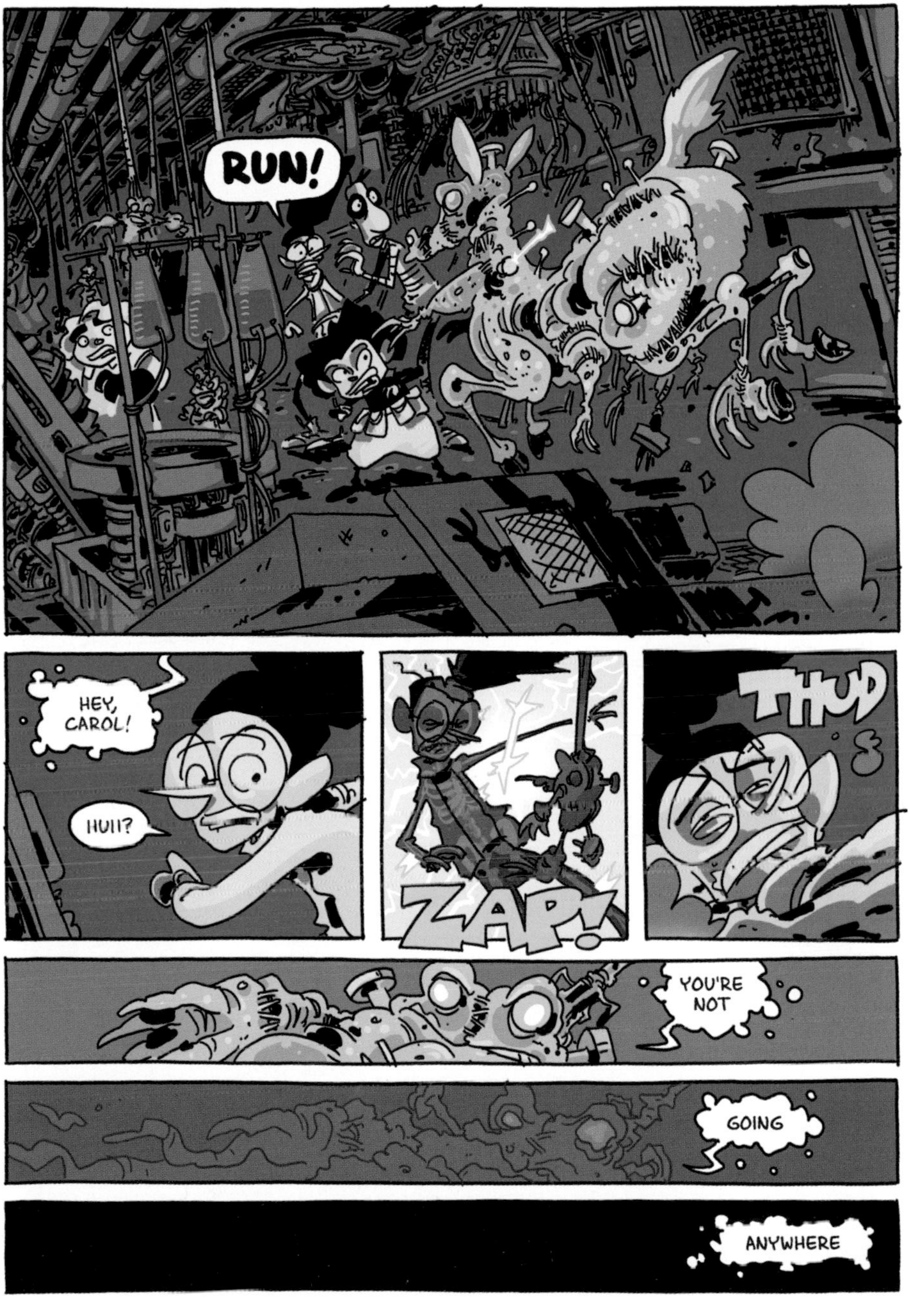

RUN!
HEY, CAROL!
HUH?
ZAP!
THUD
YOU'RE NOT
GOING
ANYWHERE

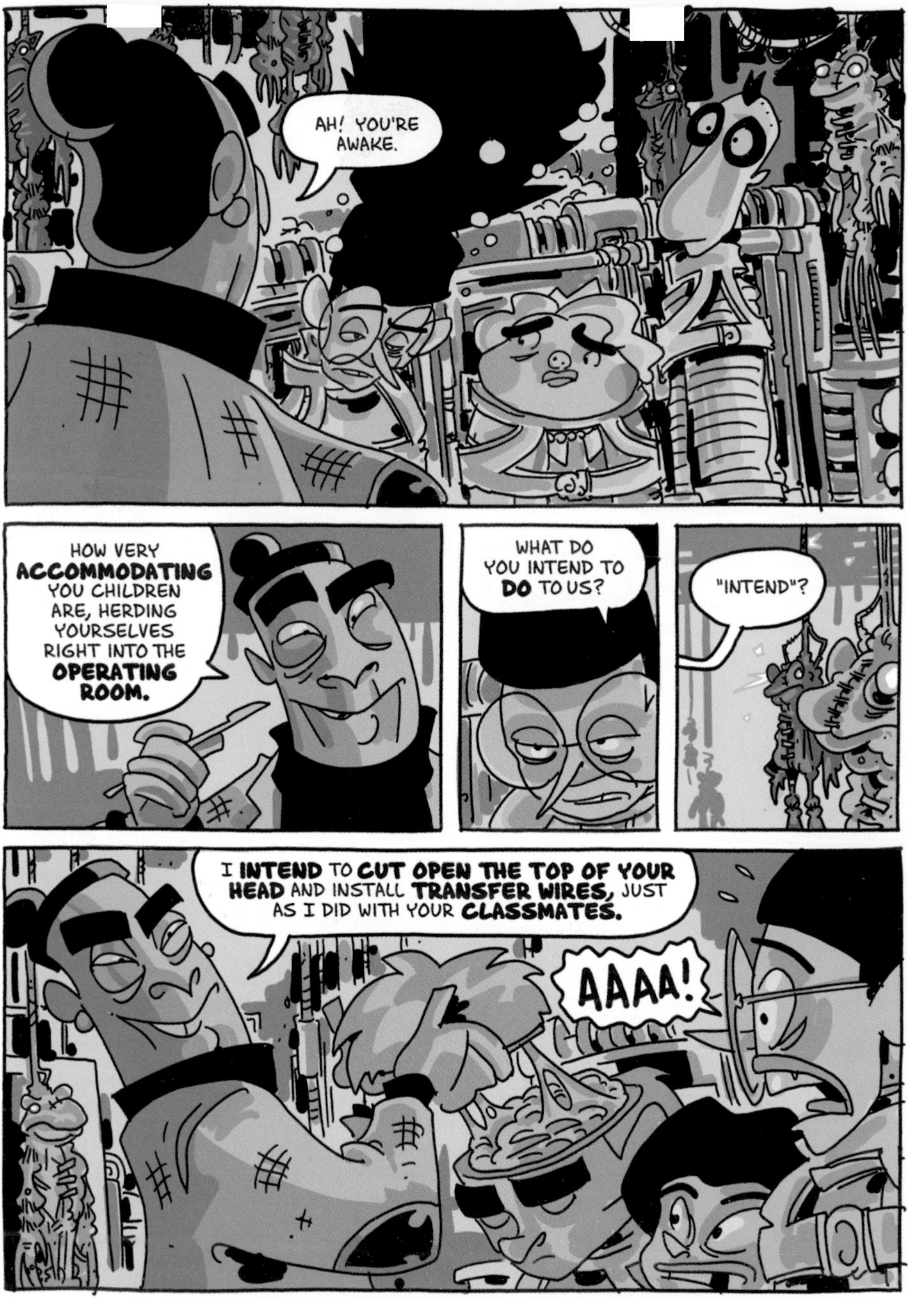
AH! YOU'RE AWAKE.
HOW VERY **ACCOMMODATING** YOU CHILDREN ARE, HERDING YOURSELVES RIGHT INTO THE **OPERATING ROOM.**
WHAT DO YOU INTEND TO **DO** TO US?
"INTEND"?
I **INTEND** TO **CUT OPEN THE TOP OF YOUR HEAD** AND INSTALL **TRANSFER WIRES,** JUST AS I DID WITH YOUR **CLASSMATES.**
AAAA!

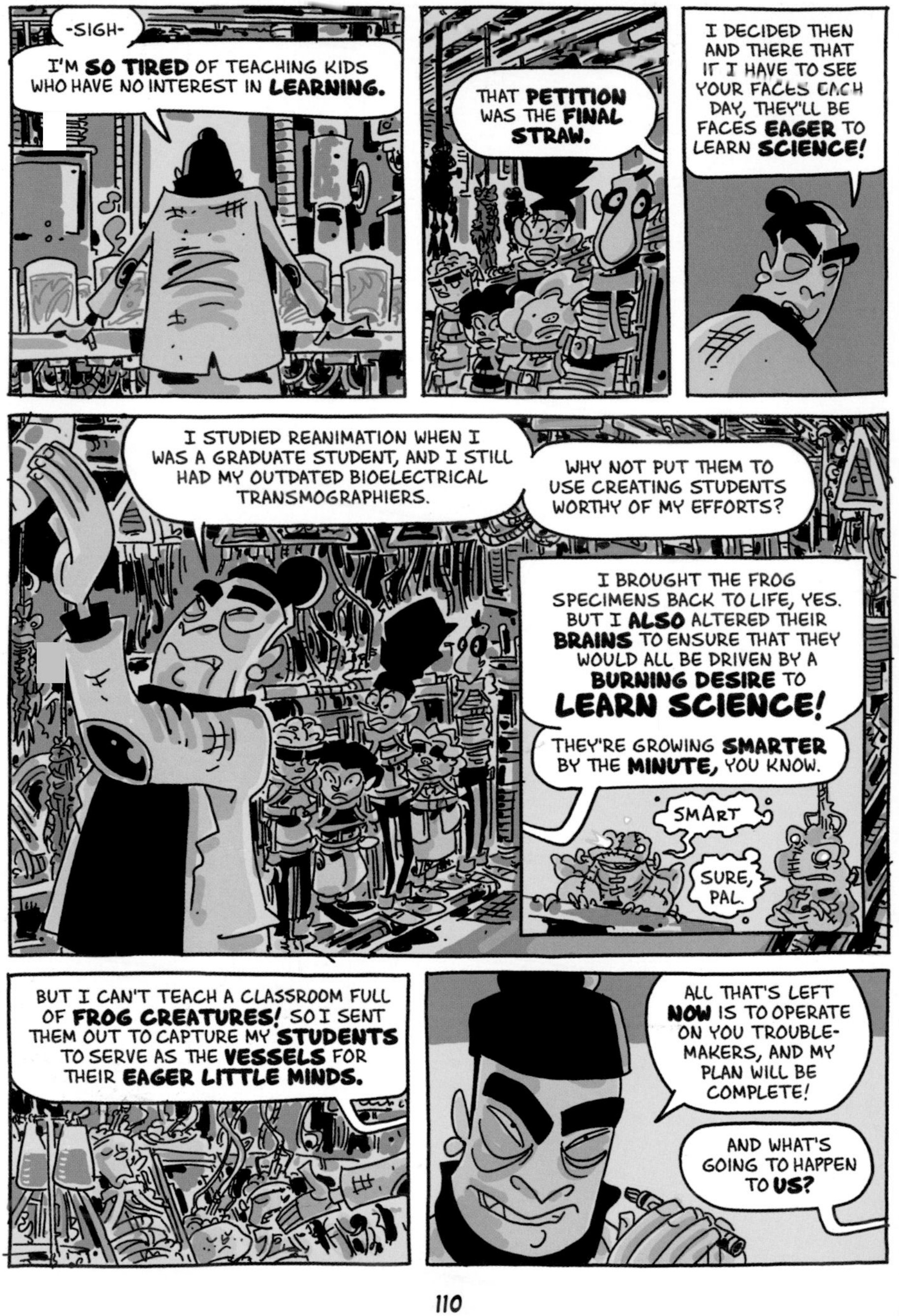
-SIGH-
I'M SO TIRED OF TEACHING KIDS WHO HAVE NO INTEREST IN LEARNING.
THAT PETITION WAS THE FINAL STRAW.
I DECIDED THEN AND THERE THAT IF I HAVE TO SEE YOUR FACES EACH DAY, THEY'LL BE FACES EAGER TO LEARN SCIENCE!
I STUDIED REANIMATION WHEN I WAS A GRADUATE STUDENT, AND I STILL HAD MY OUTDATED BIOELECTRICAL TRANSMOGRAPHIERS.
WHY NOT PUT THEM TO USE CREATING STUDENTS WORTHY OF MY EFFORTS?
I BROUGHT THE FROG SPECIMENS BACK TO LIFE, YES. BUT I ALSO ALTERED THEIR BRAINS TO ENSURE THAT THEY WOULD ALL BE DRIVEN BY A BURNING DESIRE TO LEARN SCIENCE!
THEY'RE GROWING SMARTER BY THE MINUTE, YOU KNOW.
SMArT
SURE, PAL.
BUT I CAN'T TEACH A CLASSROOM FULL OF FROG CREATURES! SO I SENT THEM OUT TO CAPTURE MY STUDENTS TO SERVE AS THE VESSELS FOR THEIR EAGER LITTLE MINDS.
ALL THAT'S LEFT NOW IS TO OPERATE ON YOU TROUBLE-MAKERS, AND MY PLAN WILL BE COMPLETE!
AND WHAT'S GOING TO HAPPEN TO US?

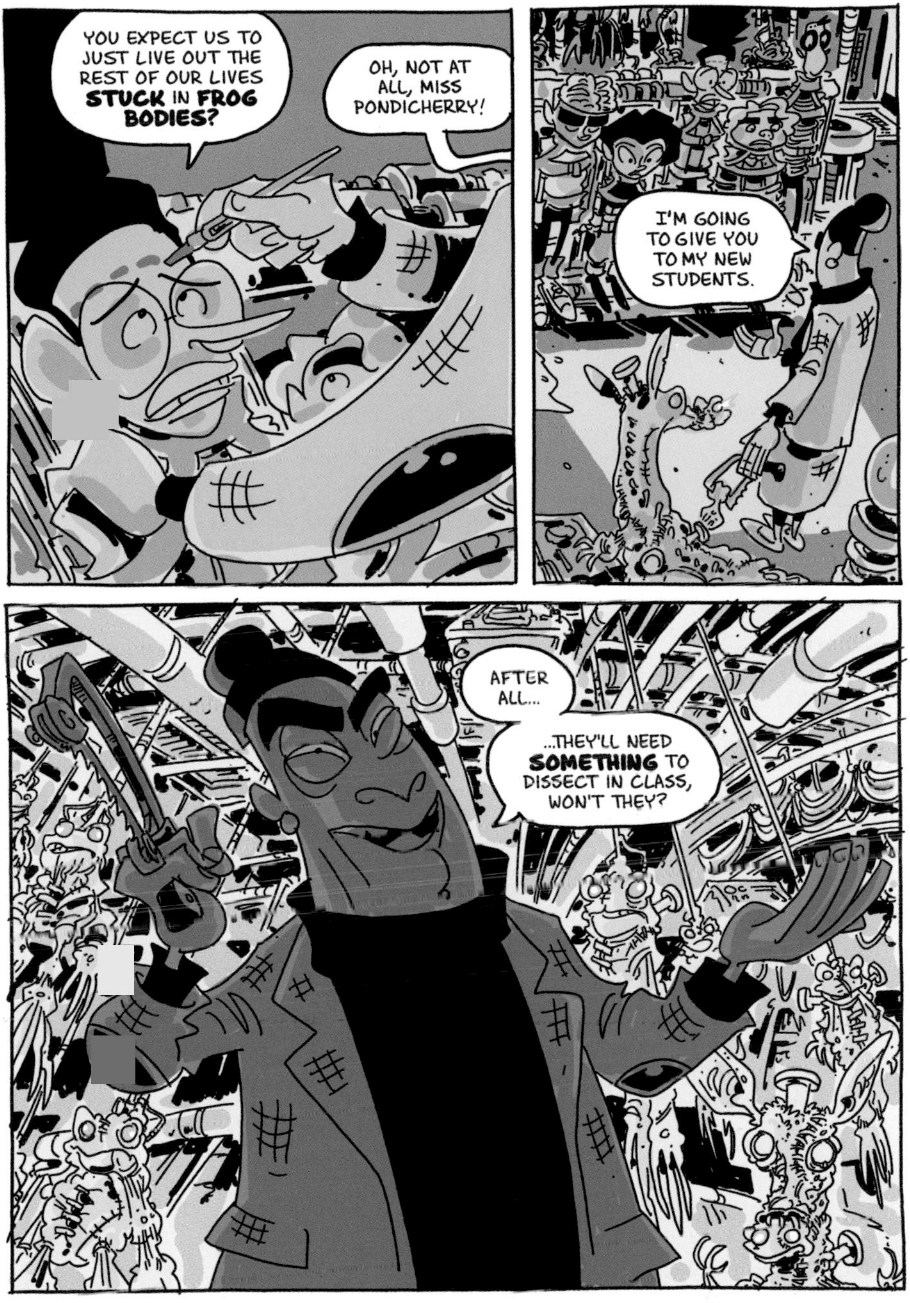
YOU EXPECT US TO JUST LIVE OUT THE REST OF OUR LIVES **STUCK** IN **FROG BODIES?**
OH, NOT AT ALL, MISS PONDICHERRY!
I'M GOING TO GIVE YOU TO MY NEW STUDENTS.
AFTER ALL...
...THEY'LL NEED **SOMETHING** TO DISSECT IN CLASS, WON'T THEY?

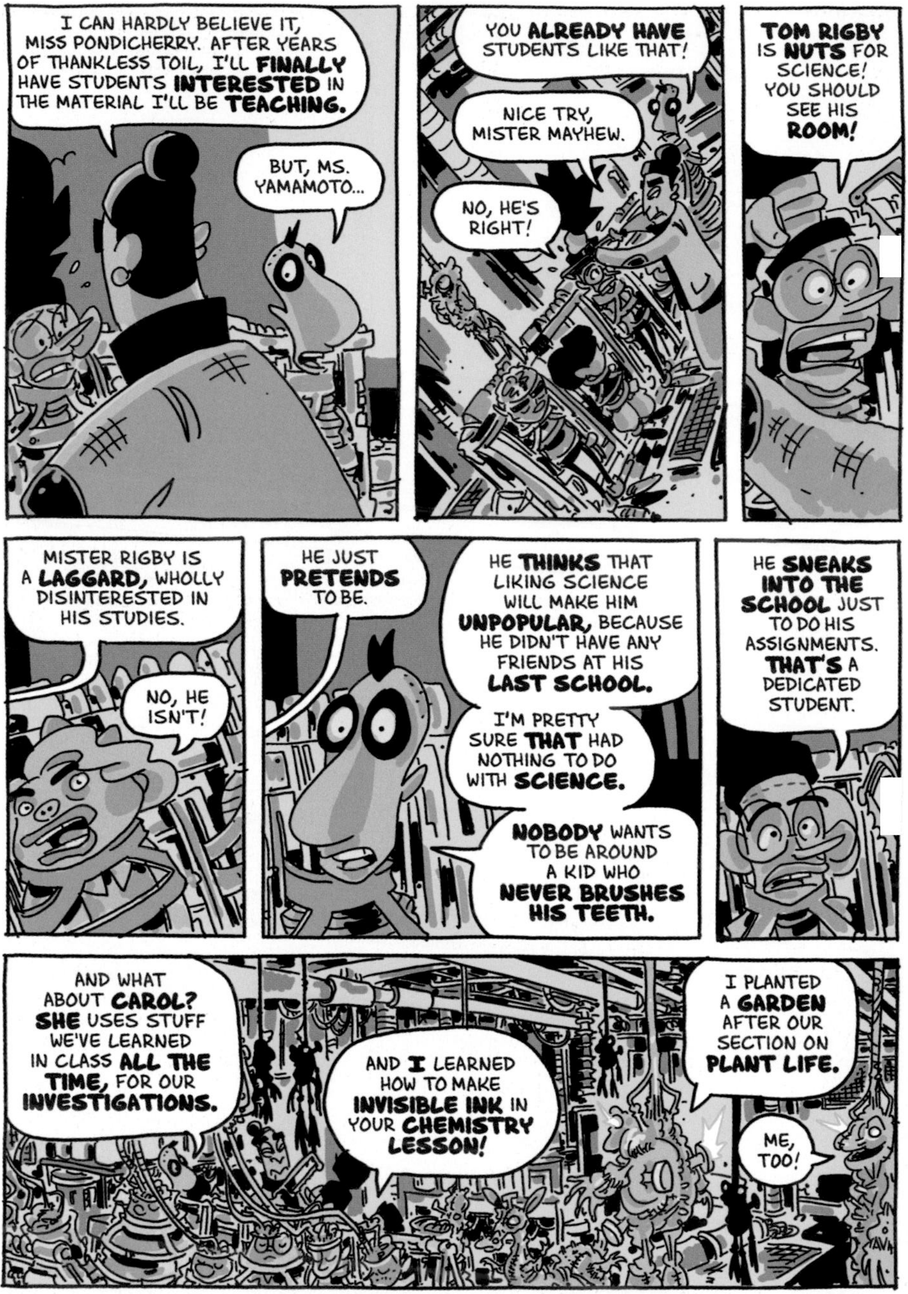

I CAN HARDLY BELIEVE IT, MISS PONDICHERRY. AFTER YEARS OF THANKLESS TOIL, I'LL **FINALLY** HAVE STUDENTS **INTERESTED** IN THE MATERIAL I'LL BE **TEACHING.**
BUT, MS. YAMAMOTO...
YOU **ALREADY HAVE** STUDENTS LIKE THAT!
NICE TRY, MISTER MAYHEW.
NO, HE'S RIGHT!
TOM RIGBY IS **NUTS** FOR SCIENCE! YOU SHOULD SEE HIS **ROOM!**
MISTER RIGBY IS A **LAGGARD,** WHOLLY DISINTERESTED IN HIS STUDIES.
NO, HE ISN'T!
HE JUST **PRETENDS** TO BE.
HE **THINKS** THAT LIKING SCIENCE WILL MAKE HIM **UNPOPULAR,** BECAUSE HE DIDN'T HAVE ANY FRIENDS AT HIS **LAST SCHOOL.**
I'M PRETTY SURE **THAT** HAD NOTHING TO DO WITH **SCIENCE.**
NOBODY WANTS TO BE AROUND A KID WHO **NEVER BRUSHES HIS TEETH.**
HE **SNEAKS INTO THE SCHOOL** JUST TO DO HIS ASSIGNMENTS. **THAT'S** A DEDICATED STUDENT.
AND WHAT ABOUT **CAROL? SHE** USES STUFF WE'VE LEARNED IN CLASS **ALL THE TIME,** FOR OUR **INVESTIGATIONS.**
AND **I** LEARNED HOW TO MAKE **INVISIBLE INK** IN YOUR **CHEMISTRY LESSON!**
I PLANTED A **GARDEN** AFTER OUR SECTION ON **PLANT LIFE.**
ME, TOO!

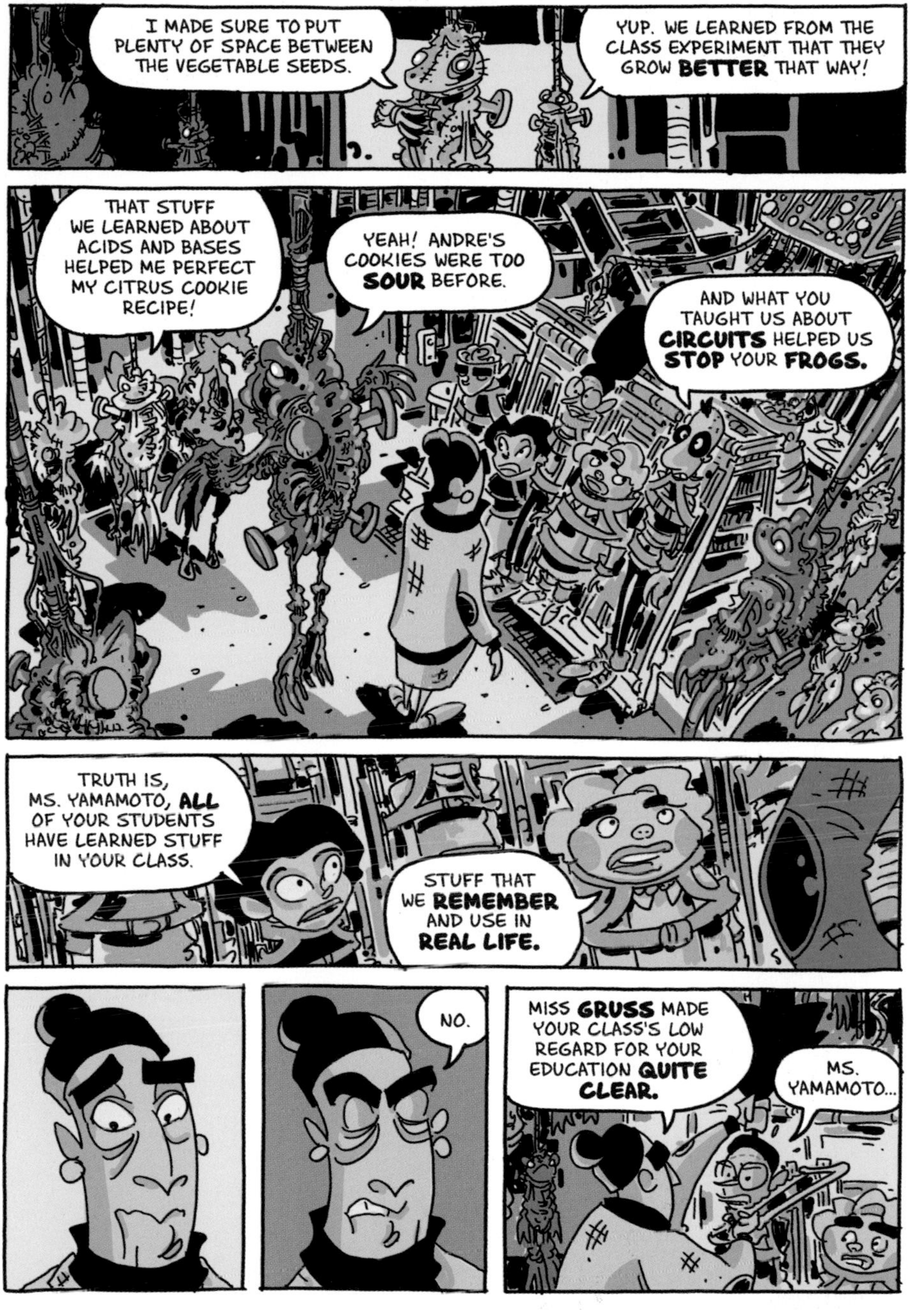
I MADE SURE TO PUT PLENTY OF SPACE BETWEEN THE VEGETABLE SEEDS.
YUP. WE LEARNED FROM THE CLASS EXPERIMENT THAT THEY GROW **BETTER** THAT WAY!
THAT STUFF WE LEARNED ABOUT ACIDS AND BASES HELPED ME PERFECT MY CITRUS COOKIE RECIPE!
YEAH! ANDRE'S COOKIES WERE TOO **SOUR** BEFORE.
AND WHAT YOU TAUGHT US ABOUT **CIRCUITS** HELPED US **STOP** YOUR **FROGS.**
TRUTH IS, MS. YAMAMOTO, **ALL** OF YOUR STUDENTS HAVE LEARNED STUFF IN YOUR CLASS.
STUFF THAT WE **REMEMBER** AND USE IN **REAL LIFE.**
NO.
MISS **GRUSS** MADE YOUR CLASS'S LOW REGARD FOR YOUR EDUCATION **QUITE CLEAR.**
MS. YAMAMOTO...

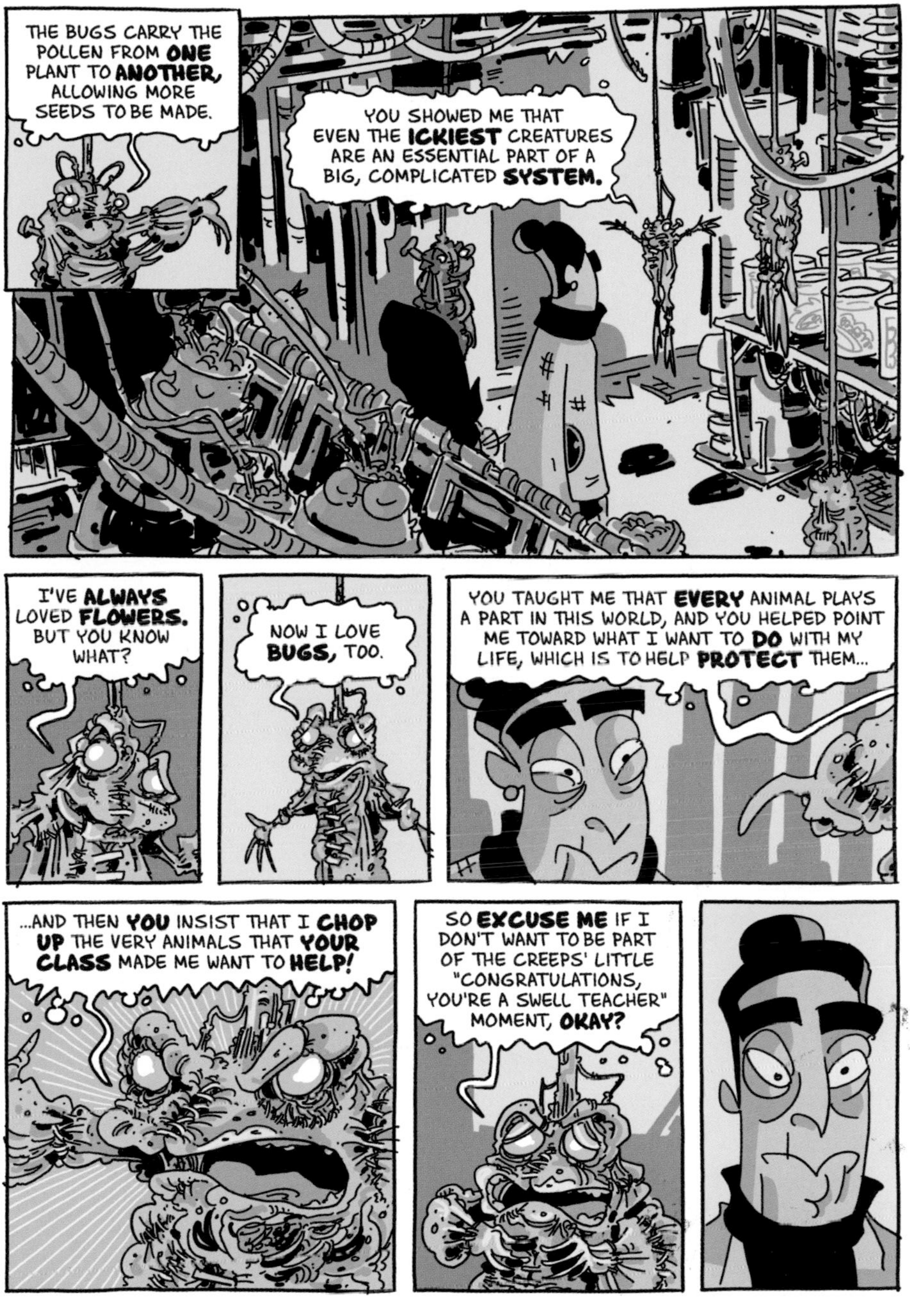
THE BUGS CARRY THE POLLEN FROM ONE PLANT TO ANOTHER, ALLOWING MORE SEEDS TO BE MADE.
YOU SHOWED ME THAT EVEN THE ICKIEST CREATURES ARE AN ESSENTIAL PART OF A BIG, COMPLICATED SYSTEM.
I'VE ALWAYS LOVED FLOWERS. BUT YOU KNOW WHAT?
NOW I LOVE BUGS, TOO.
YOU TAUGHT ME THAT EVERY ANIMAL PLAYS A PART IN THIS WORLD, AND YOU HELPED POINT ME TOWARD WHAT I WANT TO DO WITH MY LIFE, WHICH IS TO HELP PROTECT THEM...
...AND THEN YOU INSIST THAT I CHOP UP THE VERY ANIMALS THAT YOUR CLASS MADE ME WANT TO HELP!
SO EXCUSE ME IF I DON'T WANT TO BE PART OF THE CREEPS' LITTLE "CONGRATULATIONS, YOU'RE A SWELL TEACHER" MOMENT, OKAY?

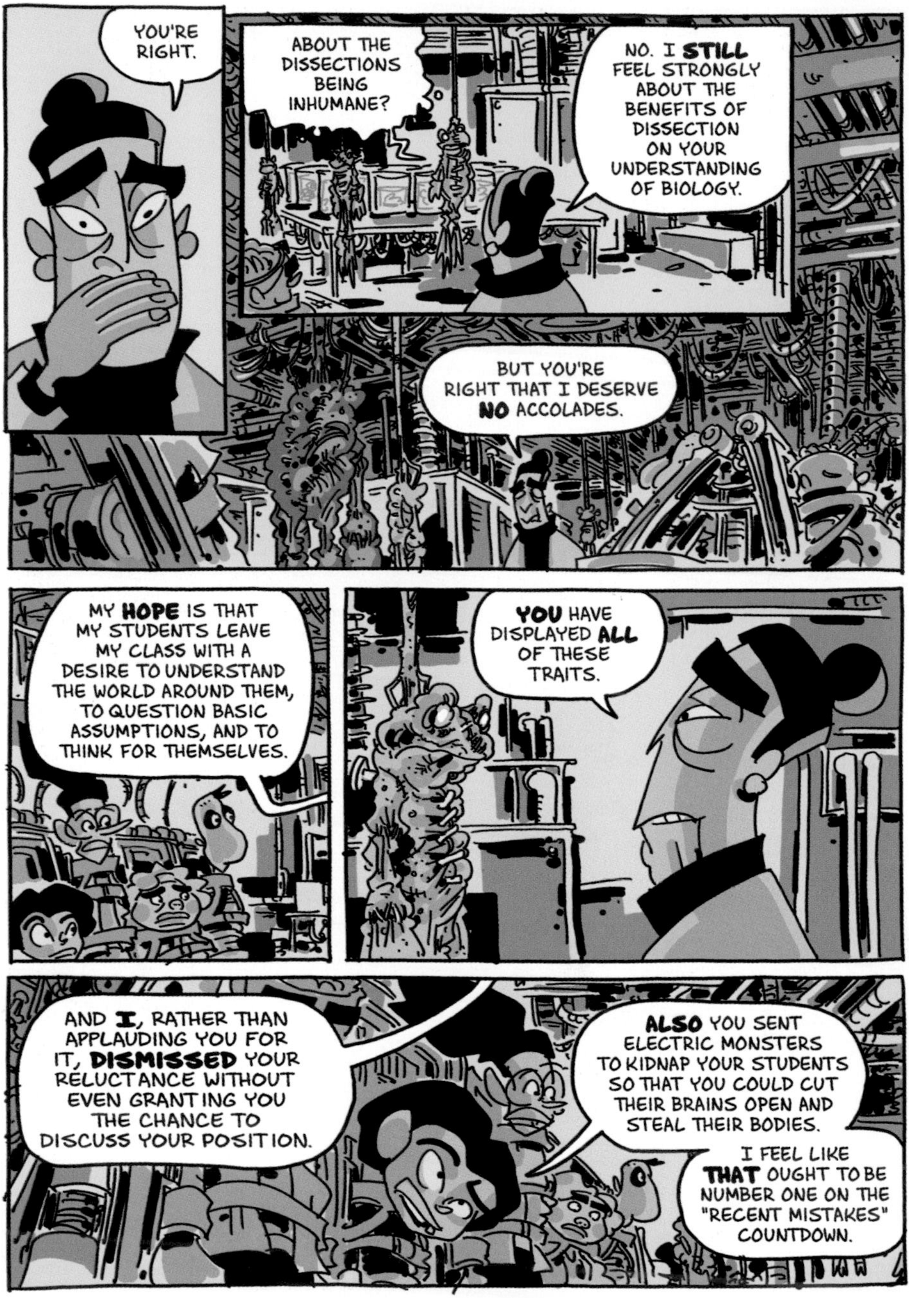
YOU'RE RIGHT.
ABOUT THE DISSECTIONS BEING INHUMANE?
NO. I **STILL** FEEL STRONGLY ABOUT THE BENEFITS OF DISSECTION ON YOUR UNDERSTANDING OF BIOLOGY.
BUT YOU'RE RIGHT THAT I DESERVE **NO** ACCOLADES.
MY **HOPE** IS THAT MY STUDENTS LEAVE MY CLASS WITH A DESIRE TO UNDERSTAND THE WORLD AROUND THEM, TO QUESTION BASIC ASSUMPTIONS, AND TO THINK FOR THEMSELVES.
YOU HAVE DISPLAYED **ALL** OF THESE TRAITS.
AND **I**, RATHER THAN APPLAUDING YOU FOR IT, **DISMISSED** YOUR RELUCTANCE WITHOUT EVEN GRANTING YOU THE CHANCE TO DISCUSS YOUR POSITION.
ALSO YOU SENT ELECTRIC MONSTERS TO KIDNAP YOUR STUDENTS SO THAT YOU COULD CUT THEIR BRAINS OPEN AND STEAL THEIR BODIES.
I FEEL LIKE **THAT** OUGHT TO BE NUMBER ONE ON THE "RECENT MISTAKES" COUNTDOWN.

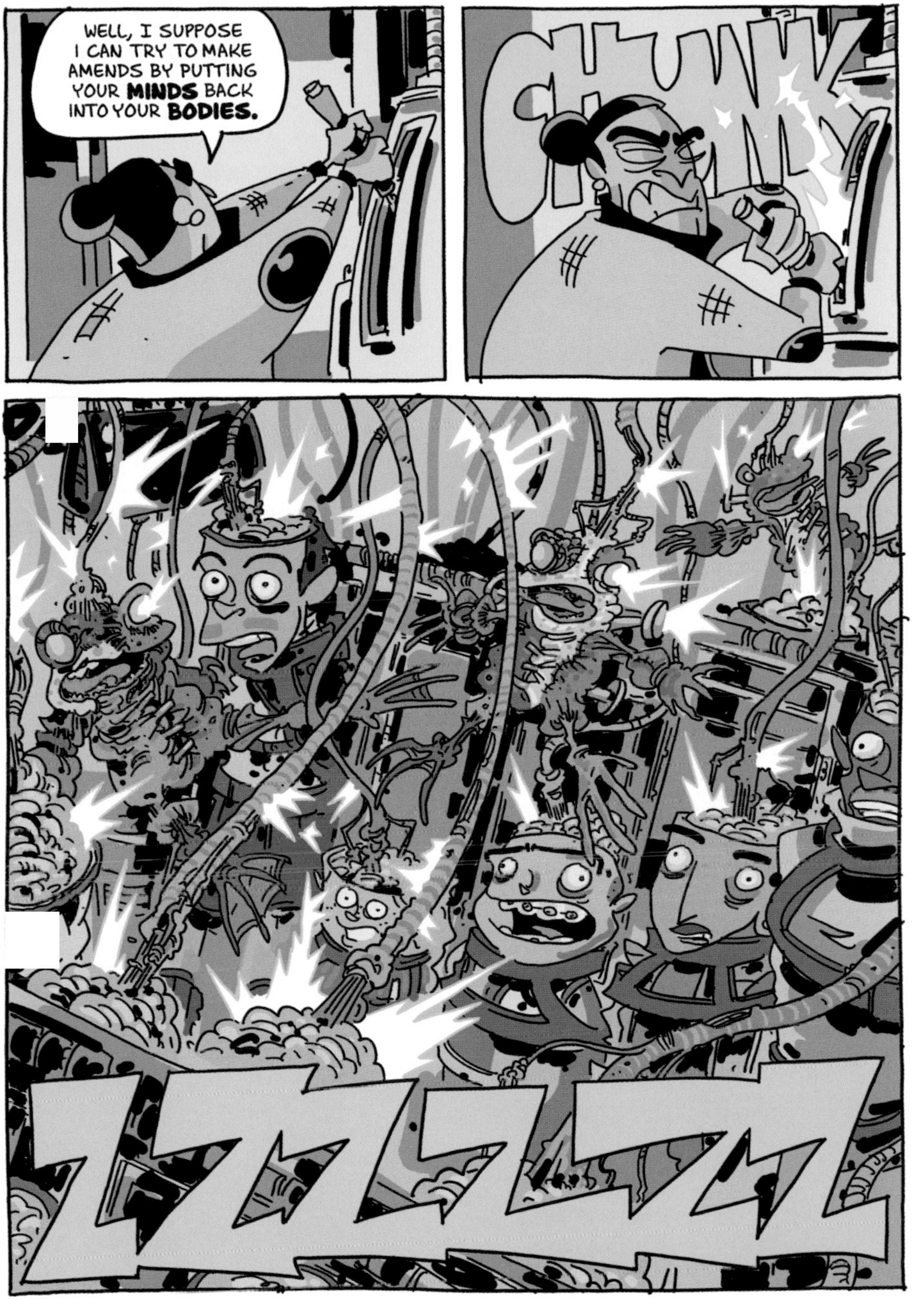
WELL, I SUPPOSE I CAN TRY TO MAKE AMENDS BY PUTTING YOUR **MINDS** BACK INTO YOUR **BODIES.**
CHUNK
ZZZZZZZ

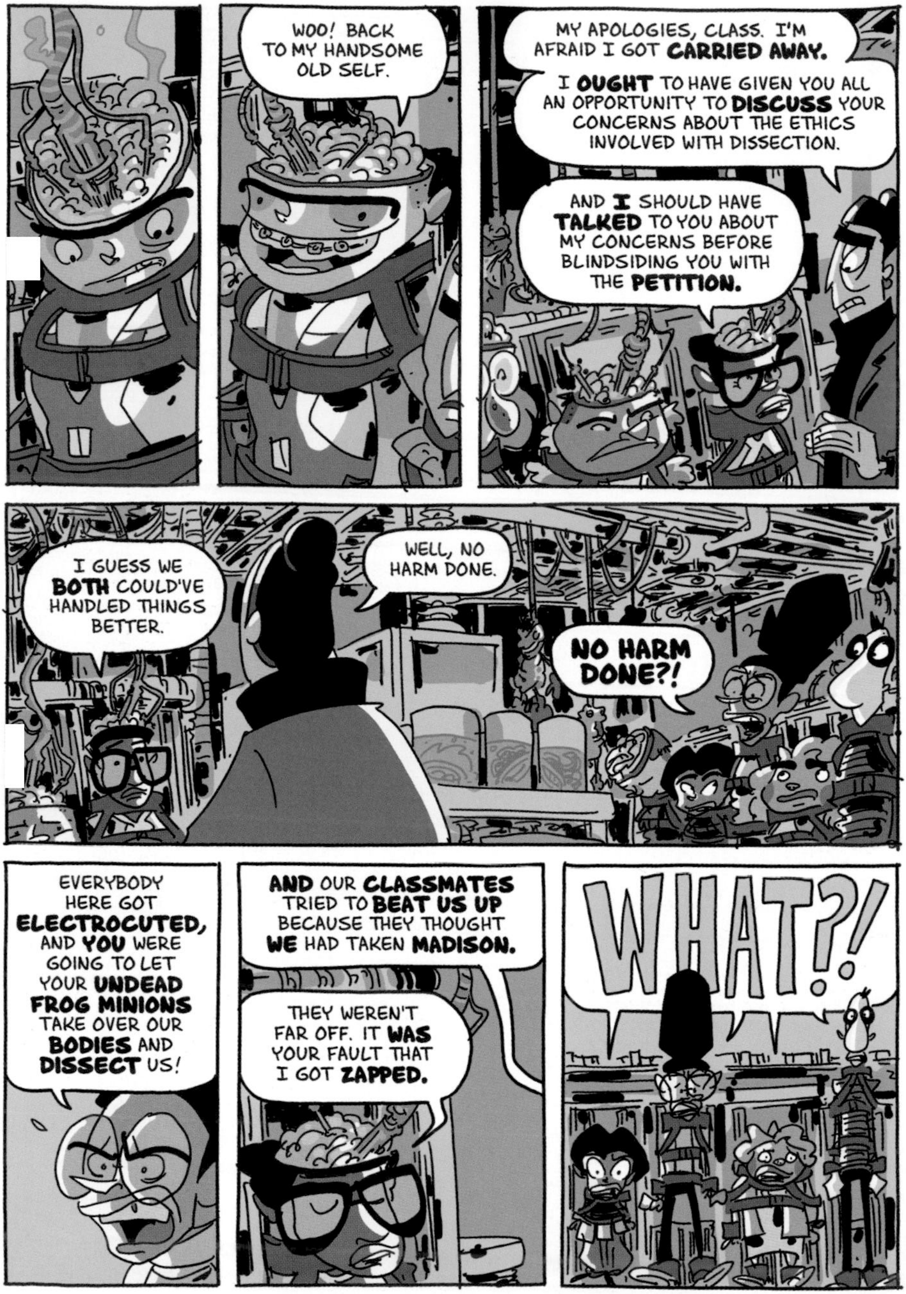
WOO! BACK TO MY HANDSOME OLD SELF.
MY APOLOGIES, CLASS. I'M AFRAID I GOT **CARRIED AWAY.**
I **OUGHT** TO HAVE GIVEN YOU ALL AN OPPORTUNITY TO **DISCUSS** YOUR CONCERNS ABOUT THE ETHICS INVOLVED WITH DISSECTION.
AND **I** SHOULD HAVE **TALKED** TO YOU ABOUT MY CONCERNS BEFORE BLINDSIDING YOU WITH THE **PETITION.**
I GUESS WE **BOTH** COULD'VE HANDLED THINGS BETTER.
WELL, NO HARM DONE.
NO HARM DONE?!
EVERYBODY HERE GOT **ELECTROCUTED,** AND **YOU** WERE GOING TO LET YOUR **UNDEAD FROG MINIONS** TAKE OVER OUR **BODIES** AND **DISSECT** US!
AND OUR **CLASSMATES** TRIED TO **BEAT US UP** BECAUSE THEY THOUGHT **WE** HAD TAKEN **MADISON.**
THEY WEREN'T FAR OFF. IT **WAS** YOUR FAULT THAT I GOT **ZAPPED.**
WHAT?!

120

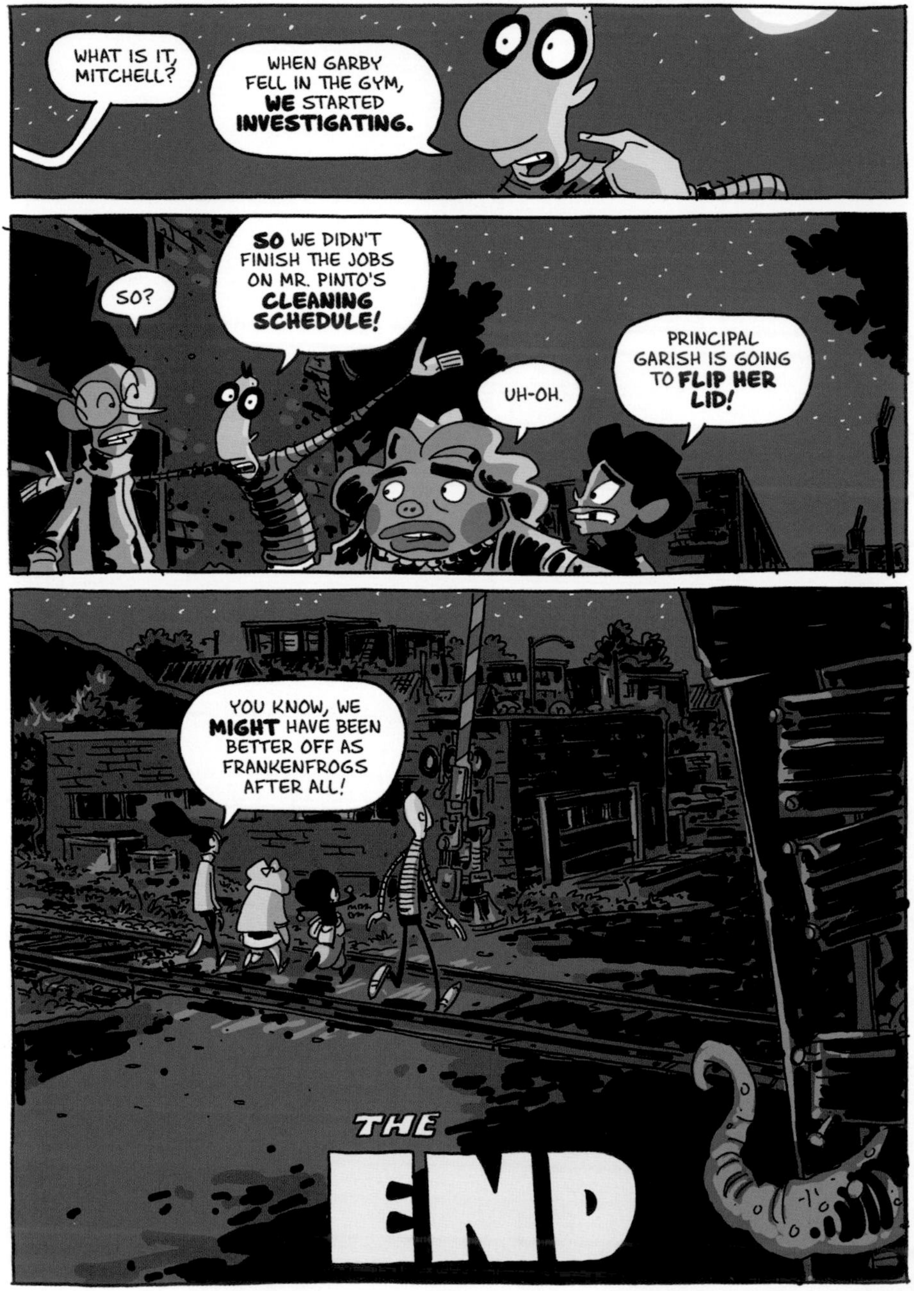
WHAT IS IT, MITCHELL?
WHEN GARBY FELL IN THE GYM, WE STARTED INVESTIGATING.
SO?
SO WE DIDN'T FINISH THE JOBS ON MR. PINTO'S CLEANING SCHEDULE!
UH-OH.
PRINCIPAL GARISH IS GOING TO FLIP HER LID!
YOU KNOW, WE MIGHT HAVE BEEN BETTER OFF AS FRANKENFROGS AFTER ALL!
THE END

ACKNOWLEDGMENTS

Thanks first and foremost to my wife, Liz, and daughter, Penny, for their patience and understanding during my erratic schedule while completing this book. Liz helped considerably with the book's execution by taking on the task of coloring the main characters throughout, saving me significant time and effort.

Thanks to Charlie Olsen of Inkwell Management, who placed this series with Amulet Books. Charlie has made it possible for me to devote all my work energies toward comics, and that has been a gift of immeasurable worth.

And thanks to everyone at Abrams who had a hand in the launch of this series and the creation of this book in particular, including Charlie K., Erica, Pam, and Carol, who helped to make this book far better that it would have been under my clumsy hands alone.